The Girl
Next Door

Phoebe Morgan

ONE PLACE. MANY STORIES

HQ
An imprint of HarperCollins*Publishers* Ltd
1 London Bridge Street
London SE1 9GF

This paperback edition 2019

1

First published in Great Britain by
HQ, an imprint of HarperCollins*Publishers* Ltd 2019

ISBN: 978-0-00-841210-4

Printed and bound in Great Britain by
CPI Group (UK) Ltd, Croydon, CR0 4YY

For my family, and for Alex.

Prologue

Clare

Monday 4th February, 7.00 a.m.

I'm not coming home tonight. The thought hits me as soon as I wake up, fizzing excitedly inside my brain, like one of those sherbets Mum used to buy me from miserable Ruby's corner shop. I won't be sleeping in this bed, I won't be wearing these red and white pyjamas, I won't be by myself.

It's so cold outside; I can see misted condensation on the windows of our house and the room has a filmy, damp feel because Ian's so bloody tight about the heating. Under the duvet, I wiggle my toes to warm up and reach an arm out for my iPhone, on charge by the side of the bed like it always is. Three new messages – two from Lauren, and one from him. The smile cracks open my face as I read it, and I feel a little shiver of anticipation run through me. Today's the day. I have been keeping my secret to myself all weekend, but tonight, I'm going to tell him. He's waited long enough.

'Clare? Are you out of bed yet?'

Mum's calling me from downstairs, I can hear Ian thudding around, making too much noise as he always does. Their bedroom is down the corridor from mine, but I never go in there. I hear the shower spray on, the sound of water hitting tiles, then his whistling begins – out of tune, like always. It'll be like this until the front door slams and he goes to work; until then, the house is full of his loud voice and Mum's anxious fussing. I've got an alarm, of course, but she insists on shouting for me every morning as though I'm six, not sixteen. Reluctantly, I swing my legs over the edge of the bed, wincing as the freezing floorboards touch my feet. My phone, still in my hand, vibrates again and I feel another bubble of excitement, deep in my stomach. Just the day to get through and then it'll be time. I can't wait to see his face.

Chapter One

Jane

Monday 4th February, 7.45 p.m.

I'm sitting in the window with a glass of cool white wine, watching as one by one, the lights in the house next door to ours flicker on. It's dark outside, the February night giving nothing away, and the Edwards' house glows against the gloom. Their walls are cream – not a colour I'd choose – and their front garden runs down to the road, parallel to ours. Inside, I imagine their house to be a mirror image of my own: four spacious bedrooms, a wide, gleaming kitchen, beams that date from the fifteenth century framing the stairway. I've never been inside, not properly, but everybody knows our properties are the most sought-after in the town – the biggest, the most expensive, the ones they all want.

There's a creaking sound from upstairs – my husband Jack, moving around in our room, loosening his tie, the clunk of his shoes dropping onto the floor of the wardrobe. He's been drinking tonight – the open bottle of whiskey sits on the counter, sticky drops spilling onto the surface.

Quietly, so as not to wake the children, I stand, move away from the window and begin clearing it up, putting the bottle back in the cupboard, wiping the little circle of stain

3

off the marble countertop. Wiping away the evidence of the night, of the things he said to me that I want to forget. I'm good at forgetting. Blanking the slate. Practice makes perfect, after all.

The house is tidy and still. The bunch of lilies Jack bought me last week stand stiff on the windowsill, their large pink petals overseeing the room. Apology flowers. I could open up a florist, if it wasn't such a tacky idea.

There's a sound outside and, curious, I move to the front window, lift the thick, dove-grey curtain to one side so that I can see the Edwards' front garden. Their porch light has come on, lighting up the gravel driveway, the edge of their garage on the far side, and the stone bird bath at the front, frozen over in the February chill. I've always thought a birdbath was a little too much, but each to their own. Rachel Edwards' tastes have never quite aligned with mine.

We've never been close, Rachel and I. Not particularly. I tried, of course. When she and her first husband Mark moved in a few years ago, I went round with a bottle of wine – white, expensive. It was hot, July, and I imagined us sitting out in the back garden together, me filling her in about who's who in the town, her nodding along admiringly when I showed her the wisteria that climbs up our back wall, the pretty garden furniture that sits around the chimera on the large flagged patio. I thought we'd be friends as well as neighbours. I pictured her looking at me and Jack wistfully, envying us even – popping round for dinner, exclaiming at the shine of the kitchen, running a hand over the beautiful silver candlesticks when she thought I wasn't looking. We'd laugh together about the goings-on at the school, the lascivious husbands in the town, the children. She'd join our book club, maybe even the PTA. We'd swap recipes, babysitter numbers; shoes, at a push.

But we didn't do any of those things. She took the wine from me, naturally, but her expression was closed, cold even. My first thought was that she was very beautiful; the ice queen next door.

'My husband's inside,' she'd said, 'we're just about to have dinner, so… Perhaps I can pop round another time?'

Behind her, I caught a glimpse of her daughter, Clare – she looked about the same age as my eldest son, Harry. I saw the flash of blonde hair, the long legs as she stood still on the stairs, watching her mother. She never did pop round, of course. For weeks afterwards I felt hurt by it, and then I felt irritated. Did she think she was too good for us? The other women told me not to worry, that we didn't need her in our little mothers' group anyway. 'You can't force it,' my friend Sandra said. Over time, I let it go. Well, sort of.

When Mark died, I went round to see Rachel, tried again. I thought she must be terribly lonely, rattling around in that big house, just her and Clare. But even then, there remained a distance between us, a bridge I couldn't quite cross. Something odd in her smile.

And then, of course, she met Ian. Husband number two. After that, I stopped trying altogether.

I see Clare every now and then, grown even prettier in the last few years. Jack thinks I don't notice the way his eyes follow her as she walks by, but I do. I notice everything.

I hear footsteps on the gravel, and recoil from the window as a figure appears, striding purposefully towards our front door. I open it before they can knock, thinking of my younger children, Finn and Sophie, tucked away upstairs, dreaming, oblivious.

Rachel is standing on our doorstep, but she doesn't look like Rachel. Her eyes are wide, her hair all over her face, whipped by the wind.

'Jane,' she says, 'I'm sorry to bother you, I just—' She's peering around me, her eyes darting into our porch, where our coats are hanging neatly on the ornate black pegs. My Barbour, Jack's winter coat, Harry's scruffy hoodie that I wish he'd get rid of. Finn and Sophie's little duffels, red and blue with wooden toggles up the front. Our perfect little family. The thought makes me smile. It's so far from the truth.

'Have you seen Clare? Is she here?'

I stare at her, taken aback. Clare is sixteen, a pupil at Ashdon Secondary. The year below Harry, Year Eleven. I see her in the mornings, leaving for school, wearing one of those silky black rucksacks with impractically thin straps. She can't possibly get all her books in there.

Like I said, we don't mix with the Edwards much. I don't know Clare well at all.

'Jane?' Rachel's voice is desperate, panicked.

'No!' I say, 'no, Rachel, I'm sorry, I haven't. Why would she be here?'

She lets out a moan, almost animalistic. There are tears forming in her eyes, threatening to spill down her cheeks. For a moment, I almost feel a flicker of satisfaction at seeing the icy mask melt, then squash the thought down immediately. Just because she's never been neighbourly doesn't mean I have to be the same.

'She's not with Harry or something?'

I stare at her. My son is out, a post-match pizza night with the boys from his football team. He took Sophie and Finn to school today for me; the night out is his reward. If I'm honest, I've always thought he might have a bit of a crush on Clare, like father like son, but as far as I know she's never given him the time of day. Not that he'd tell me if she had, I suppose. His main communication these days is through grunts.

'No,' I say, 'no, she isn't with Harry.'

Her breath comes fast, panting, panicked. 'Do you want to come inside?' I ask quickly. 'I can get you a drink, you can tell me what's happened.'

She shakes her head, and I feel momentarily put out. Most people in Ashdon would kill to see inside our house: the expensive furnishings, the artwork, the effortless sense of style that money makes so easy. Well, it's not totally effortless, of course. Not without its sacrifices.

'We can't find her,' she says, 'she didn't come home from school. Oh God, Jane, she's disappeared. She's gone.'

I stare at her, trying to comprehend what she's saying. 'What? I'm sure she's just with a friend,' I say, putting a hand on her arm as she stands at the door, feeling her shake beneath my fingers.

'No,' she says, 'no. I've called them all. Ian's been up and down the high street, looking for her. She's normally home by four thirty, school gets out just after four. We can't get hold of her on the mobile, we've tried and tried and it goes to voicemail. It's almost eight o'clock.' She's clenching and unclenching her fists, blinking too much, trying to control the panic. I don't know what to do.

'Shall I come round?' I ask. 'The kids are asleep anyway,

Harry's not here, and Jack's upstairs.' If she thinks it odd that my husband hasn't come down, she doesn't say anything.

'Rachel!' There's a shout – Ian, the aforementioned hubby number two. He appears in my doorway, a large, oversized iPhone in his hand. His face is red, he looks a bit out of breath. He's a big man, ex-army, or so people say. Works in the City, takes the train to Liverpool Street most mornings. I know because I see him through the window. He runs his own business, engineering, something like that. Always a jovial tie. I've heard him shouting at Clare in the evenings; I can never make out what he's saying. I suppose it must be hard, being second best. I know I wouldn't like it.

'The police are on their way,' he says, and at this Rachel breaks down, her body curling into his, his arms reaching out to stroke her back.

'If there's anything I can do,' I say, and he nods at me gratefully over his wife's head. I can see the fear in his own eyes, and feel momentarily surprised. It takes a lot to unsettle a military man. Unless he knows more than he's letting on. He never did get on well with Clare.

Chapter Two

DS Madeline Shaw

Monday 4th February, 7.45 p.m.

'It's my stepdaughter, Clare. She hasn't come home from school.'

The call comes in to Chelmsford Police Station just after 7.45 p.m. on Monday night. The team are polishing off a tin of Quality Street left over from Christmas; DS Ben Moore is hoovering up the strawberry creams while DS Madeline Shaw targets the caramels. It's the DCI who answers the phone, holds up a hand to silence the room.

When she sees the look on Rob Sturgeon's face, Madeline picks up the handset, presses the pads to her ears. Ian Edwards' voice is gruff, but she can hear the urgency in it that he's trying to control. Immediately, she knows who he is – the Edwards family live in Ashdon, in one of the big detached houses off Ash Road. His wife Rachel works at the estate agency in Saffron Walden. She's got one child from her first marriage: Clare. Madeline lives three streets away from her: they are practically neighbours.

'She's normally home long before now, school finishes at ten past four,' Ian says, his words coming fast. 'I'm afraid my wife is getting a bit worried.' A pause. 'We both are.' DS

Moore is making a face, delving back into the chocolate, but Madeline listens carefully. The DCI is asking questions, his voice calm – how old is Clare, when did you last see her, when did you last hear from her.

'We've tried her phone, dozens of times now,' Ian says. 'It's just going to voicemail. It's not like her to do this—' He breaks off.

Madeline is about to chip in, to tell Mr Edwards that she can come round – after all, she'll be going home anyway – but the door to the MIT room swings open and Lorna Campbell pops her head round the door, her coat on even though she normally works until eleven.

'Detective Shaw?'

Madeline slips off her headset. 'Everything okay?'

Lorna raises her eyebrows at the team. 'Report just in of a body found in Ashdon, in the field at the back that borders Acre Lane. Female victim. Guy called Nathan Warren phoned it in, says he was out walking, stumbled across her. You ready?'

The DCI's face changes. Wordlessly, Madeline follows Lorna outside.

The girl is lying on her back in Sorrow's Meadow. In the summer, despite its miserable name, the field is full of buttercups, bright yellow flowers shining in the sun, but in the winter it's dark and barren. Clare Edwards' golden hair is fanned out around her head like a halo, blood is soaking into the frosty grass around her skull. Madeline's torch beam picks out the places where it's already darkened, highlights the silvery trail of saliva that has frozen on the girl's cheek. It's freezing, minus two. She's in her school uniform: jumper and skirt, a little blue puffer coat over the top.

'Call forensics,' Madeline tells Lorna, her breath misting the air, little white ghosts forming above the body.

'They're on the way already,' Lorna says, 'the DCI too.'

'Clare,' Madeline says aloud, but it's pointless; when she bends to touch the girl's neck, her gloved fingers meet ice-cold skin, no hint of a pulse. For a moment, the policewoman looks away. She's never had a case where she knew the victim before, even though her interaction with Clare Edwards has only been brief. A school assembly last December; Madeline had been called in by the head to do a routine safety chat. Clare had approached her afterwards, wanted to know more about her job, a career in the police. It had surprised her, at the time. Now, it makes her feel sick. Clare's future is gone, over before it began.

The forensic team arrive and begin sealing off the area, their white suits bright in the darkness.

Gently, Madeline lifts the blonde hair, exposing the wound at the back of Clare's head.

'She looks so young,' Lorna mutters quietly, and Madeline nods.

The torchlight lands on her rucksack, a black faux-leather bag, thin straps. Inside are a pile of school books; her name is all over everything, the neat blue handwriting re-emphasising Clare's youth.

'No mobile phone.' Lorna hands her Clare's wallet – a purple zip-up from Accessorize. Carefully, Madeline thumbs through her cards: her provisional driver's licence, a Nando's loyalty card, plus an old Waterstones receipt, long out of date.

'Shaw. I've been on the phone to her mother. Fill me in.'

DCI Rob Sturgeon appears at her side; quickly, Madeline

begins sliding the exercise books into evidence bags, turns to face him.

'Have you told her yet?'

He shakes his head. 'No, not until we've formally ID'd. Shit.' He runs a hand through his hair. 'Is Alex here?'

They both look around, and spot DS Alex Faulkner a few metres away, talking to one of the forensics team.

'Faulkner!'

At the DCI's shout, Alex heads over, the expression on his face grim.

'Looks like someone's repeatedly slammed her against the ground,' he says, nodding to Madeline. 'Back of her head's not a pretty sight.'

There is a blue ink stain all over Clare's left hand, and her unpainted fingernails are dirty, from where she's presumably clawed at the ground.

'You don't think there was a weapon?' the DCI says, and Alex shakes his head. 'Doesn't look like it to me.'

'Suggests unplanned, then,' Madeline adds, and he nods.

'Quite possibly. Fit of anger, perhaps. Crime of passion.' There's a pause. 'We'll be testing for rape, of course.' He swallows, spreads his hands in the semi-darkness. 'Or else it *was* planned, and our killer just decided to cut out the middle man. Less evidence that way.'

'Someone who trusts their own strength, in that case,' Rob says. The guys are placing markers on the frosty ground, marking the places Clare's blood has spilled. *Trusts their own strength*, Madeline thinks. Nine times out of ten it's a man.

'You said Nathan Warren phoned it in?' she asks Lorna, frowning.

'Yes, that's right,' Lorna says, and catching the expression on her colleague's face, 'd'you know him?'

'Yes,' Madeline says slowly, stepping to one side as they begin to erect a little white tent over her body, looking out to where the stile leads to the footpath down to the town centre, 'I do know him. I know exactly who he is.'

Clare Edwards is pronounced dead at 8.45 p.m. Madeline closes her eyes, just briefly, remembering the day Clare spoke to her at the school, their conversation in one of the empty classrooms, the curiosity in her eyes as she asked Madeline what being a police officer was really like. How can that girl be lying here on the floor, pale and lifeless? The two images will not connect in her brain.

'I want you with me, Shaw,' the DCI says, breaking the memory. 'Let's get this over with, for God's sake. Keep the tent up,' he barks, his eyes scanning the meadow, 'we don't want anyone seeing this.' Gloved hands are combing the ground for her phone, lights are picking out the spots of blood in amongst the leaves. The blood on her head is darker now, dry and blackening. Madeline's mind is already on Mr and Mrs Edwards, knocking on their front door, ready to deliver them the worst news of their lives.

'We can walk there,' she says at last, 'it's only ten minutes.'

'Right,' Rob says, 'Campbell, Faulkner – update me soon as you can. Send a car after us to the house, we'll need a family liaison officer. I want everyone on this. Jesus, sixteen. The press'll have a bloody field day.'

Madeline leads the way, back across Sorrow's Meadow, out of the wooded area and down Acre Lane towards where

Ashdon High Street meets the river. The small town is quiet; it's a Monday night. Driving through, you'd have seen nothing, heard nothing. The Edwards house looms in front of them, one of a pair set back slightly from the road, and the DCI puts his hand on her arm at the edge of their drive: a gravel affair, primroses either side, stiff with the cold. There's a bird bath to the left, frozen solid in the February air. Madeline looks to the house next door, separated from the Edwards' by a thin grass strip. Lights off, except for one. The Goodwins' place. Both houses are huge in comparison to Madeline's; security systems glow in the darkness. Behind the garage doors lurk expensive, silent cars.

'Just the basics for now,' Rob says, 'until we have the full picture.'

'Are we mentioning Nathan Warren?'

Madeline's question goes unanswered; the door opens before either of them can even knock and then there they are, framed before the police in the bright light of the house, Rachel Edwards and her husband Ian. Rachel looks like Clare – that same striking face, beautiful without needing to try. They recognise her from the town; she can see the flash of hope on their faces. Madeline steps forward.

'Mr and Mrs Edwards. This is DCI Rob Sturgeon, my colleague at Chelmsford Police Force. We have news on your daughter. May we come in?'

Chapter Three

Jane

Monday 4th February, 9.00 p.m.

The curtain is thick and warm between my fingers from my vantage point at the living-room window. The minute I closed the door on Rachel and Ian, I texted Harry to come home, my fingers fumbling slightly in my haste. I wish I hadn't had the glass of wine earlier, wish my mind was clearer, sharper, ready to help the neighbours. There is no sign yet of the police. What's taking them so long?

What's happened, Harry replied, *why do you need me home?* I told him to use the back door, to be as quick as he could. I want all my children under my roof, where I can see them.

As I wait for him at the window, blue lights spill suddenly across the pavement, illuminating our house in their morbid glow. My heart thuds. *It might be good news*, I think. But nobody comes to start a search party; I don't hear the whirr of helicopters out looking. Just two detectives crunching up the drive, followed by a third woman who quickly gets out of the police car. Then the slam of the Edwards' front door, the flicker of lights in their living room. Still, I think to myself, you never know. I keep telling myself that, although my insides feel

15

cold. Eventually, when there is no sign of further movement, I draw the curtains, blocking the police car out, then check on Sophie and Finn in their beds, listen to their breathing for a full minute. My babies. I don't go into the master bedroom; Jack has closed the door. I don't want to disturb him now, there is no point. My husband doesn't take well to being disturbed.

'Mum?' I jump at Harry's voice; the gruffness of it always surprises me now; how quickly he has lost the boyish tones of his youth. Still only seventeen, he looms above me in the corridor. He must have come up the stairs behind me, his socked feet soundless on the thick white carpet.

'I didn't hear you come in,' I say, gesturing to him to come back downstairs, away from the rest of our sleeping family.

Downstairs, I lock all the doors and windows, check them twice as Harry fetches a glass of water from the sink, drinks it greedily in exactly the same way he did as a ten-year-old.

'What's going on?' he says, 'I saw the police car outside.'

'Nothing,' I say quickly, 'false alarm next door. Something to do with their security system.' There is no point worrying him, not now, not when I don't know the full story. The houses down this end of the town are used to things like this; we have state-of-the-art security systems now which, despite their cost, are triggered unnecessarily more often than not. A small irritation of the rich. My son doesn't think anything of it.

I watch Harry closely as he pulls open the fridge door, scans the shelves.

'Didn't you just have a pizza?' I say lightly, placing my hand on the small of his back, and he turns round, gives me a rare grin.

'Well, yeah. But you wanted me home before I could finish the second. What was up?'

'Oh,' I say, 'it was when next door's alarm first went off. I thought it was the real thing. Didn't want to be alone, as it were.' One of the houses across the way was burgled last year; two men in balaclavas. It's the only crime I've ever heard of in Ashdon. Bad things don't tend to happen here.

He frowns. 'Dad not in?'

I pause, a micro-second. 'He's asleep, came home with a bit of a headache, poor thing.'

My son grunts, having already lost interest in favour of left-over pasta in the fridge. My eyes flit over the half-drunk bottle of white wine next to it, but I make myself turn away, tell Harry I'm going up to get some sleep. I avert my eyes from the windows, not wanting to see what may or may not be unfolding next door.

When I go into our master bedroom, Jack is asleep, his familiar body curled in an S shape, his dark hair vivid on the pillow. I stare at my husband for a full two minutes before climbing in next to him. The scent of whiskey on his breath makes me feel sick. *He didn't mean it*, I keep telling myself, *it was the heat of the moment. That's all.* After a while, I put in my earbuds, turn my face into the duvet. I can't help Rachel Edwards now. The police are next door, they are doing their job. I think back to what Jack told me when we first moved to Ashdon. *You will love it here.* A gorgeous little town in rural Essex. A place where bad things don't happen. A place to fix our marriage.

I fall asleep with both sets of fingers crossed for Clare.

Chapter Four

Jane

The morning dawns grey and cold, and there is a second when I forget the events of last night, think only of the soft pillow beneath my head and the brushed cotton sheets beneath my body. *Only the best for my wife,* Jack had said, presenting them to me on moving day, as though Egyptian fabric could make up for the broken rib he'd inflicted on me in our old house. He'd pleaded with me over that one, and I knew why – if it went on his record, he'd never practise as a GP again. So it didn't, and here we are. I am still the doctor's wife. My children have two parents, a happy home. We all make sacrifices, and besides, the sheets are beautiful. I run my hand over them, soft and cool beneath my fingers. The room is very still; Jack is already up.

Then I remember, and it hits me: *Clare didn't come home from school.* Immediately, I am up out of bed, racing into my children's bedrooms, flicking on the lights. I am met with a grunt from Harry, the duvet yanked up over his head, the smell of teenage boy permeating everything. Finn and Sophie are the opposite – already awake and crowing in delight at the sight of me, their little fingers reaching out for a morning kiss.

I decide to go to the Edwards' house this morning, just after I've taken the children to school. Harry likes walking by himself nowadays, usually leaves before us, just after Jack. I suppose you don't need your mum holding your hand at seventeen. I cannot concentrate on making breakfast; my hands shake slightly as I pour milk onto the children's cereal, my eyes darting constantly to the window as though expecting to see Clare waving at me through the glass. But the street is silent, the same as it always is. I allow myself a flicker of hope. Rachel will probably ring any minute, I think, although I don't think she's ever picked up the phone to me in her life; she'll ring me and tell me it was all a false alarm, and we'll laugh about what a nightmare teenagers can be, how they'll turn us grey before we know it.

Jack was bleary-eyed when he left for the surgery. He tossed and turned a lot in the night; I kept still, like a board. I hesitated a minute before going next door, but I could hardly leave things as they were last night, could I? For all I knew, Clare could've been tucked up in bed by then, sleeping off a hangover. I didn't hear anything with my earbuds in. Like I said, I still thought it might be okay, even then.

The air feels strange inside the Edwards' porch – stiff with shock. I notice Clare's trainers on the shoe rack, just inside the front door – black with pink stripes. For a moment, I think she must be home safe and sound and feel a huge wave of relief, the tension lifting out of my body, just for a second. Ian is the one who comes out to speak to me, his voice hushed.

'Rachel's not in a state to speak, Jane,' he says. 'They found our Clare last night.' *Found.*

She's not his Clare, not really, she's Mark's daughter. There were lots of whispers when Rachel remarried; people saying it was too soon, inappropriate. Mark died of lung cancer about three years ago.

I feel my face changing as he tells me, the shock seeping into my skin.

'I'm so sorry,' I say, 'I'm so sorry, Ian.' The words seem inadequate, inarticulate.

He stares at me. He looks as if he hasn't slept and his breath smells faintly of alcohol – not that I can blame him for that.

'Do they know what happened?' I ask, biting my lip, and that's when he tells me, the words pouring out of him like poison. She was found by Nathan Warren, the man who lives down by the river. She was wearing her school uniform, he says. They think someone attacked her, bashed her head repeatedly against the ground. She was alone. It was minus two. The police have closed off Sorrow's Meadow. A family liaison officer is in the kitchen as we speak.

I shudder, try not to let him see. Sorrow's Meadow runs across the back of Ashdon, surrounding us all, trapping us in. I used to take Sophie there sometimes, let her play in the flowers. I can't imagine I'll be doing that any more. And Nathan Warren – the name makes the hairs on the back of my neck stand up. Everyone knows Nathan – he lives alone, in his mother's old house, used to have a job as a caretaker up at the school. Apparently they let him go a few years ago after one of the mothers complained about him. Said he'd followed her daughter back from school. Nothing ever came of it though, as far as I know. It was all before our time. Hearsay. And hearsay can be dangerous, destructive.

I wonder if Ian and Rachel know about it, if the police have a record. Nausea runs through me, and for a horrible moment I panic that I am going to be sick, right on their doorstep. I imagine the vomit splashing onto Clare's trainers.

'Please,' I say to Ian, 'let me know if there's anything I can do. For either of you. We're just next door. We're here for you.'

He nods, his mouth a tight line. A woman appears behind him – young, short brown hair. Not exactly pretty, but she has kind eyes.

'This is Theresa,' Ian says, 'she's our support officer.'

'Family liaison,' Theresa says, stretching out a hand for me to shake. 'And you are?'

I don't like her tone. 'I'm Jane Goodwin,' I say, 'I live next door.'

She smiles at me, and immediately, I feel as though I've probably imagined the odd tone. 'The Edwards are lucky to have good neighbours,' she says to me in a low voice. 'It's times like this when communities can really pull together.'

'Of course,' I say to her, 'my husband and I will do anything we can to help.'

I think of myself tucked up in bed last night, crossing my fingers for poor Clare. It was no good, of course. By that point, she was already dead.

The police haven't spoken to us yet, though I imagine they'll come knocking. The news spread like wildfire today – everyone was talking about it at the school drop-off. No one's using the word murder, not yet, but no one thinks it was an accident either.

'I heard it was Nathan Warren that found her,' Tricia hissed at me this afternoon, as we stood by the school gates. 'I wonder what the police make of that. D'you remember that fuss a few years back, when he lost his job at the school?'

I nod. I always felt a bit sorry for him; people said he'd had an accident a couple of years ago, that it had affected his mind a bit. *He was painting the roof for his mother*, Sandra had told me, *fell off the ladder, hit his head on the stone*. But other people insist he's never been right, that there's something more sinister about him. *The way he looks at you*, one of the mothers had said once, *I wouldn't want him alone with my daughter, put it that way*.

I didn't want to let the children out of my sight today, wanted to wrap my arms around them and never let go. But Jack said we had to carry on as normal, not panic until they release more information. I didn't like the way he looked at me when he said it, like I was paranoid, overprotective.

Thank God it didn't take long to find her, at least, I said to Jack when he got home this afternoon, but he didn't reply. He said he'd had a hard day at the surgery. I told him it was okay, that I understood he was tired, that I knew he hadn't meant what he said last night. I wondered if he'd forgotten, even, in all the drama over Clare.

Harry was horribly shocked at the news; I spoke to him as soon as he got in from school.

'I'm so sorry, darling,' I said to him, 'I know this must be a dreadful shock, her being around your age. The police are doing everything they can.' His face went completely white; I got him a chocolate biscuit from the cupboard, usually reserved for special occasions. The last thing I need is multiple trips to the dentist. I put a hand on his arm but he shrugged away from me, took himself off upstairs.

'Let him be for a bit,' Jack said to me, 'he'll come around.'

I stared after Harry, wondering. My son has become closed off to me these last few months; he mentions school friends, but never girls. *It's normal for teenage boys to be private,* Tricia told me a few weeks ago, *you probably wouldn't want to know what goes on inside his mind anyway!* She'd laughed, like it was a joke. But I do want to know. I want to know everything.

Chapter Five

Jane

Tuesday 5th February

We sit at my friend Sandra's kitchen table, all of us on our third glass of wine, red for them, white for me. Easier to clean. I'm considerate like that. She texted Tricia and I this evening, wanting an emergency wine night. *I think we're all in shock,* her message said, *come to mine for seven?*

'You'll be good for Daddy, won't you?' I said to the children before leaving the house, hugging their little bodies tight to my chest. I didn't want to leave them, but Jack told me to go, and something in his eyes made me put on my coat, grab my handbag, close the front door tightly behind me. My rib twinged a bit as I walked the ten minutes to Sandra's house, a semi-detached place with lavender borders leading up to the front door. In the summer, the smell of them is lovely; now, they are sorrowful-looking husks, scentless and dead.

My hand is underneath Sandra's; she grabbed it as she was talking, wanting the comfort even though I know part of her loves this gossip, despite the morbidity of what's happened. Our wedding rings chink against each other. Tricia tops up our glasses, although we've had too much already. Everyone drinks more these days, even the PTA. It takes the edge off.

'This used to be a safe place,' Sandra is saying drunkenly, her lips blackened from the drink. Another reason I chose white. Moving her hand from mine, she clutches at her skinny chest, her palm smacking the centre, where people think their heart must be. They're wrong, obviously, usually by a good few inches. That's what Jack says, anyway.

'My heart,' she says, 'it feels like it's breaking for that little girl. Is that silly? But it really does.'

'I know,' I say. I thought this *was* a safe town, a nice place, a community of do-gooders. It's how my husband sold it to me. A home for us, for our little family. *You will love it here*, he said, his lips curving into mine. A memory comes to me, of just before we moved: the steep drop of the staircase in our old house, the spirals in the ceiling above my head as I lay on my back, my rib broken and bruised. The way they looked at me in the hospital, before I smoothed it all away.

'Tell us again how it happened, Mrs Goodwin,' they'd said to me, and I watched as the nurses looked at my husband, their eyes slightly narrowed, their pens poised above my notes.

'Perhaps you'd feel more comfortable without Mr Goodwin in the room?' one of them had suggested to me, but Jack was standing by her side and so I shook my head no, told them I was fine.

'I slipped,' I said, 'I slipped and fell as I was carrying the children's washing upstairs. Roll on the day they can do their own laundry!' The youngest nurse had laughed at that, smiled at me kindly, adjusted my pillows. I could almost sense the goodness radiating out from her, the purity. I wanted to be like that too. For just a brief moment when Jack went to the bathroom, I wanted to reach out to grab her arm, tell her the truth. But I thought of the children, their little eyes blinking up at me, and I didn't.

A fresh start, he said on the drive home from the hospital, *for both of us*. Shortly after, we moved here.

Sandra takes another sip of wine, shoves a handful of Kettle Chips into her mouth. The gesture smudges her lipstick a bit, but no one says anything.

'I can't imagine how you're feeling, Jane,' she says, 'her being next door to you guys.' She gives a little shiver. 'You can't believe it, can you?' She lowers her voice, looks at me and Tricia, her eyes darkening just a little. 'You don't think – well, you don't think the obvious, do you?' She's almost whispering now, and I know what she's going to say even before she opens her mouth, her white teeth flashing in the kitchen light. She uses strips to whiten them; I've seen them in her bathroom. £19.99 for a pack, bright white teeth for a lifetime. 'You don't think she was *raped*?'

The word changes the atmosphere in the room, as though the walls are tightening slightly, hemming us in. I put a hand to my throat, thinking of Clare's long legs, of my son's eyes on her golden blonde hair.

'I think we ought to let the police be the judge of that,' I say, 'but I hope to God she wasn't.'

'It would be a motive though, wouldn't it?' Sandra presses on, oblivious to my discomfort. Rather than reply, I take another sip of wine, press my hand to my stomach, feel it rumble with hunger. We haven't eaten dinner. Liquid calories.

'I know what you mean,' Tricia chips in, eyes gleaming with the promise of more gossip. 'It does seem odd, doesn't it, for someone to target her like that, without a reason?' She shivers.

'And Nathan Warren being the one to find her – well, it doesn't exactly inspire confidence, does it? Poor, poor Rachel. And after losing Mark, too.' She pauses. 'I hope she isn't thinking anything stupid.'

'I took her a lasagne round this afternoon, after the police left,' I say, and the women nod appreciatively. I did *think* about taking her one, which is almost the same thing. The curtains on Rachel and Ian's bedroom window were pulled tight when I left to come to Sandra's; I couldn't see inside. Their bedroom faces into our bathroom; when I'm in the shower, I can see the full sweep of their bed, their his and hers wardrobe, the suit Ian hangs up before a big meeting in the city. They can't see me, I don't think. Anyway, a lasagne might have disturbed them. Overstepped the mark.

'You're such a good neighbour, Jane,' Sandra says, hiccupping as she takes another sip of wine, and I smile, look away. Her house is a mess; kids' toys clutter the floor.

'We'll get through this,' Tricia says, nodding decisively, the effect ruined only slightly when a spill of wine slops from her glass, splashing onto her expensive cream blouse. 'We all will. This town needs to stick together. We're a team.'

The clock on the mantelpiece chimes – it's an old-fashioned one, like my grandmother would own. Sandra never did have much style.

'I'd better get going,' I say, 'Jack will be waiting.' I glance at my watch, feel a rush of anxiety as I picture him looking at his phone for messages, annoyed now that I'm later than I said. Opening a beer, the soft click of the bottle cap releasing. *Jack's lucky to have you*, an old friend said to me once. How true those words are now.

'Oh, send our love,' the women say, almost in a chorus, and I nod, start gathering my bag.

'Ooh!' Tricia says as I'm nearly at the front door, 'I almost forgot to say, because of Clare. But did you hear about Lindsay Stevens, from the Close?' She lowers her voice, even though we're the only ones in the house apart from Sandra's kids upstairs. 'Apparently, her *divorce* papers came through. Supposedly she's devastated.'

'Goodness,' I say, trying to look shocked, arranging my face into an expression somewhere between sympathy and sadness. 'That's awful.'

Tricia nods. 'I thought I'd bake something for her, drop it round next week.' She looks at me expectantly.

'I'll help,' I say, just in time, and she beams at me, gives my arm a little squeeze.

'Thanks, Jane, you're a star. See you tomorrow for pick-up time! And get home safe, won't you? Text us when you get in. God, I won't sleep properly until we know who did that to Clare.' She looks worried, and I feel a sudden chill which I push away. It's a ten-minute walk home, and besides, I've been through worse.

I shut the door quietly behind me, thinking about Lindsay. I can't tell them how I really feel about her divorce. I can't tell them that deep down, part of me is jealous. It's too soon for them to know the truth.

I walk home, down the quiet road, using the light on my new iPhone to check the ground in front of me, even though I know the small pavements like the back of my hand. I pass the schools on the right, the primary and secondary next to each other, encouraging all our children to stay just five feet from home for the entirety of their young lives, and my torch-light catches the whips of yellow ribbon tied to the row of saplings outside, hastily erected today after the news about Clare came out. Sadness spreads fast. Quickly, I move the beam away and stumble slightly. I'm drunker than I thought.

The Edwards' house is lit up, lights blazing. As I get closer, my heart starts to jump in my chest. There are cars outside: two police, one black. Can't really pass all this off to Harry as a security breach again. It won't be long before the journalists descend. I shudder at the thought, thinking of the horror of last night. I think of my daughter Sophie, the sweet pink pout of her lips, the way her little white socks slip down her ankles. If anything happened to her, I'd die. She's our only girl, though I always wanted more. I don't have a sister, and Jack never speaks to his older sister Katherine – but we ended up with two boys. Not that I'd change Harry and Finn now, not for the world. Well. I might make Harry a touch more communicative. A touch less interested in blondes.

I walk quickly past the Edwards' house, keeping my head down, not checking to see if there's anyone sitting inside the parked cars. My keys are cold in my hand. I press the metal into my palm, harder and harder until it hurts. Our front door is heavy, a wooden slab framed by a thatched roof. If there was a fire, we'd all be up in smoke. Maybe that would be a good thing. He's suggested it more than once. Shouted it, in fact. Luckily the children had Harry Potter on, the audiobook blasting into their little ears. Drowning out Daddy. I suppose Harry might have heard.

Inside our house, I press my back against the door, force

myself to take deep breaths. Harry is home tonight; his huge black trainers are discarded inside the front hallway. I bend to pick them up, stack them neatly on the shoe rack, wanting to create a sense of order to ease my jumbled mind. I hope he's feeling better. It's horribly unsettling, having this happen so close to home. I know it's awful, I know I should be focused on our neighbours and their grief, but selfishly, I don't want the police sniffing around my family, prising apart the cracks in my marriage. Things can still change, any day now. He is usually sorry. So, so sorry. And the bruises fade fast, after all. There's never been any point getting anyone else involved. Not at this stage.

Jack is sitting up in our living room, just as I pictured him, his legs stretched out on the large grey sofa that cost us over three grand. *Three grand*, I wanted to say to him, *three grand would've sent Sophie to the private school in Saffron Walden*. The 52-inch television screen is flickering in front of him, the volume down low. He puts a finger to his lips as he sees me. My stomach clenches.

'The kids are asleep. Well, Harry's on the Xbox, I think, in his room. But Sophie and Finn went down over an hour ago.' He's staring at me. Unblinking.

'Thank you,' I say robotically, moving through the room to the kitchen, the spaces joined together by the dark beamed archway. I stand at the sink, run a glass of cold water. The basin is deep, the gold tap high above it. Modern. Trendy. The kitchen faces the Edwards' house. I wonder if Jack has been watching too.

'Were the children alright?' I ask.

'Fine,' he says, 'Sophie wanted a story, Finn wanted more juice. Harry grunted at me. Nothing too strenuous.'

I can't work out what mood he's in. Words hang between us, all the things we're not saying.

He gestures to me and I wobble towards him, fingers clamped around the water glass. He smiles up at me, puckers his mouth into the kissy shape that used to mean he wanted sex, and I grip the glass even tighter and purse my lips back at him, trying for a moment to recreate the old magic.

Later. I've swept up the broken glass, keeping a sliver wrapped in kitchen paper, up where the matches are kept so the kids don't get hold of it. Just in case. I have these little weapons hidden around the house – break in case of emergency. The knife slipped between the top row of paperbacks in our room, third from the left, next to *Wolf Hall*. The envelope of twenties nestled in with the cookbooks. My escape routes, such as they are. He doesn't know, I don't think.

In bed, we turn towards each other; I've brushed my teeth, he hasn't. I can still taste the slight fug of alcohol on my tongue, feel the beat of my heart in my ears. I picture Rachel and Ian lying in bed next door; I can't imagine they're asleep either. Maybe they're not even in, maybe they're down at the police station already. Perhaps the police are searching the house. I think of them thumbing through Clare's things, their eyes taking in every little detail. I've watched too much CSI.

'How were the PTA girls?' Jack asks, and I half smile in spite of myself. Girls. We're forty-five.

'Lindsay's divorce papers came through,' I tell him, 'Tricia spilled her wine. Sandra says her heart hurts.'

'That's impossible,' he says, and I roll my eyes in the darkness. Always the doctor. 'Why's she getting a divorce?'

I shift onto my back. The white curtain brushes my arm, ghostly in the darkness. We're trying so hard to be normal that it hurts. 'I didn't get to find out.'

I can almost feel the twist of his smirk, although his lips are barely an outline.

'Lucky her.'

There's a pause.

'Jane,' he says then, 'about last night…'

I wait. I suppose I'm waiting for an apology, but this time, one doesn't come.

I wish I could barricade the downy pillows between us, protect myself in my sleep. I want to talk more about Clare but I can't; instead I stare at the wall and think of my children, of their sweet, chubby little faces, their sweeping dark eyelashes, the soft inhale and exhale of their breath in the next room. I think of Harry, his teenage body sprawled out underneath the duvet, the smattering of newly acquired stubble on his jawline. My babies.

I don't fall asleep until Jack does. I'm too frightened.

Chapter Six

DS Madeline Shaw

Tuesday 5th February

Ashdon is a small town, population 3,193. The town sign sits in the centre, opposite the primary and secondary schools and beside the River Bourne. On it are three farmers, a sheep, and a strangely oversized ear of corn. The town has a doctor's surgery, a pub and a church, a newsagent, a ceramics place and a lot of middle-class mums. It is not the kind of town where bad things happen, and the death of Clare Edwards comes as a horrible shock.

Madeline has lived in the town for just over eighteen months. When the DCI formally assigns her to work underneath him on the Clare Edwards case, she is drinking coffee at her desk, black for the calories, and playing back the recording of Nathan Warren's phone call, made to Lorna after he came across Clare's body. She knows about the allegation made against him a few years ago, the report of him following a girl home from school, and has already asked Ben Moore about it. DS Moore had shrugged, waved a hand in the air.

'If you want my honest opinion, it was all nonsense,' he said. 'The people of Ashdon, well, the impression I get is that they don't like anyone who's not like *them*. The woman whose daughter it was never pressed charges; some people said she was making it up because she was pissed off at the school about something. They moved not long after, over to Saffron Walden.'

Madeline had nodded, noted it all down just in case.

'I want you on this, Shaw,' the DCI says now, 'you know the town, you know the people. You've got the edge.' He looks at her, eyes narrowed. 'Don't let me down, Madeline.'

She grits her teeth; not likely. She's spent the night thinking about the look on Rachel's face when they told them the news; the sound of the woman's knees hitting the floor, the way her husband's arms wrapped around her tiny waist. In her experience, the family is never quite as innocent as they look, but these two are doing a good job so far of convincing her otherwise.

'I'm so very sorry for your loss,' she told them both, the words sounding wooden in her mouth. She handed them the list of Clare's personal items, the ones they have had to take in for evidence. Clare's watch, the hair tie from around her wrist, her school things and her purse.

'We are still looking for Clare's phone,' Madeline told the parents. 'We're working on the assumption that whoever attacked Clare took it with them.'

'Can't you trace it?' Rachel asked, her breath ragged, snotty.

'My team are working on that,' the DCI said, 'and we'll be looking at the phone records too – finding out who Clare had been speaking to recently, eliminating people from our enquiries.'

Both of them looked back down at the list.

'And her necklace?' Rachel had asked, touching a hand to

34

her own throat, grasping at her neck as though she'd like to snap it in two. Ian reached up, clasped her hand in his and pulled it gently back towards the table.

The police exchanged glances. 'Necklace?'

'For her sixteenth,' Ian said. 'We gave it to her as a birthday present. It was only two weeks ago, 14th of January. A gold one, a locket with her name on.'

Madeline thought back to the sight of their daughter on the ground, her blonde hair shining in the light of the torch. Feeling for a pulse at Clare's neck. There was no necklace.

'Is there any chance your guys could have missed it?' Ian said, looking between them, colour rising a little in his face.

'No,' Madeline said, 'that's extremely unlikely. Everything that was recovered from the scene is on this list.'

'But we'll double check,' Rob added, just as Rachel began to sob again, the sound echoing around the kitchen.

'She's a good girl,' her stepdad kept saying, over and over again as the police stood to leave, the breakfast things still piled up by the kitchen sink, a stack of Clare's clothing freshly washed on one of the chairs. 'She's a good girl, our Clare.'

'We'll be in touch,' Madeline had said, 'as soon as we can be, Mr and Mrs Edwards. We'll be back first thing tomorrow.'

But she'd checked the list this morning, rang the pathologist to check there was nothing else with the body. No necklace. No phone.

The two of them spend the morning searching the Edwards' house from top to bottom. The parents don't look any better than they did yesterday – there's a bottle of wine by the front door, empty, and another half full on the windowsill.

Someone's already left a bunch of bedraggled-looking flowers on the lawn outside, red roses, no note.

Rob and Madeline go upstairs, leaving Rachel and Ian sitting downstairs with Theresa, the family liaison officer who arrived just as they were leaving last night. She's nice, is Theresa, Madeline likes her. Nice but new, good at making tea. Madeline has told her to let the police know how the Edwards are together, what they say in the privacy of their own home. Theresa looked at Madeline like she'd said something awful.

'You don't suspect them?'

'Theresa,' she'd said, 'in a case like this, we can't rule anyone out.'

Ian Edwards has told them that both he and his wife were home that afternoon, that he'd left work early with the plan of taking Rachel out for dinner. Rachel had confirmed that she'd been back from her job at Saffron Walden Estate Agency by four, following a viewing of a house in Little Chesterford, eight miles west of Ashdon. The couple had met back at home.

'The family who viewed the house weren't interested,' she'd said between sobs. 'They didn't stay long, you can check.'

'We will,' the DCI said, his voice deliberately neutral.

Clare's bedroom is tidy, everything in its place – pale pink duvet, wardrobe full of clothes. Madeline runs her hand through the hangers, her gloved fingers brushing over Clare's dresses and cardis. Her eyes scan the bookshelves, the bedside table with its cluster of hair ties and roll-on deodorant. There's a pile of jewellery, stud earrings and a silver charm bracelet, but no sign of the gold locket necklace. There's a string of photos dangling from the mirror – black and white polaroids of two girls sticking their tongues out. One of them is Clare.

Not recognising the other girl, Madeline gently tugs the strip of photos and holds it in her gloved hand. Two sets of bright eyes stare out at her.

'She was just a child,' Madeline says aloud. The DCI doesn't reply.

'No photos of her father,' Madeline says, gesturing around the room. There are none downstairs either; Mark is absent from the house altogether. Instead, Ian's face beams down at them, his arms around Rachel and Clare. The replacement.

'Odd,' Rob says, 'to have none whatsoever.'

There's nothing in Clare's bedroom to suggest anything untoward, but they photograph the entire room just in case, bundle her still-winking silver laptop into an evidence bag. Back downstairs, Theresa hands out fresh mugs of tea.

Madeline shows the parents the photograph of Clare and the other girl.

'Lauren,' Rachel says immediately, 'she's Clare's best friend.'

Madeline nods. 'Thank you – we'll need to speak to her, to find out if she knew any more about Clare's movements on the fourth. Can I take a last name, please?'

'Oldbury, Lauren Oldbury,' the mother says, her voice cracking a little. Her face is very pale, her lips look almost bloodless.

'Mind if I keep this?' Madeline asks, the photograph of the girls between her fingers. Both parents shake their heads mutely, their eyes fixed on the static face of their daughter.

'Mr and Mrs Edwards,' the DCI says, 'I'm sorry to ask this, but we're going to need you to formally identify Clare's body.' He glances at Madeline. 'One of my officers will accompany you this afternoon.'

Rachel lets out a little moan. Her hair is lank, hanging limply onto her collar; she's wearing the same clothes she was in last night. Ian nods, sets his lips together in a hard, straight line. Ex-army; Lorna's looking into the files. There is something about him that doesn't fit with this house; he is the third wheel, the cuckoo in the nest, the second husband, no matter what story the photos try to tell. Madeline wonders how Clare felt about the marriage. Whether she had much of a choice.

'Thank you,' Ian says, and the DCI nods.

'We'll send a car.'

Madeline clears her throat.

'Mr and Mrs Edwards, as you know, we have reason to believe that your daughter's death was suspicious, and in light of this I have to ask you: do you know anyone, local or otherwise, who might have reason to cause harm to her? Or failing that, to you?'

Rachel's face is anguished; tears begin to slip down her cheeks, sliding into the tracks that are already there, white against her day-old foundation. Madeline watches her. The mother without a child. Bereft.

'No,' she whispers, 'there's no one. She's sixteen, she's my baby, she's never done anything wrong, never—' She breaks off, and Ian puts an arm round her, the gesture protective. The police watch them both, noting the dynamic between them.

'What about you, Mr Edwards?' Madeline asks. 'Is there anything that comes to mind? Anything about her actions in the last few days, any behaviour that was out of the ordinary?'

The glance between them is fast, but the DCI's eyes narrow a little and Madeline tilts her head to one side.

'No,' Ian says, 'no, nothing. She was a good girl, detective. Like I said last night. Everyone liked her.'

They wait a moment, but Rachel continues to cry, and Theresa comes forward, places a box of tissues on the table.

'Alright,' the DCI says, 'thank you both for your time.' They get to their feet, and Madeline feels in her pocket, hands Rachel her card.

'If you think of anything that might help,' she says, 'you call me, anytime. Day or night. This is my direct line.' Rachel's eyes flash up at her, glassy with tears, but she swallows hard and nods. They watch as Ian closes his hand over his wife's, Madeline's card disappearing from sight.

As the police crunch back down their drive, Rob looks at Madeline.

'What d'you think?'

She takes a deep breath. She doesn't know the Edwards well – she tends to keep herself to herself in Ashdon, as much as she can, anyway. Rachel's not part of the mum chums – Jane Goodwin and the like – but Madeline has seen her a few times with Ian, having a Chardonnay in the Rose and Crown pub of a Sunday afternoon. She sells glossy new homes to moderately wealthy clients in Saffron Walden by day, and she was bereaved a few years ago – Mark, lung cancer. They have an old coroner's report on him somewhere. She remarried relatively fast.

'I don't know,' she says at last, 'but I want a background check on them both, and their alibis checked for that afternoon. And I want to talk to Lauren Oldbury. Clare was sixteen – at that age, you tell your friends much more than you tell your parents.'

The DCI glances at his watch. 'Quick sandwich before we talk to Nathan Warren?'

Madeline makes a face. 'Only sandwich you'll get round here is from Walker's corner shop, and trust me, you'd really rather not.'

Nathan Warren sits in interview room three at Chelmsford Station, his hands splayed on the table, his big brown eyes darting around the room like a trapped animal.

Madeline slides into the seat opposite him, hands him a cup of filter coffee and pours them all a glass of water. The DCI winces as Nathan's hand grips the polystyrene cup too hard, splashing liquid onto the grey-coated table.

'Sorry,' he says immediately, stuttering slightly, and Madeline grabs a couple of paper towels from the corner of the room, dabs up the mess.

Nathan Warren has been standing on Ashdon High Street corner nearly every day for the past eighteen months. He's been a part of the town for as long as anyone there can remember – he used to be the school caretaker, and before that he delivered the paper, the *Essex Gazette*, popping it through the inhabitants' letterboxes (usually late, but no one ever complained). Most of the time now, no one knows *what* he does. Madeline has seen him wandering around on the green before, sometimes wearing a hi-vis jacket. There's a traffic cone he moves around, left over from an old accident – the council turned a blind eye to it, figured it gave him something to do. Kept him out of trouble, and the police have never bothered to get involved. Until now, that is.

'Thanks for coming in, Nathan,' Madeline begins, smiling

at him. The nastier women in this town say he's '*simple, not all there,*' but she is reserving judgement until they know the full story. People are capable of one hell of a performance when they want to be.

'I know you already gave a statement to DS Campbell on Monday, Nathan, but we wanted to run through a few things with you, if that's alright.'

He doesn't speak, just stares at them both, one hand anxiously clenching and unclenching.

'Where were you on the afternoon of Monday the 4th of February, Nathan?' the DCI snaps, and Nathan visibly blanches.

'I was at home,' he mutters, 'just at home.'

'Can anyone verify that?'

The police already know that they can't – Nathan lives alone, in the house his mother left him when she died five years ago. As far as they know, he has no other family.

'Nathan,' Madeline says gently, casting a look at Rob, 'it would help us if you could walk us through that afternoon – what you did, up to and after finding Clare Edwards in Sorrow's Meadow.'

He scratches behind one ear, the movement fast, sharp.

'I was home,' he says again, 'and then I went for a walk.'

'And what time was this?'

He looks panicked, and Madeline shifts her wrist slightly, allowing the watch face to point in his direction, wondering if he struggles with the time. The pathologist thinks Clare died some time between 5 and 7 p.m.

'About seven,' he says then, nodding as though pleased that he's remembered, 'after the news finished. I always walk around up there, I like the flowers.'

'There *are* no flowers in February, Mr Warren,' the DCI says, and Madeline presses her lips together, takes a deep breath. She can't shake the feeling that she'd be handling this better on her own.

'Okay Nathan,' she says, 'so you went for a walk. And did you see anyone else while you were walking?'

He shakes his head.

'Just me.'

'And you saw Clare lying on the ground?'

He nods, looks away from them, starts jiggling his left leg underneath the table. He's a big man; his hands are like spades. They know that Clare weighed around eight stone – she'd have gone down like a feather if someone of his size was involved.

'And what did you do when you saw her?'

He looks back at them, and his eyes look sad, huge in his face. His skin is very pale, but his lips are full, like those of a child.

'Told her to wake up,' he mumbles, 'but she wouldn't.'

'And did you touch her?'

'No, no, no,' he says, and he starts shaking his head then, quickly from side to side, too fast.

'There's no need to be upset, Nathan,' Madeline says firmly, 'we're just trying to establish the events in the run-up to Clare's death. You've been very helpful.'

The DCI exhales.

'Are you sure you didn't touch her, Nathan?' he asks, leaning forward slightly in his chair, lacing his hands together on the table. His wedding ring glints in the overhead lights and Madeline feels a bite of dislike. Just because Rob Sturgeon wants this case cut and dried as quickly as possible doesn't mean they can go pinning it on Nathan.

He doesn't answer.

'I'll tell you what I think, shall I Nathan?' the DCI says softly. 'I think you might've followed Clare Edwards when she came out of school. I think you tried to talk to her. I think that when she didn't give you what you wanted, you didn't like it. You pushed her. And then you panicked.' A pause. 'It wouldn't be the first time you'd followed a girl home from school, would it?'

Madeline feels a flash of anger – the DCI has no right to bring up an old, and possibly false, allegation. They need to show Nathan Warren that they're on his side. In her experience, people don't tend to talk much otherwise.

He's shaking his head even faster, putting his hands to his ears as if horrified by what they're suggesting.

'No,' he says, 'no! I didn't touch her, I didn't touch her.' He looks frightened, murmurs something else under his breath.

Madeline leans forward. 'What was that, Nathan?'

'She was pretty,' he says, without looking at them, and Madeline feels a jolt of unease.

The DCI is glowering. 'Yes,' he says, 'she was a pretty girl, wasn't she, Nathan? Did you like that about her?'

Nathan gives a little moan. He glances at Madeline as if for help, and she puts a hand on Rob's arm, wanting him to calm down.

'Is it possible you were in Sorrow's Meadow a bit earlier than you thought, Nathan?' she asks him. 'If you tell us, we'll be able to help you. If you don't, things might get harder.' A pause. He just keeps shaking his head, back and forth like one of those toys people put in the backseat of cars. Madeline resists the sudden urge to reach out, tap him on the top of the

43

head with her pencil to see if his head will bob the other way. They are not getting anywhere today.

'Let's pick this up at another time, sir,' Madeline says quietly.

Rob glares back at her, but she meets his gaze head-on. As they exit the room, she thinks once more of Ian, covering his wife's hand, putting his arm around her waist. People can put on one hell of a performance. It is too soon to know who to trust.

Chapter Seven

Clare

Monday 4th February, 8.00 a.m.

*M*um has made crumpets with butter for breakfast and I eat quickly, eager to get out of the cold house and let the day begin. I know I should tell Ian and Mum that I'll be staying at Lauren's or something tonight, but they'll have a go at me and I just can't face it today. Yesterday's argument was bad enough. I'll text Mum later on, when it's too late for them to stop me.

'Have a good day today, Clare,' Mum says as I eat the last bit of my crumpet and swallow more tea, feeling it burn my tongue because I've drunk it too fast. I nod.

'I've washed your blue coat and your black skirt,' she says, pointing to the pile of washing on one of the kitchen chairs, 'in case you wanted to wear that this week. I know it's your favourite. And I got the stain off the coat.'

'Thanks,' I mutter. I can feel Mum watching me, feel her eyes burning into my face. She probably feels bad for yesterday, but that's tough luck.

'You have a good day too,' I say, a bit reluctantly, and at that moment Ian comes in, whistling in that annoying way he does first thing in the morning, a repetitive, grating tune that now pops into my head at random times throughout the day. His hair is still a bit wet from the shower and little droplets of water glisten in his beard.

'Morning, my two lovely girls!' he says cheerfully, shoving a piece of toast in his mouth and pulling open the fridge. I stiffen, push my chair back and reach for my blue puffer coat from the pile of washing, shrugging it on.

'I've got to get to school.'

Ian pauses at the fridge; I see Mum looking at him, her expression almost pleading. The fridge door swings shut and Ian clears his throat, swallows down a mouthful of peanut butter toast, and looks at me.

'Listen, before you go, Clare – I'm – well, we're sorry for what happened yesterday. Us rowing with you about the exams. Your mum and I talked and, well, we think we've probably been pushing you a bit too hard, love. It's a stressful time, isn't it, and we know you're doing your best.' He stops for a second, then opens his mouth as though about to say something else. I can see peanut butter clinging to his teeth.

'We are sorry, Clare,' Mum chips in, and I stare at them, surprised by this sudden show of togetherness. My tongue still feels weird, like sandpaper where the hot tea has burned it.

'Don't worry about it,' I say at last, wanting the moment to be over. Ian looks visibly relieved, a smile breaking out on his large face.

'That's our girl,' he says, and to my horror he pulls me towards him, gives me an awkward half hug, my face pressing up against his shirt, my gold necklace pushing into the dip in my neck as I'm crushed against him. He smells of Mum's new

46

shower gel that she got for Christmas, and too much Lynx. I want him off me.

'Be good, Clare,' Mum says, and I breathe a sigh of relief when Ian releases me and turns back to the fridge, his already-short attention span reduced even further by the lure of bacon.

Quietly, I let myself out of the front door, take a deep gulp of air. At least they've apologised. Sort of.

I close the garden gate behind me and shove my hands in my pockets, ignoring a WhatsApp from Lauren asking if I've done our English homework. She'll be panicking, she always does, but I'll just let her copy mine. I pull my hat down over my long blonde hair, hoping it won't look too flattened by the time I get there, then set off down Ash Road towards school. It's only a ten-minute walk. I can never decide whether I like the claustrophobia of this town – I've lived here ever since I can remember, since Mum and Dad left London for somewhere smaller, quieter, safer. You'll love it here, Dad said. They certainly got what they wanted – nothing dangerous has ever happened in the history of this place. Other than what went on within the four walls of our house, of course, but no one talks about that. Especially not my mum.

Chapter Eight

Jane

Wednesday 6th February

'Can we have porridge the way Dad makes it next time?' Sophie, my daughter, is pouting, her spoon halfway to her mouth like Goldilocks caught in the act. The bowl I've made her for breakfast is almost untouched – I make it with water, Jack makes it with full-fat milk. You'd think a doctor would know the dangers of cholesterol, but there you go.

'Next time,' I say, using a damp J-cloth to blot the orange juice that Finn has spilled on the table. My eyes prick from tiredness, my mouth feels dry from last night's wine with the PTA girls. I checked my phone every time I woke up in the night, shading it from Jack's eyes, wanting to see if they'd made any arrests for Clare Edwards. The news is sparse, the details vague. I've set an alert for it on my phone, so that if anything new comes in I'll see it straight away. I can't bear the thought of being separated from my children today. Not when this has happened next door. I want to lock the front door, tuck them up in their beds and throw away the key.

I can't stop myself from glancing at the window, at the painted cream walls of the Edwards house. When I had a shower this morning, I wiped the steam from the glass and looked across the gap that separates our houses. Their bedroom curtains were open, but neither of them were in bed. As I watched, I saw Ian enter the room, go over to the wardrobe. I shifted slightly, making sure he couldn't see me. I only had a towel on. Water was dripping down my neck. He bent down, took something out and slipped it into his pocket. Then he left the room. I waited a few seconds, but he didn't come back.

Downstairs, everything is silent. The family liaison officer is still there, or at least her car is. Their kitchen curtains are open too and I notice there are wine bottles on the windowsill. An oddly neat row of them, three empty, one half full. The recycling men come on Wednesdays. Theresa ought to have put them outside, really.

Behind me, I hear my husband coming down the stairs. I turn back to the hob, where the remainder of the porridge is bubbling over, waiting for Harry. He's going to be late for school.

'What's that I hear about the best porridge in the world?' Jack says, entering the room dressed for work: blue shirt, the cufflinks I bought him last Christmas. Little crossed ribbons; the silver glints in the light filtering through the kitchen window. He's doing the false voice he uses for the kids. I look behind him for Harry, but there's no sign of my eldest son.

Jack kisses me on the cheek, takes a sip from the cup of coffee I proffer. The mug says: 'Best hubby in the world.' A cruel joke, courtesy of Hallmark. Sophie is beaming, and I reach out to touch her hair, feel the soft brown curls of it underneath my palm. The curls were a surprise when they came; my own hair hangs straight down my back, or it used to when I was younger. Now it sits on my shoulders, trimmed once a month at Trudie's Salon in the town. The name makes me shudder every time I go in; the epitome of parochial.

The toaster pings and I flip the bread onto a plate for my husband, watch as he spreads it with too much butter. He won't put on weight, he never does.

'What are you up to today?' Jack asks me, pulling a silly face at Finn, and I take a deep breath, steel myself.

'The usual, Jack. You don't need to worry.'

He doesn't reply. We both know that second sentence is a lie. The only person who needs to worry is me, as long as I'm married to him.

'Where's Harry?' I ask, and Jack shrugs.

'Coming down, I guess.'

I go to the foot of the stairs, place my hand on the bannister. 'Harry!' As I stand there I think of how many times I have done this, the familiarity of it. Rachel will never call for Clare again, never feel the frustration that comes with having a teenager in the house, never sigh and look at her watch as the breakfast goes cold.

'Harry!'

'Coming, I'm coming.' I hear him before I see him, and then he is there; my boy, his black hair hanging scruffily down towards his shirt collar, the smell of Lynx Africa emanating towards me. His school bag trails behind him, bumping on each stair until he's in front of me. His skin is pale, his eyes look a little bloodshot.

'Darling,' I say, reaching out before I can stop myself, running my hand along his jaw and straightening his collar, 'how are you feeling today?' I can see the expression hidden beneath his features; I saw the way he used to look at Clare.

He shifts away from me, just a little, the movement as hurtful as it always is. It's not that we don't get along, Harry and I, it's that we've stopped knowing each other, somewhere along the way. But he's my firstborn, my surprise baby, born years before the others, when Jack and I were young.

Tying us together.

'I'm fine,' he mutters, not meeting me eye.

'Breakfast is ready,' I say, for want of anything else, and he finally looks at me, nods.

'Thanks, Mum.' I watch as his school bag drops to the floor and he lopes into the kitchen, hear the squeal of Sophie as she sees him. He's good with her, and with Finn. It's us he's grown distant from, me and Jack.

As he pulls out a chair at the table, I see his eyes flicker to the window, to where the Edwards house stands silently in the cold February light. He stares for one second, two, then his gaze moves away.

After breakfast, Harry leaves, headphones in as always, bag slung across his right shoulder. On the doorstep, I catch him, my hand on the sleeve of his blazer.

'Harry,' I say, 'be careful, won't you?'

My eyes lock onto his. The moment hangs between us, and suddenly I feel foolish. He is seventeen – but then I remind myself that Clare was sixteen, on the cusp of adulthood too. Age isn't always a protection.

'Of course,' he says, 'I'm always careful, Mum.' A half smile, blink and you'd miss it. 'Don't worry.'

He closes the front door behind him and I watch him cross the street through the window, his cheeks immediately beginning to redden in the cold air. The sky is grey, giving nothing away. As I watch, a car pulls up beside him, then swings left, coming to a stop outside next door.

'Mummy!' Finn calls behind me, pulling my attention away, 'I can't find my shoes.'

Ten minutes later, and we are finally ready to go. Sophie and Finn are bundled up like two little snowmen, their reading folders clasped tightly in their hands. Jack is still sitting at the kitchen table; I glance at my watch. He should have left fifteen minutes ago.

'Jack,' I say, 'you'll be late.'

My husband's gaze doesn't move, his eyes focused on the now-congealing bowls of porridge that I've yet to clear up. Sophie is staring at me, confused. Quickly, I pull my face into a smile and blow a kiss at Jack, making a loud smacking sound which makes the children laugh.

'Say bye bye to Daddy!' I say, and we all wave at him, two snowmen and a wife.

Turning away from him, I step outside, a child in each hand, and that's when I see them: the flowers. They're on the ground outside the Edwards house, lining the front of their lawn. Pink flowers, red flowers, yellow flowers, wrapped in cellophane, handwritten notes damp in the morning chill. Overseeing them all is a large teddy bear, grotesque and unseeing. Glassy eyes stare blankly into mine.

Quickly, I pull the children across the road, just as a blue van slows down in front of us and pulls up alongside the car I saw. Both are emblazoned with the words *ITV News*. I swallow. It hasn't taken long.

'Mummy?' Sophie says, catching the expression on my

face, but I quickly bend down and wrap her scarf around her even more tightly, re-do her zipper so that it's right up to the chin, blocking her view of the Edwards' front lawn. Finn isn't concentrating, he's fiddling with something in his pocket. I hurry them down the road towards the school, trying desperately not to look back over my shoulder. Our feet slide a little on the pavements; they should have gritted the roads again, it's cold enough.

For the next ten minutes, I listen to Sophie chatter about her art class, soaking up her innocence, her total oblivious-ness to the fact that a dead teenager has been found not five minutes from where we're standing. She loves art, it's her favourite subject. Like mother, like daughter. On Mondays I wash her uniform in a hot spin; there is always paint on her shirt. I'd complain to the teacher, but I don't want to draw attention to us. Not anymore. I saw the way the headteacher looked at me when I had to cancel the PTA dinner last month; the concern in her eyes, the questions about life at home. I guess walking into a door doesn't quite cut it these days.

'Jane!' Sandra grabs my arm after I've waved goodbye to the children. She's wearing a thick woollen scarf and too much mascara, and her nose is red in the cold. She leans close to me. 'Have you seen the news vans? One drove right past our house this morning. That'll be it now, it'll be everywhere.' She shivers, stamps her feet on the ground in an attempt to warm them up. 'God, imagine, Ashdon on TV. Well, we've all seen the way they cover cases like this, they're like vultures, aren't they?' She eyes me beadily. 'Your house might be on the news too. Or at least in the frame.'

'Sandra,' I say to her, 'don't tell me you're jealous of that.'

She looks admonished. I put a hand on her arm. 'Don't think about it, not for now anyway. News coverage might help the police, help them catch whoever did it.'

'You're right,' she says, her face brightening, 'you're right, Jane. God, I hope they catch him soon. Has your Harry heard anything more? The older ones must be devastated.'

'No,' I say, 'Harry didn't really know Clare very well.' My throat tightens, ever so slightly.

'Book club this week?' Sandra says, changing the subject, and I pause, then nod.

'We ought to keep going, keep a sense of normality,' she says, 'perhaps we could do it at yours? I've almost finished the Zadie Smith.'

Before I can answer, she's waving her gloved fingers at me, then turning to go. I stare after her for a moment, watching her slightly stocky frame make its way across the tarmac, stopping to talk to other mothers on the way. The book club invitation will have made its way through half the town by the time she's finished. Sandra knows everything about everyone, or she thinks she does, anyway.

I move away from the school, tucking the strands of hair that have escaped from my scarf back inside the soft grey material. It's cashmere; Jack bought it for me last Christmas. *For the one I love,* it said on the gift tag. I put the tag in my bedside drawer, along with the dried rose he gave me when we first started dating, and the faded yellow boarding pass from our honeymoon in Thailand. I look at them sometimes, my little mementoes, to remind myself of his love. Sometimes it's hard to remember. I didn't put the hospital tag in there;

I cut it off my wrist the day after the incident on the stairs and buried it in an old handbag, stuffed at the very back of our wardrobe. Some mementoes aren't worth looking at.

I pull out my phone as I walk back down the high street, send Jack a text. *Off to work. See you tonight.* A pause. *Love you.* I keep it on vibrate, in case he replies, but although the little tick tells me he's read it, the phone stays resolutely silent and still.

When I get into work five minutes later, Karen, my boss-stroke-colleague, is on the phone. Her voice is sombre and her face looks serious, but despite that, I feel it – the wash of freedom that comes when I am here, in this light-filled shop, away from my husband, away from the house. We're a tiny little place, selling ceramics and cards mainly; I only took the job part-time because it gave me something to do. I used to work in advertising, back when I lived in London, before the children and Jack, and part of me has always craved that creativity. Sometimes I think of myself, sitting in a London boardroom, MacBook in front of me, and I don't recognise myself at all. They say marriage and kids don't have to change you: whoever said that is a liar. I'd say a broken rib changes a lot of things.

It wasn't always like this in the beginning, Jack and I. When I met him, I was won over. Jack, for me, presented a life I never thought I could have: money, stability, the house and kids, all in one fell swoop. And for a while, it was perfect. Better than perfect. We were obsessed with each other; I was his little project, the girl he took on and made good. And like any good subject, I rose to the challenge. Made myself into the woman he wanted. Before long, you couldn't even see the divide between who I was and who I am now. And if it's up to me, I'll keep it that way. No matter what.

That's all I'm trying to do.

'Morning!' Karen mouths at me, still on the phone, and I wave my fingers at her, unwrap my scarf from around my neck and hang it on the peg. There's a small studio-cum-office at the back where Karen and I work, and everything we make is placed at the front of the shop. Art as therapy; I thought something like this would help me deal with life at home and it does, sometimes. The kettle bubbles happily and I tune the radio as I get my teacup down from the shelf: a painted ceramic mug Sophie and Jack made me for Mother's Day last year. Wobbly hearts adorn the sides and my own heart stretches.

I make coffee. When I first met Jack, he warned me off it, well they all did there, told me about what it does to your heart rate, your nervous system, your cortisone levels. But he breaks his own rules now. I can break them too.

'Sorry about that, Jane,' Karen says when she hangs up the phone. The shop belongs to her, and we rub along together, although I find it hard to get as stressed out about ceramics as she does. Most of our income comes from Jack, these days. Good old Jack, Jack the doctor, Jack the breadwinner. The old rhyme goes through my head, *Jack be nimble, Jack be quick*. There's nothing fairy tale about our marriage. *But it's what I wanted*, I remind myself. *What I still want, even now*.

I settle down next to Karen, power up my computer. The screensaver flickers on: Finn and Sophie on the beach, Harry pulling a silly face behind them; our holiday in Cornwall last year that ended in one of the worst fights Jack and I have ever had. I can't even remember what started it now. In the photo, Sophie has ice cream around her mouth. Bright yellow; quickly, I click onto one of my latest designs, feel a bubble of relief as it replaces the image on the screen.

'No worries,' I say to Karen, taking a sip of caffeine – it's too hot, it burns my tongue. Burning off the wine from last night. I feel it again: the impact of the glass, the hideous sadness when I saw the bruise this morning. Purple, the colour of heather. It'll be green soon.

Karen tuts. 'It was Beth again, calling from school. She didn't want to leave the house this morning – well, who can blame her! After the news. She's in the same year as Clare Edwards. That poor girl. It's just so awful. It feels like the whole town is in shock.' She frowns, rubs a hand across her eyes. I feel a stab of empathy, make a sympathetic noise in my throat. Beth is her daughter at the secondary school, sixteen last week. I helped decorate the birthday cake at work that afternoon, stabbing the little candles into the thick white icing.

'Actually,' I say, 'they live next door to us.'

The reaction is immediate. Karen gasps, her hands flying to her mouth, the silver band on her wedding finger glinting in the light.

'No! Jane! I didn't realise. I'm so sorry. I—'

I wave my hand in the air. 'No,' I say, 'really, it's fine, well, it isn't, but…' I pause. 'Obviously it's horrible, having it happen so close to home.'

Karen shudders; I can actually see the shiver going up her spine, snaking its way through her thin stripy shirt, across her narrow shoulder blades. 'I just can't believe it Jane, next door to you! In our town! Right after Christmas, too, who would

57

do a thing like that? Beth says she was a pretty girl, was she? One of the popular crowd. Well, you can tell that from the photo. I expect it won't be long before it makes the nationals.'

She nods towards the town paper, splayed on the desk. *Schoolgirl found dead in Ashdon field.* Clare Edwards' blonde hair shines like a halo, her white teeth grin out at us, frozen in a smile. My eyes fill, and I look back at my screen.

'It's terrible,' I say, 'it's the very worst thing.'

I buy a paper of my own from Walker's corner shop on the way to get the children from school. I don't know why, but I want to read the details, pore over it all in my own home. I need to be alert, prepared – my children are the most important thing on the planet. I have to keep them safe. My heart thuds as I stare at the headlines – I can't believe it, I can't believe she's dead. One of our own. It fills me with horror. Ruby Walker smiles grimly at me from behind the counter. Leader of the local girl guides, most miserable woman on the planet. I've seen her lips move in prayer before, when she thinks no one's watching.

'Anything else?' she says, her face one of permanent despondency, and I grab two KitKats for Sophie and Finn, a Twix for Harry, and a bottle of wine for us. Jack likes Merlot; I like Sauvignon. The paper folds between my hands, hot with ink.

'Dreadful,' Ruby says, shaking her head at the figure on the front, and I nod, look away from her to the row of bright sweet wrappers. It is dreadful. We all know it is.

'You knew her, didn't you?' she says, staring at me. 'You and your husband. You must have.'

I clear my throat. There's something weird about the way she says 'husband', or am I imagining it? Half the mothers in this town are in love with Jack. I don't want to have to add miserable Ruby to the list. Although I suppose she's not exactly competition.

'Not very well,' I say, 'the Edwards family kept themselves to themselves.' I'm exhausted with saying the same thing.

'How was Ray-of-Ruby?' Jack will say to me later, and I'll smile in spite of myself. It's been our name for her since we moved to the town; in all this time she's been nothing but a misery. Sophie will be going to Brownies soon, but I've told her she's exempt from Guides. Karen says Beth used to hate it – endless knot tying, constant prayers about the end of the world. Some people thrive on disaster. Ruby is loving all of this drama.

At the school gates, I stand with the other mums on the verge of grass between the primary and the secondary. Harry doesn't get out until ten past four, but I pick Finn and Sophie up at three thirty. I love seeing their little faces as they toddle towards me, love the moment I can envelop them in my arms again. Especially now, when tragedy is so close.

Both the schools are Church of England, of course. There's a noticeboard pinned to the gates, and a new poster flaps in the wind. I lean forward, stare at the black font. The priest is doing a special service tomorrow night, in memory of Clare. *Please join us,* it says, *as Ashdon comes together in the face of adversity.* It must be the most excitement Pastor Michael's had for ages.

Normally, the mums and I would grin at each other at a

missive from the church, but today, you can almost sense the nerves, feel the shockwaves radiating around us all. Nothing like this has ever happened before. Not in Ashdon. Not next door. Briefly, I close my eyes, think back to that morning, the very last time I saw Clare. I watched as she left for school, slamming the front door behind her, or did I imagine the slam? Harry wasn't down yet, Finn and Sophie were still brushing their teeth. Clare was early, earlier than normal. Her blonde hair shone in the February sun, the ends catching the light. Jack appeared behind me at the window, and I moved away. I wonder if her stepdad was watching her too. Whether she was aware of how men looked at her. Whether she looked at anyone in the same way.

I crouch down when I see Finn coming towards me, jolting me back to the sharp February afternoon. I open my arms for his warm little body, eager to have him back. He's always at his most loving just after school. A reassuring trait. Sophie bobbles towards us and Sandra appears as if by magic at my side, smiling at me. I've only had a few hours respite. This is how it is in this town. She's gripping her own daughter Natasha tightly by the hand.

'Oof. Think the wine from last night is catching up on me, I feel a bit dreadful now. Thanks for coming though. How was work?' She doesn't pause for breath. 'The girls are best friends this week!' she mutters to me, and I nod in response. Sophie and Natasha have a love–hate relationship, it seems. As much as seven-year-olds can, anyway. I can see Tricia heading this way but I pretend not to notice, in case she remembers my promise to bake for getting-a-divorce-Lindsay. Quickly, I hustle the children towards me, grabbing reading folders and lunch boxes between my fingers. Nobody is sticking around much to talk today, all of us wanting to get home, wrap our children up in cotton wool, protect them from whatever horrible fate met poor Clare.

There's a gaggle of us who usually walk down the main street, but we're the ones who can veer off first. Our house is only ten minutes from the school, set back just slightly from the road, alongside the Edwards'. It's pink in contrast to their cream, your typical cottage pink, with a neat black roundel on the front denoting the name. *Badger Sett*. Horribly, achingly, twee. Sometimes, I wonder what on earth I was thinking coming here. Especially now this has happened. Not that Jack would want to leave; his practice is here. This is, after all, our fresh start.

Finn's little hand is clutched in mine as we trot away from the school. My heart is bumping in my chest, worrying about the pile of flowers and tributes building up on the Edwards' lawn, how I'm going to shield it all from my children. Sandra walks beside us, Sophie and Natasha up ahead. My eyes remain fixed on Sophie's purple backpack as Sandra lowers her voice.

'Have you heard anything more today?' she asks me. 'Tricia was telling me that the police think someone hit her on the back of her head, must have come up to her from behind. Can you imagine?' I shiver, and clutch Finn's hand a little tighter. The buttons on my blouse feel tight around my neck. I always dress conservatively these days. The doctor's wife.

'Have the police been round to yours yet?' Sandra asks. 'They must be going to. I bet they'll ask you all about it. Doesn't your kitchen window look into theirs?'

She knows it does. I almost want to laugh at how transparent she is.

'I've been in the shop,' I say, nodding my head in the direction of it. Everything in this town is so close together; it's a claustrophobic's nightmare.

'Tricia says they're sending DS Shaw round,' Sandra says, 'you know, going door to door. To see if anyone saw anything. And they've questioned Nathan Warren – well you'd have to, wouldn't you? I still think there's something not right about him. I mean, what was he doing, out *walking* at that time?' She sniffs and exhales, her breath misty in the cold air. 'They've already searched the Edwards' house apparently, one of the mums saw them coming out yesterday. Did you? You didn't say.' She goes on without waiting for an answer. 'Imagine someone riffling through all your things like that.' She makes a face. 'I wonder if they found anything. Rachel's so beautiful, of course, but you just never know, do you? I wonder what DS Shaw makes of her. Chalk and cheese, those two.'

DS Madeline Shaw – Ashdon's resident detective. She's lived here for the past couple of years, in a little house just up the hill, past the schools. We don't have much to do with each other – she's not exactly the book club and wine type. How strange it must be for her, having this kind of crime happen right on her doorstep. Or fortuitous, I suppose.

Ahead of me, Sophie's backpack bounces. Her hair glows in the sunlight and I feel a wave of sickness. Sandra must see the look on my face because she sighs, makes a tutting noise. I look down at the floor, my eyes scanning the pavement, the tap, tap, tap of our feet. Sandra's wearing those hideous

Birkenstock boots; I've got my little black ones on, Russell and Bromley, last year.

'I know,' she says, 'the thought of it happening again… of it being one of our girls this time. It doesn't bear thinking about, does it? I can't abide violence.'

The shudder moves up my spine. Yellow flowers glisten behind my eyelids. The memory of the stairs in our old house, the way he pushed me, the pain in my ribs.

'No,' I tell her, 'neither can I.'

Chapter Nine

DS Madeline Shaw

Wednesday 6th February

'Madeline?'

The DCI is in front of her, his eyebrows raised. He's impatient; the story has been picked up by the tabloids, and the calls are beginning to come in thick and fast. Some journalist has dug out an old picture of Clare from her Facebook page: her posing on a beach in Barbados. The inset is Rachel and Ian, him in an England football shirt, grinning at the camera. *The grieving parents?* the caption says. And so it begins, he thinks.

'Have you got the pathology report in yet?'

'Yep. Fast-tracked it,' Madeline says, handing him the email that has just finished printing, 'just in from Christina.'

He scans it, his eyes moving so fast that he could be skim-reading.

'Cause of death identified as internal bleeding on the brain following a wound to the back of the head,' Madeline says, 'just what we thought at the time. Bruising to the shoulders, which makes sense if someone grabbed her. No signs of sexual assault. They've tested.' It was the first thing they'd looked at; without it, one obvious motivation is gone.

The DCI sighs. 'Well, at least that's something. Though

we'd have stood more of a chance of getting the perpetrator's DNA if he'd fiddled with her. No obvious motivation, if you rule out rape.' He runs a hand through his hair, wincing as the phone begins to ring again. This always happens when there is a crime of this nature – people coming forward with false leads, psychics, nutters wanting their five minutes of fame. The media make things worse; he wishes they didn't need them so much.

'We're testing her clothing for DNA; should be in in a few days. The only thing I'm sure of at the moment is that this wasn't an accident.' Madeline stands up, looks over Rob's shoulder and points to the pictures of the body, scanned in by Christina, the pathologist. 'Look at this. Someone had a hold of her – my bet is they slammed her head against the floor, or hit her from behind and then flipped her round onto her front. It wasn't done by an expert.'

'No,' he says, 'not exactly methodical.' The pair of them stare at the photos. There's another bruise too, further down Clare's arm, blossoming purple, edged with green.

'Where does the name come from?' Rob says suddenly, 'Sorrow's Meadow. Unusual.'

Madeline shakes her head. 'No one knows really. Ruby Walker the newsagent always insists it's to do with the river. The sorrow collects in one place and then the water flows it away, some rubbish like that.'

Rob grunts, stares back down at Clare's bruises. 'Right. And where are we with the door to doors? The neighbours?'

'I'm about to get going now with Lorna.'

'Make sure you speak to everyone,' he tells her, 'anyone who saw anything that night at all. Unusual cars, out-of-towners, anyone else out "walking".' He snorts derisively as he says this, still annoyed that he can't get more out of Nathan Warren. 'And Madeline,' he says, 'find out what people think of the parents.'

'Their alibis checked out to a point, sir,' she tells him. 'We've CCTV of Ian leaving Liverpool Street Station on the early train, and arriving into Audley End a little later, but we don't have anything placing him back home. In Rachel's case, the estate agency confirmed her viewing in Little Chesterford, but again, no way of telling exactly what she did afterwards.'

'So there's a pocket of time?' the DCI asks, frowning at her.

'Well, technically,' Madeline says, nodding. 'The time during which they say they were waiting for Clare to come home, leading into the time when Ian was supposedly out looking for her.' She shrugs. 'We've no reason to suspect that that's not true, though, have we?'

Rob is still staring at the photographs of Clare, his face unreadable. 'Get a sense from the neighbours anyway,' he says. 'Find out what they – Rachel and Ian – are really like. Little town like this, people might talk.'

DS Lorna Campbell keeps up a steady stream of chatter as she and Madeline drive towards Ashdon, telling Madeline about how she's just moved in with her boyfriend, how he worries about her working in the police.

'He thinks I'll get shot or something,' she tells her, laughing nervously. She can only be in her late twenties, must be at least ten years younger than her superior. She's got a slight overbite and the movement is awkward, unattractive.

'You won't get shot in Ashdon,' Madeline says to Lorna,

trying to reassure her, but then again none of them ever thought they'd find a dead body in Ashdon either, did they? They cannot be sure of anything at this stage. The DCI's words ring in her head as they drive. *So there's a pocket of time*, she thinks.

Chapter Ten

Jane

Wednesday 6th February

We're having dinner all together tonight – I've just set the table when Jack walks in, shrugging off his jacket, earlier than expected. Our eyes lock for a second and I know he's heard the news about the door to door enquiries, probably ten different versions from every patient he's seen today. The doctor's surgery is a great place for gossip; there's nothing people love more than offloading their woes in a quiet little room. I've been a tiny bit tense all evening, waiting to see if they knock on our door. I've got long sleeves on, just in case, although I know that's not what Madeline Shaw will be looking for. Domestics don't seem to concern the constabulary these days. If they ever really did.

Finn wraps his arms around Jack's leg, hangs there like a small monkey, his feet suspended just above our shiny dining-room floor. His socks don't match: tiny elephants wave at red and blue stripes. Harry emerges as I'm plating up, blinking as though he's just made his way from a dark cave, which judging by the state of his bedroom last time I popped my head in, he probably has.

'How was your day, darling?' I ask Jack, keeping my

voice light with an edge of warning: *yes, I've heard too, don't bring anything up right now.* We're trying not to talk about Clare Edwards in front of Sophie and Finn. They know now, of course – the school told them all this morning, the kiddie version, one classroom at a time, but they don't really understand. We all got a text message about it; the new way of communicating with parents, or so it seems. *Your child's well-being is of the utmost importance to us,* it said. Well that's good to know, I thought.

Sophie is mainly sad about the buttercup field, as she calls Sorrow's Meadow – we used to go there a lot on Saturdays, especially when she was younger. She liked to test us all, hold the flowers underneath our chins, reveal our culinary appetites. I've got a photograph of her with a buttercup crown twisted into her hair, smiling up at the camera – it used to be on the mantelpiece but I took it down before I went to bed last night. She looked too vulnerable, it made my head spin. Clare was someone's daughter too. Well, she was Rachel's. Beautiful Rachel Edwards. Perfect Rachel who thinks too highly of herself to ever attend our book clubs or wine evenings. The thought pops into my head before I can stop it, and I chastise myself. That happens sometimes.

'It was fine,' Jack says, going to the fridge. His eyes flick to the window, but the Edwards' curtains are closed tonight, the wine bottles hidden from view. I watch as he takes a brown bottle of beer from the side door, flicks off the top. It skitters across the work surface and I close my fingers around it before he can.

'Can I have—' Harry says, and I shake my head before he can finish the sentence.

'Not tonight, Harry,' I say, 'it's a school night.' We – or rather Jack – lets him have a beer sometimes, on special occasions only. I'm keen to keep it that way.

'How many people did you make better today, Daddy?' Finn asks, back in his seat at the table, head tilted back, trying to balance his dessert spoon on his nose. He fails; it clatters onto the table, clanging against his plate. Harry rolls his eyes.

Jack laughs, but it's mechanical, practised; it's not the warm chuckle he had when we met. It makes my stomach churn. 'Ooh, about five today. Careful with that spoon, buddy. You don't want to end up with bogeys in your pudding, do you?' He sniffs the air. 'Smells like Mummy's made apple pie.'

Of course I've made apple pie: it's Wednesday. God forbid I went off-piste.

Jack smiles at me. I smile back.

Sophie slides into the room, her socked feet skidding on the wooden floor. White with frills, matching. At least something's gone right. Her hands grab my waist and I lay my palm on her curly head.

'Careful, missy. We don't want any accidents. Have you washed your hands for dinner?'

Jack is religious about hygiene – we wash hands before and after eating, anti-bacterial gels dot the house. I flout the rules occasionally, but he's right about the children.

Sophie runs her hands under the tap as I finish serving up our meal – shepherd's pie with a side of green beans. Finn makes a face. Jack swigs his beer. The bottle's half empty already; I catch Harry eyeing it longingly.

'Beans are good for you,' Jack says, pre-empting Finn's complaint, and I breathe a sigh of relief. I am too tired to take this one on today. I need to save my energy for later, for when the children have gone to bed.

I want to ask Harry what they've said at the secondary school, how they're dealing with Clare's death, how *he* is dealing with it, but he's eating his dinner in near silence, one eye on his phone which sits on the table alongside us all.

'Shall I set a place for your iPhone next time?' I ask him when it vibrates yet again, the words coming out more snappily than I meant them. Jack frowns but Harry barely reacts, and somehow, it's worse than a retort. Since when have I become invisible?

'Harry,' Jack says, and finally our son looks up. 'Do as your mother says – no phones at the table please, mate.'

He slips it into the pocket of his trousers, but not before I see another eye roll. I feel a little bubble of frustration, then remember that Rachel Edwards will never see her daughter roll her eyes at her again. The thought silences me, and for a moment I lose myself, thinking of next door.

The food tastes funny in my mouth; no matter how hard I try, I'm not a good cook. Forks scrape rhythmically across the plates, white china from our wedding. I don't believe in saving things for special occasions, everything gets lumped in together in this house. Besides, I'm not sure our wedding is really something to celebrate any more. It doesn't feel much like it to me.

'Jane?' Jack is looking at me strangely, his eyes narrowed. 'Did you hear what Sophie said?'

'Hmm?'

Looking across at my daughter, I see her blue eyes are milky with tears. My heart drops.

'What's the matter, darling?'

Sophie whispers something, so soft that I can't hear it. Her head is bowed now, the ends of her curls dangerously close to the whipped peaks of mashed potato. I frown.

'Sophie?'

'A boy at school said there's a monster in the buttercup field,' she says, louder this time. Her little voice breaks, turns into a sob. 'He said he's been let out and he's coming back to get me.'

It's at that moment that the doorbell rings.

Jack and I go together, a united front, leaving Harry to put the television on for Sophie and Finn. I gesture to him to go into the back lounge, away from the front door. My heart's racing; I didn't even hear the car pull up.

DS Madeline Shaw has dark blonde hair that looks like it might grey soon, and lines on her face that suggest she doesn't bother with the rituals I subject my own skin to every night. Cleanse, tone, moisturise. *Repeat ad infinitum, Mrs Goodwin.* There's a younger woman with her, someone I've never seen before.

'Mr and Mrs Goodwin,' Madeline says, 'sorry to disturb your evening. This is DS Lorna Campbell from Chelmsford Police.' She gestures to her colleague and I extend my hand, careful to keep my arms covered. The latest bruises aren't a pretty sight. I can see Jack watching me, and I want to scream at him that the police have got bigger things to worry about than a less-than-perfect couple. They've got a dead girl, and that trumps us, doesn't it?

'I expect you've heard the news, Jane,' Madeline says, and I nod, bite my lip.

'Can I offer you some tea, officers? Would you like to come in?' I ask, but Madeline shakes her head, her ponytail flicking from side to side.

'We just need to check a couple of things with you both, please,' the other woman says, and Jack turns to her, all smiles, his handsome face shining in the half light spilling from our house. If I look right I can see the pile of flowers and teddies outside the Edwards' – it's doubled in size. Rachel and Ian have left it all in the cold. I wonder if it'll rain. There are more cars on the road now, their headlights highlighting the pavement; I can't see whether there are figures inside. Suddenly, I'm overcome by the desire to shut the front door, drag the curtains across the windows, hide us all away from the glare of the events unfolding next door.

'Of course,' Jack says to the policewoman, 'anything you need. Jane and I were so devastated to hear the news. I think the whole town is still in shock. We've been looking out for Rachel and Ian, of course, but – well, we didn't want to pry.'

If they've clocked how good-looking my husband is, neither of them show it yet.

'Did either of you see anything or anyone out of the ordinary on the night of Monday the 4th?' Madeline asks, her face serious. I wonder whether this is her first really big case here, whether she's out to prove herself. God knows she doesn't seem to have much of a personal life, from what I can gather. No kids. No partner. Maybe this is her chance to shine.

I shake my head, thinking back to that night, pushing away the more painful parts, Jack's words. The way he looked at me, the disgust. *He didn't really mean it.*

'I didn't, I'm afraid. My friend Sandra did the school run,

73

took the kids to hers for an hour or two while I made dinner. Jack got home from the surgery just after five. I went to get Sophie and Finn. Then we were here all night.' *Arguing*.

'I'm a doctor,' Jack interjects, mainly for Lorna's benefit I think, but to her credit, her face doesn't change at all. Most women go weak at the knees for a handsome doctor. I should know – I was one of them.

'And your eldest son, Mrs Goodwin?' Madeline asks, her face turned towards me. 'Was he in all night with you both too?'

She's smiling at me, her face open, calm. She may as well have *You can trust me* tattooed on her forehead.

'Yes,' I say quickly, 'Harry was upstairs. He went out with some friends from the football team after school, but he was back early on.' The image comes to my mind: a flash of blonde hair, my son's eyes watching her from the window. I'm talking too fast.

The policewoman nods, makes a note in her pad. I don't look at Jack.

'And did you see Clare that day, Mr and Mrs Goodwin? Monday morning, around 8 a.m.? Her parents say she left for school after breakfast.'

'I think I saw her leave at the usual time,' I say slowly, 'but she was in a hurry, going to school I suppose, like you say. I was busy with the children's breakfast. You know how it is.' Madeline nods at me and I look away; she obviously doesn't. I see again the swing of Clare's black rucksack as she walked down the front path, not knowing it would be the last time she ever would.

The younger woman is nodding along. I wonder how she

sees me. A boring mother? A rich wife? Do I have the life she wants to emulate?

'No unusual cars round here? No one hanging around the school that morning? You're usually there, aren't you Jane?' Madeline asks, smiling at me. I try to think, although I know Sophie and Finn will be wanting a bedtime story round about now; I can almost feel their pull dragging me back inside the house. Jack's presence beside me hums.

'I didn't see anyone,' I say. 'My eldest son took the little ones to school that day, as a favour to me. I'm sorry. I'm so sorry for her poor parents.'

'Do you know them well?' Madeline asks, focusing her gaze on me. 'Ian and Rachel, I mean. Would you say you were friends?'

I shake my head. 'I wouldn't say we were close,' I say, 'I mean—' I pause, glance next door. 'I would have liked to be,' I say at last, 'but it never really happened.'

Beside me, Jack nods. 'My wife's pretty involved with the town,' he says, with a little laugh. 'PTA, book club, you name it. But some people don't join in in quite the same way, I suppose.' He looks down at me and I smile at him as he puts an arm around my waist.

The younger detective, Lorna, makes a note on her pad.

'And did either of you see Mr or Mrs Edwards that afternoon?'

I frown, Jack's arm still tight around me.

'I didn't notice,' I admit. 'I wouldn't normally pay attention – like I said, we weren't close or anything. Their cars came and went all the time, and their garage is around the other side – well, you'll have seen.'

Lorna nods. 'Thank you, Jane. And don't worry. We knew it was a long shot, coming down this end of the town, but we wanted to make sure we covered all bases, spoke to all the neighbours. We're hoping someone a bit closer to Sorrow's Meadow saw something.'

'Don't you live up near there?' Jack asks Madeline, and she nods, the ponytail bobbing again. Her face is pale, tired-looking. I wonder who looks after her, if anyone does. I want to ask her if they've got any leads, but I don't want to sound hysterical. I don't want Jack to laugh at me when we get behind closed doors.

'Yep. First major crime I've ever had on my doorstep. And yours, too.' She smiles grimly.

'We had word just now from your receptionist, Dr Goodwin,' Lorna says, clearing her throat before looking down at a notepad in her hand. 'Danielle Andrews. Saying she thinks she might've seen Nathan Warren that night, on her way home from work. He was the one who reported the body.' She pauses. 'Did you leave at a similar time? The meadow's not far from the surgery, is it?'

There's a split second; perhaps only I can feel it. 'No,' Jack says then, 'I was a bit earlier, I'm afraid. Danni tends to stay late, we've a bit of a backlog at the moment with the records.' He shakes his head, looks down. 'She's a star for doing so. But I didn't see anyone on my way home.'

Madeline nods. 'OK. Worth a shot. Thanks for your time, both of you,' she says, and Jack reaches out, shakes both their hands again.

'Thank you,' he says. 'We hope you bring whoever did this to justice.'

The words are formal, they stick in my mind. Justice. Justice for Clare. What does that word mean? I don't think Jack even knows.

'If you think of anything relevant,' Madeline says, reaching into her jacket pocket, 'will you give me a call?'

I take the card from her. 'Of course.'

Back inside the house, we don't speak, except to the children. Sophie is still at the table, little tears rolling down her cheeks, and I feel awful for leaving her like that. Finn has scampered off to the living room with Harry and I hear Jack coaxing him away from the television, the sounds of CBBC echoing through the wall.

After I've calmed Sophie down and taken her upstairs, I sit by her bedside for a bit. The light has fallen outside and the familiar room is shrouded in darkness, save the little white rabbit nightlight plugged into the wall. She won't sleep without it on, these days. I look out onto the quiet road, thinking of Madeline Shaw's questions. Thinking about Clare and her family.

Carefully, I stand and draw the curtains across, the coloured balloon pattern Sophie chose herself covering up the dark sky. Sitting back down on the soft chair beside the bed, I stroke her hair, wind a curl around my finger, careful not to tug. Finn is sleeping now in the next room; we moved them into separate bedrooms when he started school. I miss the days when they shared, when I could listen to them both breathing at once, make sure they were both safe. There are no guarantees. I know that now.

I don't know what Sophie's heard at school, what's really being said about Clare's death. They've released hardly any details, save for the fact that Clare was found dead in the wooded area of Sorrow's Meadow by Nathan Warren on Monday night, and that anyone who saw anything is asked to please come forward. I think back to that evening, sitting on the sofa with Jack, the whiskey bottle on the floor beside us. I wonder if anyone *did* see anything, if the police will act quickly. I hope so, for all our sakes. I can't stop picturing that smile of hers in the paper; so confident that she'd live for ever. So horribly, heartbreakingly wrong.

Sophie stirs slightly in her sleep; I watch her little chest rise and fall in her bright pink pyjamas. As I watch her, I feel a shadow fall behind me and turn to find Harry framed in the doorway of the bedroom, tall against the yellow of the hallway light. Startled, I get to my feet, pressing one finger to my lips.

We step out into the corridor and I pull Sophie's bedroom door gently shut behind me.

'Are you alright?' I say to my son, placing one hand on his arm. He's still wearing his school shirt, there's an ink stain on the hem.

'Mum,' he says, and his voice is different to the teenage grunts we've become accustomed to; it's softer somehow, more childlike, more like the Harry of old, before hormones hit.

I stare at him. 'What is it?'

He's holding something in his hand, a piece of paper, crumpled slightly as if it's been in his jacket pocket.

I hold out my palm, and he hesitates.

'I found it,' he says, 'yesterday morning. I was looking for Dad's headphones, mine broke, and it was on his desk in the study.'

My heart is beating a little too fast as I stare at the piece of paper. I can tell Harry is worried, is trying not to be; his face at seventeen is the same as it was at seven: the tell-tale pull of his lips to the left, the wrinkling of the nose to dissipate anxiety.

Unfolding the paper, I recognise it immediately – it's Jack's schedule for the surgery. His secretary Danielle sends them every night, and he prints them in his study. I used to laugh at him for it, tell him he was old-fashioned, a dinosaur, that most people would just look at their phone. *What can I say,* he always said, *I'm a paper kind of guy. All those years in medical school poring over books. It makes me feel more organised.*

The chart is as it always is, a list of names and times, ten-minute slots, half an hour for lunch. No rest for the NHS, Jack always says. I run my eyes down the list. Dongal, R. Andrews, C. Wilcox, S. And then I see it. Edwards, C. 4.30 p.m. My heart clenches as I see her name.

'Look at the date,' Harry says, and then he reaches out, touches the paper, the right-hand corner denoting the figures. February 4th 2018.

'It's not long before she was found,' Harry says, 'is it, Mum? Why hasn't he told us?'

I stare at my son, the paper hot in my hands. The blood is thrumming a little in my ears, and I take a small step towards my son, praying that my husband doesn't walk in at any point. I can see how much he wants my reassurance.

'Oh, darling,' I say, smiling at him, trying to think fast, 'how unfortunate – I'm sorry you found this.' I pause, my mind racing as I think what to say. 'You know he can't tell us his appointments, though, don't you? He never does. Patient confidentiality is important.'

'But,' Harry says, and I can see his mind working, my clever son, 'wouldn't that have made him one of the last people to see her? Alive, I mean?'

Our voices are low, but I can hear the sound of Jack downstairs, the tread of his footsteps, the opening and closing of the kitchen cupboards.

'Harry,' I say, 'please, this is nothing to worry about. The police already know.' I glance at my watch. 'It's late already, you should go to bed. We can talk more in the morning, if you like.'

He looks unhappy, his teenage features twisting uncomfortably, caught between the lure of the Xbox in his room which he must know I won't tell him off for tonight, and the unease of what he's found, the piece of paper not quite linking his dad to a dead girl just hours before her death.

I smile at him again, touch my hand to his hair. It feels greasy, unwashed. I make a mental note to buy him more shampoo, not that he will notice.

'Goodnight, Harry,' I say, and then I lean forward and kiss his cheek, my cool lips grazing the teenage stubble on his jaw. 'Forget about this – I promise it's nothing to worry about.'

He retreats, and I see some of the tension slip from his face the burden is passed from him to me, the slip of paper nestling between my fingers now. His bedroom door closes and I hear the electronic noise that denotes the start of another video game; for once, I will let it go. Out on the landing, I take deep breaths, my back pressed against the white wall. *Edwards, C.* I open the page once more, just to check, but the words are there in black and white, the NHS logo emblazoned across the top. I think of Madeline Shaw on my doorstep, the pile of disintegrating flowers on the garden next door. Why didn't my husband mention it to the police? A bite of panic pushes its way up my throat but I force myself to count to ten, inhaling through my mouth, breathing out through my nose. *It must have slipped his mind*, I tell myself.

Carefully, I fold the piece of paper in half, slip it into my back pocket.

Downstairs, I hear the sound of the fridge door shutting, the hiss and flick of another beer. I stand in the half light of the corridor for another few seconds, listening to the sounds of our house around me, the life I've worked so hard to create, then I turn to go downstairs to my husband. My heartbeat quickens with every step. My rib, though outwardly healed now, still twinges with pain. I think of the way Clare looked at our house that last morning, of the way Jack paused before answering the police. Before my mind can go there, I push the thoughts away, to the back of my brain, where I store the things I'd rather not think about. I know my husband. I know what he's capable of.

Don't I?

Chapter Eleven

DS Madeline Shaw

Thursday 7th February

'What kind of picture did you get of the parents?' Rob asks Madeline. It is early, the sky almost dark. He hates the winter months, the lack of daylight hours. Makes cases like this so much harder; people don't see things as much in the dark. They go home, tuck themselves away. Especially in towns like this.

Madeline hands him a coffee, cupping her own. 'Not much of one,' she admits, 'the neighbours sort of implied that they never made an effort, were a bit unfriendly almost.' She sighs. 'Then again, Jane Goodwin isn't everyone's cup of tea. One of those overachieving types; you can't blame Rachel for not being a fully-paid up member of the fan club.'

'Any signs of friction between them and Clare?'

She runs a hand down her notes. 'Hmm. The Bakers on Church Street said they'd seen Ian arguing with her once, outside the pub one night. Late home or something; he had to come out to get her. One of the women in the Close said she knew Rachel, apparently she implied once that the remarriage was a bit tricky, that Ian was hard on her daughter. I guess it's difficult, taking on someone else's child like that. Specially at that age.'

He nods, thinking. 'Not enough to commit murder, though, is it? Unless it was accidental. Lost his temper.' He pauses. 'He's an engineer, right? Got his own business in London.'

'Right,' she says, 'in the city.'

The DCI whistles. 'Must make a packet to afford a house like that too.'

'I'm going to the school this morning,' Madeline says, 'to speak to Lauren Oldbury, and anyone else the school thinks Clare was close to. She's more likely to have talked to people her own age about any problems at home.'

Clare's school locker – 46B – is full to the brim. Madeline snaps on a pair of white gloves, Lorna at her side, and the pair of them begin sifting through her pens and pencils, her gym kit that is slowly growing stale, her painstakingly inked English books. She had tons of gel pens, all the colours of the rainbow. Madeline puts one to her nose and sniffs it. Raspberry.

'Anything?' Lorna asks, and she shakes her head. There's an iPhone charger, curled like a snake under the gym bag, but no phone. It still hasn't surfaced, even though Ben Moore and one of the new recruits are combing the area for it, searching through the bins. Not that they were really expecting to find it here in her locker – most teenagers are glued to them. She'd have had it with her.

There's nothing else in the locker to suggest anything untoward – they find a long, blonde hair caught in the zip of her pencil case but the station have already got a DNA sample from her toothbrush, which Madeline quietly lifted from the Edwards' bathroom on Monday evening. Pink, well used.

'The students will be out of registration in two mins.'

Andrea Marsons, the headteacher, appears at Madeline's side and she turns to her with a smile.

'No problem. We'll get out of your hair. If I could just get that list?'

The teacher hands her a piece of paper. 'This is – was – the girl we think Clare was closest to. Her best friend – the two of them were always together, thick as thieves.'

Madeline looks down at the name on the slip of paper. Lauren Oldbury, Form 10B. She thinks of the smiling polaroids in Clare's bedroom, the pair of them with their arms around each other. Those faces are now smiling out of an evidence bag at the police station.

'That's it? No one else?'

The headteacher shrugs, nods. 'She was well liked, but she didn't have many close friends. Shyer than she looked, we always thought.'

'Any boys?' Lorna says, and Andrea gives a rueful smile.

'You've seen the photo, detective. All the boys had a bit of a soft spot for Clare.'

'But no one in particular?'

She shakes her head. 'Well, not that we saw. But Mrs Garrett was Clare's form tutor, she may know more.'

'We'll need to speak with her too, if that's okay.'

'Of course.' There's a pause. Madeline waits for a beat, then loses patience.

'Now, Mrs Marsons.'

She blushes a little and apologises, flustered suddenly, then leads the officers down the corridor towards the staff room, where Mrs Garrett is sitting in a pink armchair, clutching a cup of tea in a mug with the town crest on it. Madeline clocks the furnishings, the sense of class that pervades the whole place. Ashdon is a nice school – well run, affluent. But they're all out of their depth now.

'Emma? The police are here to see you.'

She jumps, her tea spilling slightly over onto the knuckles of her hand.

'Sorry to disturb you, Mrs Garrett,' Madeline says, nodding to the headteacher, who disappears back out into the corridor. The atmosphere in the staff room feels strange, dampened, as though a cloud of sadness hangs over the school.

'We gather you were Clare Edwards' form tutor?'

Emma Garrett is quite pretty; young, with a neat dark bob of hair, red polish on her fingernails. Lorna smiles at her and sits down.

'That's right, and I taught her Maths,' Emma says, setting down her mug of tea and clasping her hands together worriedly. 'It's such a terrible thing, I can't get my head around it. I haven't slept for days.'

'Our condolences,' Lorna says, 'it must all be a horrible shock.'

'I only started in September,' Emma says, pulling at the skin around one of her bright red fingernails, and Madeline feels a wave of sympathy for her. What a bloody start to her teaching career.

'Mrs Garrett,' she says, 'we're trying to put together a picture of Clare Edwards – who she was, who she spent time with, what kind of mood she was in over the last few weeks. Is there anything you can tell us?'

Emma picks up her tea again, takes a small, delicate sip. Her hands are shaking as she puts it back down.

'She was a lovely girl,' she says at last, and it is clear in her voice that she means it. 'Really kind-hearted, a good pupil, excellent at English. Everybody liked her – the boys used to stare at all that long blonde hair.' She half laughs, then stops abruptly. 'I can't imagine why anyone would want to hurt her, really I can't. It doesn't make sense.'

'Did she seem different at all in the last week or two?' Lorna interjects, and Emma thinks for a moment.

'If anything, I'd say she maybe seemed happier,' she says, narrowing her eyes as if casting her mind back. 'She was on her phone a lot, that was something – it went off in registration a couple of times and I had to remind her of the school's policy on mobiles. I wondered if she might be seeing someone, actually, but she never showed any interest in the boys in my class. Not that I could tell. Occasionally you do notice it – people partnering up, flirty glances, you know, but there was none of that with Clare. She spent most of her time with Lauren; she's in 10B.'

'Yes – we know. We'll be speaking to her too,' Madeline says, making a note on her pad.

'Did Clare ever mention her parents?' Lorna asks, leaning forward a little towards Emma. Madeline watches the teacher's face closely, but Emma shakes her head.

'Not really. You know her dad died? About three or four years ago, I think it was – it was before I qualified. She lived with her mum and stepdad, but she never mentioned them much. They tend not to, at this age. Too fussed with boys and booze.'

'Did she drink, do you think?' Madeline asks, and Emma looks taken aback.

'Oh – well, sorry, that was just an expression, really – I never *saw* her drinking. I mean, I'm sure they do, out of hours, but that's not really any of my concern. I'm sure she and Lauren occasionally…' Her voice tails off and her face looks momentarily panicked, as though the police are about to haul her down to the station for lack of care of her students.

'And you – did you get to know Ian and Rachel much? At parents' evenings, something like that?'

She makes a face. 'A little – as I say, I'm new here. Rachel was always nice, very polite, quite quiet, I suppose. We only ever had good news for them – Clare worked hard, like I said. I always thought—' She stops speaking, bites her lip.

'Go on,' Madeline prompts, shifting forward in her chair.

'Well, I always thought Ian was hard on her – you know, he went on about exams a lot, her grades. She was never failing but you'd think she was from the way he spoke. I guess he just wanted the best for her, but it felt a bit harsh sometimes.'

'Do you think it upset her?' Lorna asks, and Emma pulls a face.

'I don't know – maybe. She always seemed happier when he wasn't there, when it was just her and her mum.'

'Okay,' Madeline says, 'thank you, Mrs Garrett. You've been very helpful. There's just one last thing – could I trouble you to fetch Lauren Oldbury?'

She hesitates, still looking worried. 'I'm not sure if— her parents might—'

'Of course,' Madeline interrupts smoothly, 'if she'd like a parent here, we can wait. But we're assuming a member of staff will sit in with us too – yourself or Mrs Marsons, perhaps? We'd like to keep this as discreet as possible, avoid too much fuss.' She lowers her voice a little. 'The school is under enough pressure already, I imagine?'

'I'll get her now,' Emma says, rising hurriedly to her feet, 'and I can sit in with you, no problem. I'll pop a sign on the door, make sure none of the other teachers come in for a bit.'

While she's gone, Lorna helps herself to a chocolate hobnob from the little side table in the staff room.

'Coffee?' she asks, jerking a head at the kettle on the side, but Madeline shakes her head.

Lauren Oldbury is more adult in person than she looked in the photographs. She is taller than Clare was, harsher looking somehow. Her eyes are slightly bloodshot, rimmed with dark kohl, as if the girl has been crying but wants to cover it up. Her wrists glitter with expensive bracelets – Madeline spots a Pandora, a Links of London. In her ears are little silver studs that glint in the staffroom lights.

'Sorry to drag you from lessons,' Lorna tells her. 'I'm Detective Campbell and this is DS Shaw. We want to ask you a few quick questions about your friend Clare.'

She looks like she's chewing gum; Emma gives her a look but they're not here to admonish her for that – they're here to find out what she knows about Clare Edwards.

'You were close to Clare?' Madeline begins, and Lauren nods quickly.

'Very.'

'Did you notice anything different about her recently, anything at all? We understand she was a popular, well-liked pupil – had it always been that way?'

Lauren nods again, chewing her gum a little faster. Her school blouse is unbuttoned too low; Madeline can see a hint of purple lace bra, no doubt for someone else's benefit but inappropriate all the same.

'She was always a bit of a queen bee, I suppose,' she says, not quite meeting either of their eyes. There is none of the sadness that radiated from Clare's parents – this girl seems almost defiant, sure of herself. Comfortable putting her friend into the past tense.

'Was Clare seeing anyone, Lauren? Did she have a boyfriend?' Lorna asks, and Lauren half laughs, shrugs.

'I mean, not that I know of. Everyone fancied her. But she was never interested, she was silly – always saying they were just kids, immature, you know.' She shrugs again. 'I thought it was a bit weird, to be honest. Harry Goodwin was always keen, but she didn't show much of an interest.'

Lorna makes a note at this, and Madeline's ears prick up. Harry Goodwin. Neither of his parents had mentioned that. A blush stains Lauren's chest, begins to spread up towards her cheeks.

'I kind of thought she could be seeing someone older,' she says suddenly, fiddling with the bracelet on her wrist. Madeline catches a glimpse of a silver charm, half of a heart. Best friends for ever. She pictures the other half on Clare's dressing table, unworn.

'What makes you think that?' Lorna asks.

Lauren crosses and uncrosses her legs. 'Dunno, she was just a bit of a dark horse. I never understood why she didn't go for Harry. I mean,' she shrugs, 'he's pretty hot.'

'Did you notice her being on the phone a lot, the day she was killed?' Madeline asks, and Lauren looks nonplussed.

'We're always on our phones,' she says, and sure enough,

her own silvery iPhone is winking at them all, tucked beside her thigh on Emma Garrett's vacated armchair.

'Did she talk about her life at home with you?' Lorna says, trying a different tactic, and at this Lauren stiffens slightly, her spine upright on the squishy chair.

'Dunno. A bit. Her stepdad pissed her off. But, like, I'm not saying he did it.'

'No,' Madeline says, 'don't worry. Everything you tell us is confidential at this stage.' They wait for a beat, two. 'What do you mean, he pissed her off?'

She shrugs. 'Usual stuff really. Went on at her about exams. They both did. Her mum's a bit weird, always was. Even when her dad was alive. 'Specially then, actually.'

'Weird in what way?'

'I dunno. Control freak, maybe. Wanted to know where Clare was all the time. Treated her like she was a baby, you know?' She gives a little snort. 'And she was always so dolled up. Almost like she and Clare were in competition.'

It doesn't really match up with their initial impression of Rachel Edwards, but then, maybe they're wrong. *People are capable of one hell of a performance.*

'And that bothered her? The controlling stuff?'

'Well, course. It'd bother me. My own mum's not much better.'

Somewhere in the school, a bell rings, loud and shrill.

'I really don't think Lauren should be kept too much longer, detectives,' Emma Garrett says, glancing anxiously at the staff room door. Madeline nods, smiles at Lauren, and they get to their feet.

'Of course,' Madeline says, 'we won't take up any more

of your time. If you think of anything else, Lauren, anything that might be useful, it's really important that you tell us. Even if you think Clare may not have wanted you to.' She puts a hand on the girl's arm. 'Is that clear?'

'Sure,' she mumbles, not looking at them, and Madeline removes her hand and shakes Emma's, thanking them both for their time.

'D'you think *he* did it?' Lauren's voice is louder than it has been throughout their interview, more forceful, as she suddenly raises her chin and looks Madeline in the eye. The policewoman frowns.

'Who?'

'Nathan,' the girl says, and the detectives see the visible curl of her lip at the mention of his name, 'Nathan Warren. He's a weirdo. Everyone knows it.'

Madeline and Lorna exchange a quick glance.

'We've no reason to believe that at present,' Madeline says eventually, 'but we are looking into everything at this stage.' There's a pause, and for a moment she thinks Lauren is going to say something else, but then her mouth closes, forms a hard, tight line once more.

The teacher is apologetic as the three of them watch Lauren walk away.

'Not very emotional,' Lorna remarks quietly, 'for someone who's just lost her best friend.'

They see themselves out, exiting through a back door to avoid the hordes of students craning their necks at them. Lorna's frowning, her forehead creased in that way she gets when she's got a theory.

'Wonder if it *was* a boy?' she says as they get back into the car. 'Someone she'd rejected?'

'Harry Goodwin?' Madeline says. 'Not that his parents had noticed. Nor the teachers.'

Lorna sights. 'The teachers in my day hadn't got a bloody clue what any of us got up to.' She pauses. 'Strange comment about the mother. *All dolled up.*'

Madeline flicks the radio on as they drive, thinking. It's beginning to rain – sharp, grey lashes on the windscreen. They pick up the local station and it's Clare again, her name echoing out in the clipped tones of the newsreader.

'Police investigating the death of schoolgirl Clare Edwards have said the case has been officially upgraded to a murder enquiry. Detective Constable Inspector Rob Sturgeon told Radio Essex that they are treating this as a very serious investigation, and appealed to the public to come forward with any information they might have. Sixteen-year-old Clare was found dead in a field in the town of Ashdon, North Essex, on Monday the 4th of February. Her next of kin have been informed. Members of the public are reminded to remain vigilant, and to not approach anyone who they believe could be dangerous. The number to call with information is...'

'Christ.' Madeline switches it off angrily. 'Would've been helpful if the DCI had warned us he'd spoken to the press.'

Lorna shrugs, looks out of the window. 'You know what he's like, Maddie.'

There's a pause. The rain feels like it's getting louder. 'Hey,' Lorna says, 'slow down a minute. It's Nathan Warren.'

They slow slightly and peer out of the window – and there he is, shuffling along the road. Madeline watches him, thinking about the venom in Lauren's voice, the suddenness of her question. They have his statement already – he is adamant that he didn't touch Clare, stumbled across the body whilst out walking on the night of the fourth.

He looks soaked to the skin, staring down at the pavement as he walks, seemingly unaware of the weather. Madeline frowns.

'What's he doing out in the wet like this?'

'There's something not right about him,' Lorna says, 'you know, besides the usual. Something about him feels funny to me.' She pauses. 'You know he lost his job as the school caretaker? D'you think we should speak to him again?'

Just as they draw level to him, Nathan stops walking, turns to face the road, and as Madeline drives past, her gaze is distracted from the road. His face is one of utter despair, and his eyes connect with hers – that desperate chocolate brown visible even in the rain. A chill goes through her, cold and deep. He reminds her of an animal, caught in the headlights – hunted, vulnerable.

'Christ, he looks traumatised,' Lorna mutters. Madeline doesn't reply, but the word spins in her head. Trauma affects people in all kinds of different ways. Even people like Clare.

Back at the station, Lorna starts ploughing through the CCTV records, such as they are. The police have got the tape from Ruby Walker's newsagents; the one at the doctor's surgery was axed two years ago in the cuts. The school doesn't have any. That's what you get in a small place like Ashdon.

Rob crashes over to Madeline's desk, angry. 'I've had Danny Brien from the *Daily Mail* on the phone this morning, they're lifting more pictures of Clare from her Facebook page.'

He comes round to her side, wiggles the laptop mouse to

bring it to life and clicks into Facebook. Clare's face stares out at them both – she's with Lauren, laughing into the camera. He clicks again, and she's with Lauren again in what looks like Pitcher and Piano in Saffron Walden, their faces pressed together, straws between their lips in that faux-provocative way that only teenage girls can quite manage. They have already been through everything on Clare's social media; she didn't do much on Twitter, but her Facebook and Instagram are full of photos of Lauren. No boys. None of her family.

'Shit,' Madeline says, 'I'll speak to Alex, get it closed down.'

He nods. 'Get her mother to make a formal request. And Shaw? Chase up that Harry Goodwin lead. If he liked her as much as her friend implied, he's worth speaking to.'

Chapter Twelve

Clare

Monday 4th February, 9.00 a.m.

I wrap my puffer coat tightly around me, shove my hands into my pockets as I walk to school. I love this coat. It was only twenty quid in Oasis, the last time Mum let Lauren and I go into Saffron Walden. Lauren nicked hers – put that thin grey jacket under her jumper and just walked out. She thought it was funny, and I just laughed along even though my heart was going a million miles an hour thinking a security guard would be after us. I know it sounds stupid but I don't like breaking the law – I don't like things being unfair. There's enough goes on that's not right without people like us adding to it.

I turn the music up on my headphones, louder and louder, thinking about Ian and his face with the peanut butter breath up close to mine. As I reach the crossroads I feel them, the hands grabbing my shoulders: big hands, much larger than mine, spinning me around. I almost scream, my gasp of breath misting the cold February air, but catch myself just in time.

When I turn, he's laughing at my momentary panic, wag-gling his gloved hands at me like a joker. I laugh too, but my heart is thudding and my hands, when he releases me, are shaking, just a little bit. I don't like surprises, and I don't like violence, not even fake violence. It brings back memories, memories of a time I don't want to think about.

'Alright?' Harry Goodwin is in front of me, grinning, his little sister Sophie trailing a few feet behind him. He's the best-looking boy in the school, everyone knows it, but I've never really liked him that much, despite the fact that he seems to like me. They live next door but we never go round; Mum and Mrs Goodwin aren't really friends. Ian laughs at her behind her back, calls her Little Miss Perfect. I always thought that was a bit mean, but then he is mean sometimes.

'You scared me.'

'Ooh, touchy,' Harry says, grinning. 'Why's that then Clarey? Getting tired of resisting my charms?'

He nudges me in the ribs. 'You're looking good today.' His dark hair hangs across his forehead – he's so far from being my type that it's ridiculous. Strong jawline, blue eyes, wears those trainers everyone wants, but I wouldn't go near him.

'Oh, Harry,' I say playfully, 'you know I'm just too good for you.' I'm trying to be flirty, funny, casual, but I walk a bit faster, relieved that it's only metres to the school gates. As Harry is swarmed by a crowd of Year Twelve boys, I look behind me, to see the small figure of Sophie, trailing behind her brother, alone on the pavement, one hand raised up to her mouth as though holding back tears. For a split second as I stare at her, I get a flashback so intense that it frightens me: myself, crouched by the bed upstairs, listening to Mum below. My heartbeat pounding in my ears, panicked saliva gathering in my mouth. Sophie reminds me of myself.

Harry turns around. 'Soph! Come on.' He catches my eye once more, a quick flash, and then they are both gone.

Chapter Thirteen

Jane

Thursday 7th February

St Mary's Church is full to the brim for Clare's memorial service. Candles light the aisles, casting a golden glow across all of us, and Pastor Michael stands at the front, hands outstretched. He's been in this town ever since we've lived here, and long before that, too – he must be nearing his eighties. Jack and I are standing near the front, the children on either side of us, Harry and Sophie to Jack's left and Finn next to me.

Harry has been quiet since he got home from school, despite the little word I had with him when he came in.

'I've spoken to Dad,' I said, 'he feels awful about you finding that appointment list, but honestly, it's nothing to worry over.' He looked at me. 'Okay?' I said.

'Right,' he mumbled eventually, 'yeah, that's good.' There was a pause, and for a second, I wondered if he knew, if he could see right through the lie. Because I haven't spoken to Jack, not yet. I have to pick my moment. Our years together have taught me that.

'Was there anything else you wanted to talk about?' I said. His reply surprised me.

'Are *you* okay, Mum?' At that, my throat got a bit tight, but I smiled at him and ruffled his hair.

'Me? Of course, darling. I'm absolutely fine.'

I smiled again, just to make sure he believed me. My chest felt hollow after he walked away. Perhaps my eldest son is more perceptive than I realised. The thought makes me feel ashamed.

What I have done is spoken to Danielle, Jack's receptionist. She came past the shop on her lunch hour; we had a little chat. She's quite pretty really, if a bit drab. I used to think he was screwing her. Perhaps he is. She's the one who alerted the police to Nathan, apparently.

'Whereabouts did you see Nathan that night, Danni?' I asked her, and she described it, over by the entrance to Sorrow's Meadow.

'Goodness,' I said, 'it's a good job someone has a keen eye for detail. Jack really values the work you do, too. Well, we all do. The NHS is such an integral part of our lives.'

She smiled, but she looked exhausted. 'Thanks, Jane,' she said, 'that's a kind thing to say.'

'You do look tired,' I said sympathetically. 'Is that husband of mine working you too hard?'

She shook her head. 'It's not that, really – it's just long hours, you know, and the pay – well.' She looked embarrassed. 'The last round of cuts haven't exactly benefited people like me.'

I wondered what she must think of us, in our big fancy house. 'I do see,' I said, putting my hand on her arm. 'I do feel for you, Danielle.'

She smiled at that, blushed. I watched as she walked away in her drab little coat, thinking of the time when I couldn't afford nice clothes either. The good news was that she agreed with me; there's no point bringing up old surgery records at this point, not until I've spoken to my husband.

I'm holding Finn's hand in the church now, trying to stop him fiddling with the dark red prayer book in front of him. He doesn't fully understand what's going on. I've told him it's a memorial service, but he thinks it's a funeral.

'It's sad, Mummy,' he said to me on the way here, 'it's a sad day, isn't it?'

'It is, darling,' I told him, reaching out a hand to touch his newly brushed hair, feeling the soft, downy strands at the nape of his neck. My baby boy.

'They can't release her body yet,' Sandra hisses at me from the pew behind, her sickly-sweet perfume lingering beside my ear. She always tells me it's Yves Saint Laurent, but I'm fairly sure her husband buys it in Superdrug and pretends. 'Not until they find out who did it. That's what Ruby Walker said.' She nods a head over to where the newsagent is standing, hands clasped together, eyes tightly shut, lips moving in a prayer of her own. Her face is set in misery, as if she has taken Rachel Edwards' pain and claimed it for her own.

I can feel Jack quiver a little beside me.

Finn is tugging on my hand, his little face screwed up.

'Mummy,' he whispers, 'I need to wee.'

'Ssh, Finn, try to hold it,' I say, as quietly as I can, and just then Pastor Michael steps forward. I glance sideways at my family, taking in my husband's handsome profile, Sophie's beautiful rosebud mouth, Harry's white collar, strong shoulders. Despite the setting, I feel a flicker of pride.

'We are gathered tonight,' he begins, 'to pray for one of our own. The loss of Clare Edwards is a tragedy, an act of God that is sent to test the patience and the faith of us all. In taking Clare from us at this tender age, our Father has selected an angel; may she rest in peace, for now and for always.'

The candles flicker; the church is silent. It reminds me of coming as a child, holding my grandmother's hand as we said Mass. My parents were never up in time to come too.

I see Mrs Garrett from the secondary school crying, little tears trickling down her cheeks and pooling on her chin; next to her, a man who must be her husband gives her a reassuring squeeze. My own eyes prick a little. Jack doesn't move. I remember Sandra behind me, and slide my free hand into his. My fingers curl around his familiar palm. One squeeze, two.

The least he can do is squeeze back.

'It is at times like these,' the pastor continues, 'that God asks us all to search deep within ourselves, to within the very fibres of our being, and to renew our faith in Him, to place in Him all our anger and our sorrow and to move towards the light.'

He lifts his hands, gestures to the candles. I feel as though I am holding my breath as I listen to his words. Beside me, Finn squirms.

'I ask you all to keep in your hearts tonight two most beloved members of our community – Rachel and Ian Edwards,' the pastor continues, and I move my head an inch or two to the right, see the hunched figures of our neighbours standing in the very front row. Ian is supporting Rachel, as though she can't stand up on her own any more. Maybe she can't. Behind me, I can feel Sandra doing the same thing, craning her head to see the stars of the show.

'Join me,' Pastor Michael says softly, 'join me as we pray for Clare's soul.'

There's a hush; the small church is deadly quiet. The large white candles stand solemnly as the congregation bow their heads; flames flicker against the cold stone walls. Then there is the sound: a low, raw whimpering, like an animal in pain. A girl, about Clare's age, has her head bowed in the second row. The soft noise echoes a little off the walls. I lean forward, recognising her as she lifts her head slightly, the crying getting slightly louder. It's Lauren Oldbury, she's the year below my son. I've seen her coming out of the house next door a few times, usually wearing something low cut.

There is more murmuring around us all now, and I feel a bite of irritation – can't she be quiet, in a church of all places? Her drama is erasing the calm of the pastor's little speech. He raises his head, and I see his eyes flick to Lauren.

'Thank you,' he says quietly, 'thank you for joining me in prayer.' He crosses himself. It is over.

I clutch Finn to me, and Jack picks Sophie up, pulling her against his hip as though she's a baby again. Her legs dangle down by his thighs, her little black tights and patent shoes making her seem strangely adult. She didn't want to wear those shoes, said they pinch her feet. I told her the whole town would be there, and she had to look her best.

Around us, the crowd is surging forwards – I can see Tricia beavering her way to the front, ostensibly holding a little packet of Kleenex which she'll no doubt offer to Lauren, while Sandra has disappeared from behind me only to emerge by the pastor's side. I almost smile, even though it's wildly inappropriate. That's my girls. Right in the action.

Lauren is still crying, louder now, and although the church has become a hustle of voices, I can still hear her voice, babbling the same thing over and over again.

'What's she saying?' I say to Jack, my heart thudding beneath my black jacket at the adrenaline of it all, and he frowns, his handsome face contorted as he listens to her. Harry's face is stricken.

'She's saying "it's my fault",' he says slowly, 'she's saying that it's all her fault.'

Pastor Michael, his creased old face white in the half light, is trying to reassure her, trying to calm her down, but still she continues to whine. The annoyance within me grows. Has she always been this attention-seeking? It must have been difficult for Clare, living in her shadow. I give myself a little shake. I don't know anything about their relationship, I'm projecting, imagining.

I watch Rachel Edwards, moving my gaze from Lauren. Tears are rolling silently down her cheeks but she is as still as a statue, staring ahead meekly as though all of this is happening to somebody else, as though her daughter's best friend hasn't just made a little show of herself in front of the whole of Ashdon. Something bubbles unfairly inside me as I look at her – where is her fight, her emotion? How well would she have protected Clare if it came to it? If someone close to her was threatening her daughter, how capable would Rachel be of taking action? Beside her, Ian stands tall, his back a stiff, straight rod in the half light of the church. Perhaps he takes action enough for them both.

Later. Sandra and the other PTA women have formed a little gaggle outside the church, heads bowed together in what looks like prayer but I know is probably gossip, endless chatter spewing from their mouths about the car crash that is poor Lauren. *Looked to me like she was whimpering like that for attention,* Sandra mutters to me, *I always thought she was a bit of a minx, that one. She certainly dresses the part.* I don't say anything; I'm still thinking of Rachel's face, silent and passive as the service unfolded around her. Was she the same at home?

Jack and I say our goodbyes outside; I watch the way the women smile at Sophie, still in Jack's arms, at the way he cradles her against him, her curly hair spilling onto his jacket. Model father, model husband. *Edwards, C.*

Maybe one day I'll tell them.

Harry has disappeared; when I look around I see him standing with a couple of other boys from the school, leaning against the side of the church. I catch a glimpse of orange embers and tense, but my son isn't the one smoking, his hands rest by his sides. As I watch, he moves to stand a little apart from the other boys, maybe a metre or so away. He's looking upwards, to where the moon casts a milky light over the churchyard. His expression is sad. I wonder, briefly, whether my son knew Clare more than he is letting on. After all, he couldn't have been immune to her looks. Not many people were.

Tricia's husband Hugh grunts at us all, says something about getting home to watch the last bit of *Grand Designs*. Rachel and Ian are nowhere to be seen. I wonder briefly if we ought to offer to walk them home, guide them through the pile of flowers to their front door. When we left to come to the service there were four journalists outside, huddled around the Edwards' porch, hulking black cameras slung over their shoulders. We crossed the road to avoid them, kept our heads firmly down.

Finn is sleepy, his sudden desire for the toilet forgotten. I go over to Harry, who starts when he sees me.

'Your brother is tired,' I say, 'are you ready to come home?'

His friends stare at me curiously, and I suddenly feel small next to their tall teenage bodies. I wonder if any of them knew Clare, if any of them were close to her. I think of Lauren in the church crying, her dark hair spilling over one shoulder, her eyes rimmed with black. No sign of the police, but I saw the family liaison officer comforting Rachel, rubbing her back in slow, circular movements.

Eventually we walk home as a foursome, with Harry promising to follow in a little while. I don't like the thought of him staying out but he's seventeen now, I can't make him come home. Besides, I don't want to upset him. Not after yesterday, the confusion over Jack's papers, on top of the shock of Clare.

We use the torches on our phones to light the short walk back to the house. As we round the corner, there is a little rush of noise – a man and a woman running towards us, cameras bouncing, their faces falling when they realise we're not the couple they want.

'You want the couple next door,' Jack says to them, holding up a hand to shield me and the kids, being the protector, for once. The journalists' lights shine on his face, making him look more handsome than ever in the half light.

'Do you think there is anything suspicious about Rachel and Ian Edwards?' the male journo asks us. His teeth are white, like those of a shark.

'How well did you know Clare Edwards? How was her relationship with her stepfather?' the woman asks. Sophie and Finn are standing stock-still, confused, dazzled by the sudden rush of attention on our dark little lane.

'Please, we're with our children,' I say, reaching for them both, feeling for their soft little heads. Sophie is still sleepy, her eyes crusted with tiredness.

'We didn't know Clare well,' Jack says, and only I can see the sheen of sweat on his forehead, the way his jaw is tensing beneath the surface. I need to get us all inside. Quickly, I move forward, herding my family like sheep, away from the piercing gaze of the journalists. The little light of our porch gleams ahead of me, and we push the children in front of us. My heart is hammering in my ears. The man with the camera falls back, his figure blurring in the darkness.

'Did you tell Harry to get home soon?' Jack says finally, taking his moment when the kids are ahead of us in the porch, pulling off their shoes in their rush to get back to the TV, and I pause for a moment on our doorstep, stare at the hanging basket swinging gently in the breeze, wilted in the cold. I could ask him now. *What was Clare doing at your surgery, Jack?*

'Yes,' I say quickly, 'yes, I did.' He stares at me for a second in the porch, our coats hanging beside us. I feel my insides clench, and my mind flits to my escape routes, like it does when I'm anxious. The pile of twenties in the cookbooks, the sliver of glass by the matches, the knife nestled silently next to *Wolf Hall*.

It's late when my mobile rings, gone ten o'clock at night. I don't recognise the number, but I don't want the sound to wake the kids so I press the phone to my ear, walk over to the window. Jack's made his way into the kitchen, I can hear him opening a beer.

'Mrs Goodwin? It's DS Shaw.'

Immediately, my hands start sweating; I wipe them on my black dress, hoping the material won't stain.

'Madeline,' I say, 'how are you?'

'I was wondering,' she says, ignoring the question, 'if I could pop over in the morning, have a quick chat with your son?'

I grip the phone. 'With Harry? What about?'

'Nothing to worry about,' she says, 'but a few people have mentioned him in connection to Clare, and we need to ask a couple of quick questions. Nine o'clock alright? I've cleared it with the school.'

I stand still for a minute after she hangs up, staring across at the house next door. My heart is hammering in my chest and my hands are still slick with sweat. There's a noise, and I spin around to see my son in the hallway, his keys in his hand.

'Harry,' I say, 'you made me jump.' His eyes shine bright in the dim of the room, and for a moment, he looks so like Jack that my breath catches in my throat.

'Goodnight,' he says, and I know I need to warn him, to tell him about the morning, but the words seem to stick in my throat.

'Night,' I say, 'sleep well, darling boy.' I wait a few moments, my mind racing, then I follow him up the stairs, knock on the door to his room.

'Could we have a little chat?' I say. The door closes behind me, and I am alone with my son.

Chapter Fourteen

DS Madeline Shaw

Friday 8th February

The Goodwin house is even nicer than the Edwards'. Madeline wipes her shoes on the mat before going inside, clears her throat as Jane Goodwin hovers around her. There's tea laid out on the table, three bone china cups, a plate of biscuits that remain untouched.

Harry Goodwin is sitting on the sofa in his school uniform, his hands linked on his lap. Madeline smiles at him, nods at Jane.

'Thanks for making the time to chat,' she says. 'As I said, nothing to worry about. We're speaking to lots of people at the moment, trying to build up a clearer picture of Clare.'

Jane smiles at her. 'Of course,' she says, 'we're only too happy to help.' She sits down beside her son, gestures to Madeline to take the armchair opposite.

'Did you know Clare well, Harry?' she asks, sinking down into what is undoubtedly a chair that cost more than her kitchen. 'Would you say the two of you were friends?'

He has the grace to look slightly embarrassed.

'Not really,' he says, 'but look, Madeline – can I call you Madeline? – I liked Clare, I don't mind admitting it. I thought she was, I don't know, hot.' He glances at his mother, his skin flushing slightly. 'But she was never interested in me, you have to know that. And I was only messing around – you know, tried to talk to her a few times.' He spreads his hands. 'That was the extent of it. It's not like I stalked her.' He says something else, something slightly under his breath that Madeline doesn't quite hear.

'Sorry,' she says, 'what did you say?'

Harry shrugs, looks a bit sheepish. 'I said, I'm not Nathan Warren. I don't make a habit of following girls home.' He grins, like it's a joke, and Madeline has a sudden flash to what it must be like up at the school, the rumours, the gossip.

Jane gives a little laugh, the sound tinkling in the living room. 'Darling, of course you don't. But you shouldn't make jokes. Nathan Warren never did anything – well,' she looks at Madeline, almost conspiratorially, 'nothing that could be *proved*, anyway. He's a nice man, I'm sure.'

'Apologies, detective,' Harry says, 'I spoke out of turn there. Just messing, I suppose.'

He's confident, charming even. Madeline feels wrong-footed; she'd been expecting a surly teenager, someone awkward, unsure of himself. Jane has a hand on her son's arm now, her shiny pink fingernails glossy in the morning light that shines through into the living room.

'Did Clare ever give you any reason as to why she wasn't interested in you?' she asks, deciding to move on from the Nathan Warren comments, focus on the boy in front of her. 'Any indications of someone else in her life?'

At this, Jane seems to tense a little, sitting straighter on the sofa. Harry shrugs. 'Not really,' he says, 'but you know, it'd be nice to think she had a reason, hadn't just rejected me outright.'

Madeline smiles, inclines her head. 'Of course.' She glances around the room, at the framed photographs of Jack and Jane on their wedding day, the snaps of their younger children, pulling silly faces at the camera. Everything has a sheen to it, the sheen that comes with money, and despite herself, she feels the uncomfortable tug of jealousy. Who *wouldn't* want all this?

'Is there anything else we can help you with, detective?' Jane asks her, half rising to her feet, a clear indication for Madeline to go. 'Harry really ought to get to school.'

'Just one thing,' Madeline says, her eyes focusing once more on Harry's face, the shock of black hair, the bright blue eyes. 'Can you tell me where you were on Monday the fourth, what you were doing that night?'

There's a pause; the atmosphere in the room seems to shift slightly, tighten.

'He was with the football team,' Jane says, 'as I told you, detective.'

Harry nods. 'We went for a pizza after training. Easy enough to check.'

'Thank you,' Madeline says, 'I will.' Jane is on her feet now, and the detective rises too, taking one more glance around the room. The window on the right looks directly into the Edwards' house, she realises; handy for a boy who thinks the girl next door is hot.

'I'll show you out,' Jane says, and it's as she is placing a hand on Madeline's arm that it happens: her sleeve rides up, exposing the bare flesh of her forearm, and Madeline sees the bruise: dark purple, the edges yellowing to green. It spreads across the underside of her arm, like a stain. Quickly, Jane moves her arm down, yanks at the sleeve of her cardigan, but Madeline can see a blush beginning to work its way up from her neck, spotting her skin like blood in water.

She says nothing, lets Jane walk her to the front door, leaving Harry behind in the house. On the doorstep, the detective turns. Where once she saw the face of a privileged, wealthy woman with a need for authority, she now sees something else: the face of a woman who has a secret. A secret the police have seen more times than they'd like. Halfway out of the door, she hesitates for a second.

'Mrs Goodwin,' she says, 'you do know we're here if you ever need to talk, don't you? About anything, I mean.'

For a second, Jane's face softens. 'Thank you,' she says, 'but there's no need, Madeline. Everything is fine.'

No less than six other boys confirm Harry's version of events. Madeline hangs up the phone, puts a hand to her head. If he'd been with the football team until gone eight, there is no way he could have gone near Clare.

'For fuck's sake,' the DCI says when she tells him the news, 'we're getting precisely nowhere. The Super's going to have my head. Tell me again what he said about Nathan Warren?'

'He just made a comment about him following girls home, nothing we've not heard before,' Madeline says. 'I don't think he meant much by it.'

'Hmm.' Rob frowns, and Madeline knows how much he would love to pin this on Nathan, take the no smoke without fire saying and run with it to the Super.

'Harry's mother had a terrible bruise,' Madeline says. 'Made me wonder.'

He looks at her. 'Wonder what?'

She frowns, reaches for the last of the Quality Street. 'Whether everything's as perfect as it seems in that marriage. You never know, do you? I felt a bit sorry for her today, if I'm honest. Never thought I'd say that about Jane Goodwin.'

Chapter Fifteen

Jane

Friday 8th February

I'm in the study at the rear of the house, looking out over our back lawn. I spent ages trying to cultivate the garden when we moved in, growing lilac wisteria up the side of the house, employing a gardener to carefully landscape the patio. I had visions of a vegetable patch: runner beans, tomatoes, peas. In the end we paid a company to do it all for us – turns out I'm not as green-fingered as I thought, after all. Not that I tell the PTA mums that.

It's dark in the study, the air heavy and stale. I don't come in here much, it's more Jack's terrain, set up when he got his last promotion. He said he needed somewhere to work, somewhere away from me and the kids. *Charming,* I thought. *Of course darling,* I said. I'm not stupid enough to argue with him when there's something he wants. Not any more. Especially now the police have seen the bruise on my arm. I'm cross with myself about that, I'm usually so careful. The interest in Harry unsettled me, threw me off course, but he handled it all really well, I was proud. No one ever went to jail for having a crush on the girl next door.

After Madeline left, I took the piece of paper with Jack's

surgery appointments on from my drawer, where I've been keeping it for the last few days. I burned it in the grate, once the children had gone to school. It was gone in seconds, the paper vanishing into black dust. If he isn't going to tell the police, I don't want them finding it of their own accord.

I take a sip of white wine from the glass in my hand; I can feel my muscles relaxing as I stare out of the window. At the end of our garden is a gate, set into the fence. It leads into a narrow strip of land between us and the Edwards next door. When Rachel first moved in, I thought we might use it to nip from house to house, wine bottles in hand, or stand talking quietly at the bottom of the garden when the kids were all asleep. It didn't happen like that.

Another sip of wine; I realise with surprise that the glass is almost empty. Upstairs, I can hear Harry moving around in his room, directly above me. He's been quiet all evening, won't meet my eye properly.

'You did really well with the detective,' I said to him after dinner. 'There's nothing to worry about, now.'

As I look out over the lawn, the light in the Edwards' garden flickers on. We both have sensors, security – in houses like these you'd be a fool not to. I wait, watching, but I can't see any movement on their side. Not from here, anyway. An animal, maybe. Sometimes we get foxes round here. They rummage through the bins, trying to extricate all our secrets.

Later, in bed that night. Jack insisted on staying downstairs after I'd read Sophie and Finn their story. He's as quiet as Harry is, short with me, curt. I made him a cup of tea, smiled at him as I set it down, but five minutes later I saw that he'd replaced it with a beer.

It's cold up in our bedroom, even though the central heating is on full blast. Part of me wants Jack to come to bed. Part of me doesn't.

Unable to sleep, I get up, feeling the slight twinge of pain that occasionally still gripes at me. My arm throbs. I know what all the magazines would say, *Leave at the first sign of violence*, but I've worked hard to get to where I am now. This life. This house, these children, this family. I'm not just going to throw it all away. As I stare at myself in the dressing-table mirror, I briefly see the woman I was before – a nothing, a nobody. The girl whose parents showed no interest in her, the girl with hand-me-down clothes, invisible, forgotten. I used to dream of a big house and a family, a place in society, a role to fulfil. Money to buy expensive things, to buy status, to buy class. Jack gave me all that. The thought of losing it all, losing the life I have built, leaves me utterly cold.

There's a noise to my left, a low scraping sound. I get to my feet, pad across the soft, thick carpet to our window. At first, I can't make out anything in the darkness, but then I see the amber glow in the corner of the garden, down by the gate. As my eyes adjust to the blackness, I make out two figures standing in the gloom, where the narrow strip of land between our houses connects. Tall, too tall to be Harry. I press my face to the glass, my breath misting up the pane. Jack. It is Jack and Ian, their bodies huddled close together, the orange light of the cigarette passing between them like a firefly.

Immediately, my heart quickens. What is my husband doing, conversing with our neighbour at this time of night? Consoling him, perhaps? Where is Theresa? I thought she was meant to be keeping an eye on these things.

My body is tense, taut. Still watching, I see Jack glance back up at the house, his face illuminated clearly in the moonlight. As I stare, Ian puts out a hand, touches my husband on the shoulder. I can't see his face.

He should be comforting his wife, I think to myself, *not hiding in the shadows with my husband.*

Chapter Sixteen

DS Madeline Shaw

Saturday 9th February

The phone rings at half past seven, when Madeline is alone at the station. She's already spent the best part of the weekend there. The DCI has gone home for the night, muttering something about his wife, still in a bad mood because of the fruitless trip to see Harry Goodwin.

'Madeline?'

It's Rachel Edwards. Clare's mother.

Madeline has never told Rachel about the little chat she had with Clare at the school. Clare hadn't initially struck Madeline as the type to be interested in the police, but people have their reasons. Madeline asked Clare about her mother, about whether they'd discussed it. Ashdon Secondary was hardly prepping its pupils for a career in the force; no, if the parents had any say in it, it was a school full of future lawyers, doctors, even politicians. Respectable, well-paid roles. Clare had got a funny look on her face.

'I live with my mum and stepdad,' she'd said quickly, as though keen for Madeline to know that she didn't have both parents. Clare and her mother took Ian's name when Rachel remarried, which Madeline has always thought was a bit odd.

'And what do they think of your plans to consider the police?' she asked Clare gently. The girl had looked at the floor, pulled at a thread coming from her school jumper.

'Mum doesn't mind. Ian thinks it won't pay.' She paused, then Madeline had seen it: the red flush of embarrassment creeping up her neck. 'God,' Clare said, 'sorry, I didn't mean— I'm sure you—'

'Don't worry,' Madeline said quickly, interrupting. The poor thing looked mortified. 'I'm getting by. It's not so bad once you get a bit higher up.'

'Madeline?' Clare's mother's voice is in her ear again. She gives herself a little shake.

'Mrs Edwards,' she says, 'it's good to hear from you. Is everything alright?' It's an insensitive question; of course everything's not alright – her daughter's dead.

'I need to speak to you,' she says. 'It's important.'

'Of course,' Madeline says, remembering how she'd pressed her card into Rachel's freezing cold hand on Monday, told her to call anytime.

'I'm outside the station right now. Come let me in?' The phone goes dead.

Madeline pauses at her desk. If she tilts her chair back slightly and looks through the window she can see her, her thin shape pressed up against the metal bars of the station gate. Briefly, Rachel reminds Madeline of a prisoner, on the wrong side of the door.

Madeline goes outside to meet the mother, the cold air nipping at her. Rachel's car is parked lopsidedly on double yellow lines right outside the station; she must have driven here in a hurry from the town. The family liaison officer really should have given the police the heads up – she's still at the house every day. Rachel's face is different to how it used to be, Madeline notices, like someone has taken a spoon and hollowed it out at the sides. She used to be one of the more made up mothers in the town: bright red lipstick, thick foundation, plush cashmere cardigans draped over her shoulders. But today she's bare-faced. Dark bags hang underneath her eyes. Still pretty, of course.

Madeline unlocks the gate quickly, her fingers slightly stiff.

'Come inside,' she says. This floor of the station is empty now save for them; everybody's gone home to their lives. Her desk light hums against the darkness of the other rooms.

'Would you like a cuppa?' Madeline offers her, more for something to say than anything else. Rachel shakes her head quickly, her limp brown hair fluttering around her face. There is no point in taking her into an interview room; it feels more relaxed this way, and that's what the police need.

She doesn't sit, though; instead she paces the room like a caged up animal. Her frame ricochets around, her eyes darting from the clutter of objects on Madeline's desk to the calendar on the wall made by one of the DCI's kids at school. Blobby paint faces stare back at them, children with their whole lives stretching ahead of them.

'How are you, Rachel? I heard there was a service for Clare,' Madeline starts, but Rachel shakes her head again, stops moving abruptly and turns to look at her.

'There's something we're not seeing,' she says, and her voice has a rasp to it, as though she's been crying herself to sleep for weeks.

Madeline takes a deep breath. 'Myself and the team are

working as hard as we possibly can to understand who did this to your daughter. As you know, we are currently investigating several leads—'

'No,' Rachel says vehemently, 'no. There's something else. People are talking. The gossip – I can't stand it.' She lifts her hands and holds them to the sides of her head, flat over her ears, as though trying to block something out.

'It's all my fault,' she says, and her voice has taken on a desperate tone, pleading almost. 'I never should have argued with her, I never should have pushed her so hard on the exams. Maybe if I'd been a better mother…' She doesn't finish the sentence, her eyes are fixed on the photograph of her daughter which is behind Madeline's back, pinned to the wall.

'This has nothing to do with you being a good mother, Mrs Edwards,' Madeline says, but now she is watching the other woman's face closely. Guilt in the parent is normal, to a degree. But if there was more to Rachel's mothering than met the eye, it's worth them knowing about.

'I don't think you're doing your job right,' she says, her eyes shifting focus onto Madeline. 'It's him – that lunatic – roaming around the town. *Our* town.' Her words come in staccato bursts. Madeline picks up a globe-shaped paperweight from her desk, feels the reassuring solidity of it between her fingers.

'Nathan Warren. He was there,' Rachel says, 'I know he was there. That doctor's receptionist says she saw him, she said that, didn't she? He "found" her – a deliberate ploy to throw us off the scent. He doesn't have an alibi, does he? Does he, Madeline?'

She's staring at the other woman, mouth open, face coloured with the effort of her words. Madeline thinks of the empty wine bottles in their house. Has she been drinking? She is about to ask Rachel to sit down when she steps closer, puts her face up close. 'Clare is gone,' she says, slowly and deliberately, 'she's gone, she's dead, and all people want to do is cast speculation –' the word hisses out of her mouth, ugly with consonants, '– about my husband! Do they think I'm deaf as well as heartbroken? I hear them talk!' She leans even closer, so that Madeline can feel her breath on her face. 'Ian is a good man, Madeline!'

She can feel her cheeks colouring slightly at the mention of Ian Edwards, as though she's guilty of exactly what Rachel is accusing them all of. Rachel Edwards isn't used to things not going her way. People with money usually aren't. Rachel Edwards gets her hair done at Trudie's Salon, tasteful highlights every few months, she tends her front lawn and probably cooks a roast dinner for her family every Sunday. The only blot in Rachel's life was her husband's passing, until now of course. Now, she's a remarried widow with a murdered daughter. Madeline swallows. No one deserves that.

'Rachel,' she says, the paperweight anchoring her thoughts, 'nobody in this town is accusing Ian of anything. My team know what they're doing, and we will carry out every procedure necessary to bring Clare's killer to justice and honour her memory.' Madeline pauses – Rachel flinched at the word memory – 'I know you care about this community,' she says, more gently this time. 'We all do. And we all miss your daughter every single day.' An image of her flashes into her mind then – Clare's blonde hair, her earnest eyes.

'Will you stop them?' she asks, so close that Madeline can smell it on her, the stale, tired smell of grief.

'Stop who?' Madeline says, playing for time.

'Stop them – the town – from talking. It doesn't help. All I want is to find Clare's killer. And it isn't my husband.'

Chapter Seventeen

Jane

Monday 11th February

The children are tired this morning, scratchy and irritable. I spend twenty minutes trying to coax Finn to come downstairs. His little face is red, angry, exhausted from lack of sleep, even though I put them down on time and read them *The Jungle Book* over and over again.

Jack isn't exactly helping. He looks exhausted too, but when I ask him what's the matter he gives me a look of such loathing that I jump, move away. Panic blooms within me when he is like this. I need to do something to get him on side.

I'm not working today, but I almost wish I was; the house feels oppressive. Ever since DS Shaw saw the bruise on my arm, my mind's been in overdrive, thinking. Like I said, I don't want things getting out of hand, people barging their noses into our business. I need to be more careful.

There's a new car outside the Edwards' place, more journalists arrive nearly every day. The family liaison officer is still there too – I keep seeing her move past their kitchen window. The wine bottles are gone – perhaps she's the one tidying things up, keeping it all in order. Quickly, I do a sweep of the living room, cleaning up Finn's toys, picking up Harry's sports kit which is lying on the floor.

My phone buzzes while I'm wiping down the kitchen surfaces, yellow Marigolds on to protect my nails. Jack thinks it's an extravagance, pink Shellac every fortnight, but at the moment he still lets me, and I don't want to sacrifice it. We can afford it, after all. Besides, the routine of it helps me a bit, keeps my thoughts in check. Like the way I arrange my earrings in my jewellery box, one on top of the other every night, nice and neat; the way I check the children's pockets every day when they get home from school, running my fingers around the hems, removing bits of fluff and stray sweet wrappers; the way I pour cold white wine exactly to the little white line on the side of the glass – no more, no less. I like my routines; lately, they stop me thinking about what Jack said to me, the night of Clare's death, how difficult he has been ever since. Stops me thinking about why she was on his appointment list, and why he still hasn't told anyone. Even before Clare died, I had my routines. The main plus of the Shellac is that I get to leave the town, leave this house, escape to the nail salon in Saffron Walden and sit in silence for an hour while a woman buffs and polishes and massages my hands. There's a lot to be said for that. Sometimes I think about grabbing the manicurist's hands, begging her to help me. But I never do.

I open my phone, and my heart sinks. The school is having an emergency meeting. Tomorrow, 6.30 p.m. sharp. The head-teacher Andrea Marsons called it, sent out an email to all the parents on the PTA, which, for my sins, includes me.

Sandra rings me five minutes after the email went round. We're not due a PTA meeting for a month. 'I hear it's because Clare's mother went to the police station last Friday, Andrea wants to speak to everyone,' she says, using her hushed voice, the one she's been bringing out a lot this week, since it all happened. I picture her, standing next to the big island in their kitchen, horribly modernised in contrast to the thatched roof and wooden beams. She'll be drinking a skimmed latte from their espresso machine, taking neat little sips so as not to smudge her pink lipstick. She ought to go for something a little less bright, but I haven't told her that yet.

'Went to the station?' I say. 'What do you mean?' Sandra's ability to know things before anyone else never fails to astound me. But it's useful, too.

I move over to the kitchen window, and as I do so the curtains at the Edwards' place open. My breath catches slightly in my throat. It's Ian, his large frame filling the pane. His face is blank, expressionless. I narrow my eyes, trying to work out if he might have been crying, if he looks like a man grieving for his stepdaughter.

D'you know, I don't think he does.

'Rachel,' Sandra says. 'Apparently she accosted Madeline Shaw, after hours. Tricia saw her leaving. Says she came up with some more theories, well, we can hardly blame her, can we?' *Except we are*, I thought, *we are blaming her*. But it's not really a question; Sandra is talking over my thoughts.

'I mean, I know she's grieving, of course, but I just don't think stirring things up like that is helping anyone, is it? We've got to let the police do their job. What this community needs is the time to *heal*.' There's a small sucking noise; the low-fat latte, no doubt. She sounds as though she's reading from a brochure. I picture Rachel Edwards confronting Madeline – I hadn't had her down as a fighter. Perhaps there is more to the ice queen than I thought.

I'm still wearing my Marigolds; slowly, I slide the phone onto my collar bone, hold it in place with a tilt of my neck and ease them off. My hands look funny underneath, too pale, rubbery. Ian's moved away from the window. I can just about see the shadows of their kitchen. I wonder what they'll do with all Clare's stuff – the mugs she drank tea out of, her brightly coloured trainers on the shoe rack.

'I think we should go to the meeting,' I say, my voice clearer than my head, then with my free hand I go over to the landline, press the volume control. A shrill ring bursts into the room, loud enough for Sandra to hear.

'Sorry,' I say, 'I'd better get that, it's probably Jack. He said he'd call me from the surgery today, we're making plans for this evening.'

I hear Sandra sigh, and the sound is unmistakeably wistful.

'Bet he's whisking you off somewhere nice, is he? Ooh, you lucky thing. I'll be in with the Pinot, no doubt. Roger's working late. Same as he did all weekend.' *No changes there then*, I think, but I ignore the hint of sadness in her voice. Instead, I force a tinkling kind of laugh and say, 'Something like that. Take care, Sandra. See you at school!' Honestly. Whisking me off. She has no idea. None of them do.

It's almost pick-up time when Jack does call. I'm surprised; he rarely rings me from the surgery these days.

'Jack?' I say into the phone, trying to keep my voice neutral, 'what is it? I'm just about to go get the children.' Even though I know he's at work, I know he's nowhere near me, my whole body has tensed. Flight or fight.

'Can you meet me?' he says. 'We need to talk.'

Chapter Eighteen

Clare

Monday 4th February, 10.00 a.m.

We're in Maths first thing, my least favourite subject. I know I should be concentrating for the exams but I can't stop thinking about tonight. Excitement fizzes through me when I look at the clock – only a few hours to get through. I picture it, the look on his face when I tell him what I've done. What we'll be able to do.

My mobile is in my lap and the vibration is too loud. Mrs Garrett glares at me; I make an apology face but can't resist sliding a hand under the desk, checking the screen with one hand. The message makes my smile even wider. Not long now. He's so sweet. I know it's not fair keeping it all a secret but it's the only way I know how – Mum and Ian would go mad if they knew, and the girls at school would make my life a misery. This way, it's just us, and nobody else needs to be involved.

'Clare? Could you pay attention, please?' Mrs Garrett looks cross this time and I hurriedly slide the mobile into my bag, pick up my pen. I feel bad – she's nice, is Mrs Garrett, she's my form teacher this year. She has a hard time controlling some of the boys, I think she's quite new. I'd hate to be a teacher – I'd be crap at it. For the last year or so I've been thinking about

the police, though Mum isn't keen. I think it might help me come to terms with things a bit, help me understand what happened with Mum.

'Who can tell me what topics are likely to come up in your exams?' Mrs Garrett asks, and I feel myself drifting off again, looking down at my page to avoid the question, tuning her out a bit. The numbers on the page dance giddily before my eyes. I hear my phone vibrate again against the floor. Once, twice. One for sorrow. Two for joy.

Chapter Nineteen

DS Madeline Shaw

Monday 11th February

'**P**hone records are in.'

Lorna drops a couple of sheets of paper onto Madeline's desk. 'And I've asked the family liaison officer to keep a closer eye on Ian Edwards today,' she continues. 'And give us a heads up if Rachel goes rogue again.' From what Theresa's told them so far, Rachel is a mess and Ian is angry at the force's lack of progress, *along with the rest of the world*, she thinks. Madeline makes a mental note to find out how angry.

'Thanks, Lorna,' she says, pulling the records towards her and starting to flip through. Vodafone have given them a month's worth but it's the last few days they need to focus on, Clare's final hours. As Madeline is turning the pages, she sees it – a number called over and over again, the double 5 at the end jumping out at her. February 1st, 2nd, 3rd. Whoever this person was, she was in contact with them. A lot. Quickly, she checks it against the number they have for Rachel. It's not a match.

The DCI isn't in the room. 'Lorna,' Madeline calls, gesturing to her. 'Look at these. Clare made a ten-minute phone call to this same number on the day she died, about fifteen minutes before the beginning of the potential time of death window.' She points, and Lorna leans in.

'Run it through the database, will you,' Madeline asks, and Lorna takes the paper, disappears into the next room.

They have already asked Clare's parents who she was close to, if there was anyone they could think of, but the two of them only mentioned Lauren.

'Shaw?' The DCI pushes the door open and strides towards Madeline, his shirt untucked. His brown hair is standing on end, as if he's been running his hands through it in stress. There's a copy of the *Essex Gazette* in his hand, a picture of Sorrow's Meadow on the front. So far, they have managed to keep the press under control this week, relatively speaking, although Clare's beautiful face is obviously selling. The *Daily Mail* piece hasn't appeared yet – Rob must have bribed Danny Brien somehow. Madeline wonders if anything more has been leaked – the wound to the back of her head, the speculation over Nathan. Something tells her that this isn't good news.

'I've just had bloody Andrea Marsons on the phone,' Rob says, slamming the paper down onto the desk, 'she says the schools are in chaos. Apparently some rumour's started going round about Nathan Warren now, about it being a sexual thing even though obviously we know that's bollocks. Could be Harry Goodwin starting it, after your little meeting with him. The kids are panicking that it's going to happen again, parents making the whole thing worse. One of the mothers is threatening to speak to the nationals. I've already had to beg bloody Danny Brien to hold off on the *Mail* until next week.'

'What's she planning to say to the nationals?'

Rob shrugs in exasperation. 'Apparently someone's

suggesting that we're hiding something, that we're frightened of looking discriminatory if we bring Nathan Warren back in.'

'That's ridiculous,' Madeline says, picturing poor Nathan, standing in the rain on the pavement.

'Well, you and I know that, but the bloody gossips of Ashdon don't,' Rob says. 'Honestly, Madeline, I don't know how you stand it there. It's everything that's wrong with small communities.'

He sighs. 'Look, Shaw, can you face going to the school? Andrea reckons it'd be good for "morale".' His fingers spike the air in quotation marks.

Madeline glances at the door, hoping to see Lorna. 'Actually, I've just been going through the phone records,' she says, 'it'd be good to have a bit more time—'

He cuts her off. 'That wasn't a question, Shaw. Do you know how pissed the superintendent will be if our name comes under fire? Get yourself down to the school. Damage control.'

On the way to Ashdon, Madeline switches on the radio, tries to think. Who would want to target Clare Edwards? Pretty, smart, lovely Clare. Jealousy? Lauren's face flickers into her mind, her dark-rimmed eyes. Anger? A school prank gone wrong?

The yellow ribbons on the trees outside the school are whipping in the wind. It's cold, even for February. Some of the PTA put the ribbons up the day after she died, tying them earnestly to the bare branches in memory of Clare. Most of them look dirty now; the cars that go by (not that there are many here) splash up mud; the damp curls the edges.

The headteacher greets her at the front door of the secondary school. Andrea's wearing her usual woollen jumper but she looks harried, more so than usual. There's an ink stain on the hem of her sleeve.

'Thanks for coming again,' she says, 'we've been waiting for you. I thought it might help settle things down, you know. Show them you're doing something. Through here.'

Madeline follows her down the school hallway into the big sports hall where they hold assembly. Gym equipment lines the walls: climbing ropes, crash mats. The kids stare. The secondary school is so much worse than the primary, the older kids look contemptuous. They're buying into the stuff they overhear from their parents; that Chelmsford are not doing a good enough job.

'Hello everyone,' Madeline says awkwardly. She is met with blank looks. The atmosphere is stiff, hostile.

'Most of you know me already, but I'm DS Madeline Shaw, and together with my colleague DCI Rob Sturgeon, I'm overseeing the investigation into the death of Clare Edwards.' There's a murmuring, a few whispers that she cannot quite catch. 'As you all know,' she continues, 'the loss of Clare has hit this community hard. Our job as police officers is to do our utmost to protect you all from further incidents, and to bring justice to whoever attacked Clare.' She can feel Andrea's eyes on her; is aware that she's not sugar-coating it as much as she probably should. There isn't time for that.

'The police presence in the town is still constant,' Madeline continues, 'and we are currently following up a number of inquiries. It is essential,' briefly, she locks eyes with a guy in the back row – tall, slouching, sarcastic – 'that you cooperate with us as far as you all can. It may seem as though there is nothing you can do, but in fact there are several things I'd like to run through today that I want you all to listen to.' To her right, Andrea brightens. Positive action: that's always what they want.

'Firstly,' Madeline says, warming to the role a bit, 'you can speak up. If there is anything, and I mean *anything*, that anyone here is keeping from the police, you must let us know. Even if you think it's not important, even if you think it sounds silly. Even –' she pauses for a moment, '– if you think it might get you into trouble. Chances are, you'll be in a hell of a lot more trouble if you don't tell us than if you do.'

There's the sound of sniggering at the back; Andrea makes a shushing noise.

'Secondly, I need you all to remain vigilant. If you see anything that you think could be of any relevance to this case, again, you must let us know. No matter how insignificant it might seem. No matter how long ago you think it was. Thirdly, I want every single person in this room to exercise the common sense, intelligence and responsibility that I would expect from a well-regarded school such as Ashdon Secondary. That means there is to be no idle speculation about this case, no deliberate scare-mongering, and no unnecessary gossiping. Unsolicited rumours can be very damaging to a small community such as this one, and can interfere with a serious crime case if they go too far. If you suspect any individual of involvement, the person you need to tell is me. And that's it.'

The boy in the back row is being nudged in the ribs by a dark-haired girl next to him; the movement catches Madeline's eye. He looks about sixteen – Clare's year. Year Eleven.

'What about Nathan Warren?' he shouts out, confrontation

in his voice – not a lot of it, but there, under the surface. 'Is it true you've just let him out? You've let some paedo come back for more?'

There's a sudden splash of noise in the room and Andrea steps forward. 'There will be time for questions once the DS has finished speaking,' she says, but Madeline holds up a hand to show her that it's okay.

'I can confirm that we have recently made the decision not to hold Mr Warren after a period of questioning, yes. We do not, at present, have reason to believe he was involved in the incident, other than being the one to come across the scene. However, we will, of course, be revisiting all lines of inquiry should further evidence arise.'

Muttering spins around the room, corner to corner like a Mexican wave.

'The fourth thing I ask of you all,' she says, raising her voice, 'is to remain constantly alert. Your safety and the safety of every person in this town continues to be my priority. Ashdon has long been a safe town, and that's how we want it to stay. And part of that comes down to the way you conduct yourselves. Some of you are young adults now,' she cringes inwardly at the term, 'and you have a responsibility to this community to exercise caution at all times. I trust I can expect that from you all.'

The room has gone silent now. She has got their attention. Without warning, the school bell rings to announce the end of the period and the spell breaks; the kids turn to each other, mouths opening ready to do exactly what she's just told them not to.

Andrea smiles ruefully. 'Thanks, Madeline. Hopefully some of it sinks in.'

'Any time. Have you got a minute? It'd be good to chat briefly about Rachel Edwards. I'm – well, I'm concerned about her.'

'Yes, of course. In my office?'

The sound of her mobile cuts into the air; Lorna's name flashes up on the screen.

'Campbell?'

'Hi, Madeline,' she says, 'sorry, I know you're at the school but I wanted to let you know, we've got a match for that number, the one Clare was calling.' She reels off the digits again. 'The DCI spoke to the provider and they've released the info without a hassle.'

'And?' Madeline's heart is going a little faster; Andrea is looking at her questioningly.

'Belongs to an Owen Jones, purchased in Saffron Walden last year from the Carphone Warehouse on Moor Street. The latest iPhone, pays monthly by direct debit. Name ring any bells?'

'Owen Jones.' It doesn't, but Andrea is looking alarmed, frowning.

'What's happened to Owen Jones?' the headteacher asks, clearly jumping to the wrong conclusion, and Madeline shakes her head.

'Do you know him?' she asks, and Andrea nods, a quick up and down.

'He's a pupil here,' she says. 'He's the year above Clare.' Her face is stricken.

Chapter Twenty

Jane

Monday 11th February

After Jack and I hang up, I ring Sandra back reluctantly, ask her if she wouldn't mind doing me a huge favour and bring Finn and Sophie home from school.

'Harry will be back around 4.30,' I tell her, 'he can come and walk them back from yours. But if you wouldn't mind picking them up from the gates?'

'Of course!' she squeals predictably, 'Natasha will be thrilled. We've been meaning to have Sophie round for ages, the girls always have such a lovely time together.' They don't, they're often at loggerheads, but I'm hoping they'll get on well enough for a few hours. 'Why don't I keep them for a few hours, give Harry a bit of a break?' Sandra suggests, and I don't know how to tell her no.

'Thanks so much,' I say instead, sighing down the phone in only a little exaggerated relief. 'You're a star! I'll make it up to you in wine!' We laugh. It's so easy.

When she's gone, I bite my fingernail, so hard that it bleeds. The little cracks of blood turn my stomach. Jack hasn't called back, but I know where to meet him. It's where we always used to go to talk. Despite myself, I feel a little flicker of hope.

Perhaps he's regretting what he said to me the night Clare died, perhaps this will be a turning point.

I start to think about what I'm going to say to him, planning out the words in my head.

At around four, I get into our blue Volvo, parked conspicuously in the drive to the side of the house, pull the sunshade down to check my reflection out of habit. I look the same as I always do – brown hair pulled back into a bun, dark blue eyes that stare back at me with no indication of what I'm feeling inside. I remember just after I gave birth to Harry, staring at myself in a hospital bathroom, wondering how it was that I could look exactly the same even though my whole life had changed for ever. I was no longer the girl everybody ignored, I was a mother, and that meant something. It still does. Doesn't it?

I start the car, my fingers clasping tightly around the keys, Jack's NHS keyring bouncing against my hand. At some stage, our possessions became irretrievably amalgamated. He can't separate them, separate us. Not even if he wants to.

My mobile vibrates and my heart leaps, thinking he's cancelling, but when I check, it's just Sandra, asking me if it's alright for the kids to have sausage and mash for supper. I didn't ask her to feed them. *It's no trouble*, her message says, and I feel the implicit criticism, force myself to brush it away and type out a civil response. It messes up my meal routine, when they eat at someone else's. But I mustn't panic about that.

Pulling out of the drive, I check left and right and see the curtains moving in the row of houses opposite; it'll be Mrs Drayton, silly old bat. As far as we can tell, she's lived in the town for years and has no intention of leaving. Her front garden is full of colourful little windmills that spin in the breeze and drive me insane. The curtains twitch again, the white net shifting slightly to the left. Aware that I might be being watched, I rub my lips together and switch on the radio, letting the car fill with the sound of Radio 4. Nothing to see here.

Our house is ten minutes to the right of the schools, and the town is so small that I only have to drive a few hundred metres to the left and I'm out. The hedgerows shimmer past, the green beginning to bloom now, just a little bit covering up the dry brittle branches of winter. In the summer months, these roads will whiten with nettles and cow parsley, great aureoles of it dotting the verge. It was always Nathan Warren's job to strim these rows – well, maybe it was a task he set himself. None of us ever knew if he really *had* a job, not after the school let him go. I doubt he'll be strimming the hedges this year.

Trying to distract myself, I fiddle with the radio, find our local station. As I do so, the familiar name jumps out at me. *Police investigating the death of sixteen-year-old schoolgirl Clare Edwards have reissued a statement to the public urging them to come forward with any information. Clare Edwards, of Ashdon, near Saffron Walden, is believed to have been killed on February the 4th, just five weeks into the new year. Her body was found in a local field.*

The newsreader lists the number to call for information, and then the station has moved on; the tinny sound of a pop song fills the Volvo, mindless teenage angst set to a repetitive synthesiser. The image of my children's faces swims before me and I want to stop the car, swing it back around and rush to

Sandra's, scoop their warm little bodies towards me and bury my face in the sweet scent of their hair. But I can't do that. I have to go to my husband. The last time I refused to do as he said, I ended up with a broken rib and Egyptian cotton sheets.

Instead of stopping the car, I turn right off the road, try to take deep breaths, force myself to think calm thoughts. Karen's shop, yes; I'm in the studio at the back, painting, the blue of the sea and the yellow – no, not yellow – the pinky dusk of the sky. My hands tighten on the steering wheel but I make myself imagine a brush between my fingers, the reassuring wooden thrum of it on my narrow bones. I hear Diane's voice in my head, soothing, non-confrontational. I imagine her here in the car, sat beside me in the passenger seat, her hands folded demurely in her lap. My own hands agitate on the wheel, slip slightly. I reach out and turn the radio off. The button is slick beneath my finger.

Jack's car is already there when I arrive. Wordlessly, I pull up behind him, cut the engine, walk to his window and wait as he unlocks the door.

As I climb in, he locks it behind me. In my pocket, my fingers grip my phone, my hand slippery with sweat. Just in case.

'We need to talk,' he says, 'we need to talk about us.'

My throat feels thick at the words, full of all the things I want to say. The look on his face is grim, set. But it has to be now – now is my moment.

'Harry found your records, Jack,' I say quietly, my voice hushed in the airtight silence of the car. 'Your GP schedule with Clare's name on it.'

For a moment, something like fear seems to flash across

my husband's features, but it is smoothed away almost as quickly as it appeared.

'Don't you think you ought to mention it to the police?' I ask him, but he's not looking at me now, he's gazing out of the car window at the slowly setting sun, and I cannot see his eyes. *If you don't, I will,* is what I want to say, but of course I don't.

When he turns back towards me, his face is cold.

'It was for contraception, Jane,' he says, 'it was just routine. She must have been shagging someone.'

His words are bitter. A pause. In my pocket, my fingers fiddle nervously with my phone. My eyes dart to the locked door.

'Are you happy now? I didn't tell the police because I didn't – I didn't want them—'

I finish the sentence for him. 'You didn't want them knowing what we really are.'

A swallow. When I look at him, there are tears glinting on his face.

Chapter Twenty-One

Clare

Monday 4th February, 11.00 a.m.

The rest of the morning passes quickly; English is my favourite subject but all we're doing these days are mock exams ahead of the GCSEs. I write quickly, my pen whizzing across the page, filling sheet after sheet with my neat blue handwriting.

Beside me, I can hear Lauren sighing over her papers – English has never been her strong subject. I shift my own paper slightly so that she can see.

'You can buy me lunch later,' I mouth, and she grins, winks back at me. I guess we're friends again, then.

I finish the paper early and sit back in my chair, toss my long blonde hair across my shoulder. Andy Miles grins at me from across the room but I ignore him. The boys in this class are morons, children. They're not like me and him.

Everyone else is still working – I'm the first to finish. Harry Goodwin walks past the classroom window, sees me and smiles, and I think of him in the lane this morning, his hands on my shoulders. Lauren thinks I'm mad not to go for it with him – we rowed about it last night. If I'm honest, I think Lauren's a bit jealous that Harry's not interested in her, but if it was up to me, she could have him. I've basically told her so, *anyway. Maybe I should just tell him I'm not interested, tell him Lauren likes him. But I don't know how he'd react.*

My mind drifts to Mum, her pleading eyes as she looked at Ian at breakfast time, the desperate way she always gets. I hate the way he tries to suck up to me, all smiles one minute and grumpy the next. I can't trust him, and I know some of that is Mum's fault really, but it means I'm so tense all the time at home. I stretch a little in my chair, arms over my head, trying to ease the ache in my shoulders. My necklace rises up and I reach for it, fiddle with the little gold heart. It's a nice present. I never take it off. Mum gave me a hug when I opened it, pressing me to her chest like she did when I was a little girl.

'My baby, all grown up!' she said, cupping my face in her hands and smiling at me. 'I can't believe you're sixteen now. Time goes so fast.'

At that moment, I really loved her.

I wish it could be just Mum and me. I don't know why she doesn't understand that. That way, we'd both be safe.

Chapter Twenty-Two

DS Madeline Shaw

Monday 11th February

Owen Jones is sixteen, with a pale, freckled face and a shock of red hair. Teenage acne spots his neck and his Adam's apple bobs nervously as he speaks. They are in Andrea's office, sitting across from one another, with the headteacher hovering anxiously in the background, darting glances at the door as though she expects the press to storm in at any minute and splash her school all over the tabloids.

'I'm DS Madeline Shaw,' she begins, reaching out to shake him by the hand. His palms are sweaty, damp and Madeline has to force herself not to recoil. It's not his fault that he's sixteen and full of hormones. It is, however, definitely his fault that he didn't come forward the minute Clare was found.

'Sorry to call you away from your studies, Mr Jones,' she says, her eyes on his face. His right foot is jiggling slightly; either it's a nervous habit or he's got something to hide. Either way, he looks far from comfortable.

'Perhaps you could help me clear something up.' She is keeping her voice light, sitting back in her chair as though there is all the time in the world. 'I've been looking at the people your schoolmate Clare Edwards was in contact with, right before she died.'

Andrea is almost hopping with anxiety, and there are probably only a few minutes before her common sense kicks in and she insists on Owen having a parent or other appropriate adult present. Owen says nothing.

'We don't have Clare's mobile phone,' Madeline tells him, 'it hasn't been found. We're working on the assumption that whoever killed her also took her phone, to prevent us finding evidence. But in spite of that, we're able to access the incoming and outgoing calls within the last month, and do you know whose number pops up far more frequently than most?'

'DS Shaw,' Andrea says, 'I really think there should be—'

'Mine,' Owen says, interrupting her, leaning forward on his chair, his whole face flushed now, bright red in contrast to the paleness of his neck. 'Mine.' His voice is gruff, older than his years.

Madeline pauses, wondering suddenly if he *wanted* this to happen; she was expecting more of a battle to begin with. 'That's right,' she says, 'yours. Now, Owen, at the moment you're not in any trouble, but I do have to ask you what your relationship was to Clare, and more importantly, why you did not come forward earlier if, as we're assuming, your relationship was of a significantly closer nature than we knew.'

He sits back, puts both hands to his head, and for a minute, she thinks he might cry. His right foot is still jiggling incessantly; he barely seems to notice.

'Owen,' she pushes, 'if you have any information about Clare that you're withholding from me, now would be the time to divulge it.' One last chance. 'For your sake, as well as ours.' She waits, swallows. Is he going to break? 'And for Clare's.'

'You want to look at Ian,' he says suddenly, the words blurting out as though he's been sitting on them all week. Andrea and Madeline exchange glances.

'Ian Edwards, Clare Edwards' stepfather?' Madeline repeats, wanting to be crystal clear, almost forgetting that they aren't actually on tape.

'Yes,' Owen said, and then it's as if someone has ripped gaffer tape off his mouth, the words tumble out one after the other like they've been stored up just beneath his tongue.

'Ian wasn't very nice to Clare,' he says, 'she was frightened of him.'

She is watching his face closely.

'What is your connection to Ian Edwards?' she says slowly.

'I'm not connected to that man,' Owen says, and his fists clench, curling in on themselves into hard, tight balls. 'But I know what he's like. He used to coach us at football.'

She nods – they've got that on record – Ian coached the secondary school team last year. With military precision, according to some people.

'What makes you say that?' she asks, frowning at him. He won't look her in the eye.

'Clare told me, and I knew how she was feeling,' Owen says, and that's when Madeline sees the first flash of anger across his face. 'I knew what she was feeling because I was Clare's boyfriend.'

She decides to take Owen down to the station this afternoon, after a quick phone call with the DCI. If she is honest, she's pissed off – with herself, with the DCI, with Clare's parents. How could none of them know this? Why didn't Owen come forward before?

Andrea is flustered, hopping around trying to find Owen's dad's number. He's a minor – they will have to do it all properly.

'He's away a lot, with work,' she tells Madeline, 'and his wife died about ten years ago.' She lowers her voice to a whisper. 'Owen rattles around on his own most of the time.'

Madeline dials the number she's given nonetheless, praying it's not the abroad tone. Luckily, it rings. His dad says he'll meet them at the station in Chelmsford, sounds very taken aback. *Perhaps he ought to be home a little more*, Madeline thinks, *pay a bit more attention to his teenage son.*

Owen barely speaks in the car, huddled in the backseat; his long, gangly legs look squashed. He's tall for his age, but when Madeline pictures Clare's smiling face, she can't imagine them together. For all she can tell, Clare was a bit of a golden girl, whereas he looks like the sort of kid that flies firmly under the radar. One might even go so far as to say geeky. She wonders why nobody's come forward about a boyfriend, why neither Rachel Edwards nor Ian have mentioned it at all. Something's not right here.

He's nervous at the station, even though they have told him several times that he's not under arrest. Not yet, anyway. Madeline keeps sneaking glances at him, at the size of his hands. He looks like a typical football kid, certainly not the broad rugby player type. Compared to Clare though, he's a giant. For some reason, she doesn't warm to him.

His dad arrives two minutes later, rushing in with a briefcase in one hand and his mobile in the other. He looks just like his son: messy red hair, freckles that don't manage to disguise the tell-tale signs of middle age.

'Daniel Jones,' he says, shaking Madeline's hand, 'I'm very surprised to be here.'

'Take a seat,' she says, pouring him a glass of water which he takes quickly, drinking several gulps before turning to Owen and putting a hand on his shoulder.

'Alright, O? This is a bit of a pickle, isn't it?'

Middle-class parents, she thinks. *A pickle.*

'I'd like to start by asking Owen a few questions, Mr Jones,' Madeline says, one hand reaching out to switch on the tape. Owen hasn't spoken since his dad arrived, and if anything, his skin looks even paler than before.

'Owen,' she says to him, trying to make eye contact across the table but failing. He is looking studiously at the tape recorder, unblinking. When he does look up, she realises with a swift flash of horror that his eyes are full of tears. Furiously, he brushes them away.

'Sorry,' he says gruffly, 'shit, sorry. It's just, I miss her. You know? She was mine and now she's gone and I— I can't…' He gulps slightly, his Adam's apple bobbing up and down. Suddenly, having him there in the interview room feels unnecessarily harsh, voyeuristic. Something about the whole thing feels grubby. But there are the phone records, the incessant calls. They will get his fingerprints straight after this.

'I do understand, Owen,' Madeline says, trying to be gentle. Owen's father looks awkward, as though embarrassed that his son has displayed emotion quite so readily.

'Alright. First of all, for the tape, I want to ask you how

you would describe your relationship with the victim of this case, Clare Edwards. Can you tell me a bit about that?'

He blanches, visibly, at the word victim.

'We've been seeing each other since last summer,' he says, pulling at the edge of his school shirt sleeve, as if he wants to cover his hands up, hide in whatever way he can. 'We didn't tell anyone, I don't think she – she didn't want to. But I really liked her, you know?' His voice cracks again, and his dad coughs, the sound loud in the small room. Madeline nods, encouraging him to go on.

'So you kept your whole relationship a secret?'

He nods. 'We had to. Clare didn't – well, things were tough, at home, she didn't want her stepdad getting involved.'

'That must have been a difficult thing to keep hidden from everyone.' She is watching him closely. One of the spots on his neck has formed a whitehead, surrounded by an angry red rash. Clare could have had her pick of the boys at Ashdon Secondary. Is it possible she was embarrassed by Owen?

'It was,' he says, 'but I loved her. I wanted to make her happy.'

There is a pause. The air in the room feels tight and thick.

'And how would you describe Clare, Owen? Particularly in the weeks leading up to February the fourth. Did she seem different to you? Would you say anything was upsetting her?'

He squirms uncomfortably, his eyes flicking to the door as though he wants to escape.

'I mean…not really, we were happy, we were great.' He looks at his dad, his face flushing red again. 'We were in love.'

'Was Clare coming to see you, on the night she died?'

He looks away from me. 'Yes. But I don't know why she went that way, she doesn't usually.'

'Did you worry when she didn't arrive?'

He glances at his dad. 'Yes,' he says, 'yes, of course. I tried to call her, but she didn't pick up. I dunno, I thought maybe she'd changed her mind, I didn't know. I didn't know who to tell.'

'Did you think about reporting it to us?'

He shakes his head. 'I thought I'd call her in the morning, I thought maybe she was mad at me or something.'

'Did you give her reason to be angry with you, Owen?'

He looks up at this, his expression alarmed. 'No! No, that was just a guess, I dunno. I was worried she was with someone else, you know, another guy.' He looks uncomfortable.

'Would that have been likely? Her seeing someone else?'

He shrugs, looks away. Madeline makes a note, changes tack. She can't yet get the measure of him.

'You mentioned Ian, when we spoke today – Ian Edwards, Clare's stepfather?'

He nods, and she raises her eyebrows, indicating the tape.

'Yes,' he says, his voice a bit clearer than it was before, 'yes, that's right. Ian.' A look flits across his face, a look of intense dislike. 'Clare never liked him,' he says, and everything in his body seems to straighten, as if he is warming to his theme, becoming more sure of what he is saying.

'What makes you say that?' Madeline asks the question at the same time as his father intervenes with a quiet, 'Careful, son.'

Owen shrugs. 'He just— he was mean to her. And she was weird about him, well, that's what I thought anyway. Jumpy whenever he was nearby, as if she was nervous. She didn't want to tell him about me, and I think it's because he was – you know, aggressive.' He pauses. 'That's how it seemed, anyway.'

'Did Clare ever voice these concerns to you, Owen? Did she ever do anything to indicate that her stepfather might be capable of causing her harm? Even serious harm?'

Owen's father is beginning to look nervous. Perhaps he's realising this is more than a 'pickle', after all.

'She said he'd taken over her mum's life,' Owen says, 'that she was sick of hearing about him and the business, him in the army – it was all about him. She didn't like her mum being under his spell.'

'Look, I really think that perhaps I ought to have a lawyer present for my son,' the boy's father starts to say, but Madeline holds up a hand.

'Mr Jones, at present your son is not under any suspicion,' she says. 'We are simply questioning him due to his previously undisclosed relationship with the victim, and are attempting to get to the bottom of a matter he brought up earlier today regarding Ian Edwards.'

'He used to be in the army,' Owen says, a hint of anger creeping into his voice. 'Course, he was bloody aggressive. She didn't like him, I'm telling you. He had them both under his thumb, Clare and her mum. She had to take his name and everything. And he was always bad-mouthing her dad – he died, you know – I heard him saying stuff about him, to anyone who'd listen. Back when he used to coach the football.'

'And how long did he coach your football team for?' Madeline asks, and Owen frowns.

'Couple of months, last year. He quit, no one knew why. He never liked me, either. And if he'd found out I was seeing Clare… well, I don't know what he might have done.'

Chapter Twenty-Three

Jane

Monday 11th February

The top I'm wearing is long-sleeved, but the marks Jack has left on my arms are dotting tell-tale spots of blood through the fabric. That didn't exactly go as planned. I thought, after the tears, that he was going to apologise. I thought we were going to sort out our marriage. But as always, we morphed into an argument.

Who was she getting contraception for? I asked him, but he just shrugged, told me he'd got no idea.

Some people actually have a functioning sex life, you know, he said to me, and I felt each word like a tiny sting, needling and sharp. We haven't touched each other for months.

I follow his car home, shaking slightly, trying to ignore the rushing feelings of shame that are threatening to take over, like a wave inside my head that I have to fight against all the time. I have to keep both hands on the wheel, keep focused, get home and see to the children. I lost control of that conversation. Like I always do. But at least I know why she was on his appointment list. My husband is many things, but he isn't a murderer. An image of myself lying at the bottom of the stairs comes to me; the old pain in my ribs shifts a little. I know what he's capable of. I know his limits. Don't I?

Harry texts me as I am driving back, three words, *where are you?*

When I do get home, Jack's pulled up in our drive but he's still sat in his car, head bowed. The flowers for Clare have almost taken over the Edwards' front lawn; their ornamental bird bath pokes out from the mass of colour, creating a bizarre sight. Their house looms over us, tall and imposing, the cream walls giving nothing away.

Jack doesn't move, even when my car slides in alongside his. I stare at him as I hurry past, anxious to get inside and tidy myself up before anything else happens. I wish he'd move. I don't want the Edwards to see him.

Inside, I've left the tap dripping; water is pooling in the sink. I turn it on full and run my arms underneath it, the thin lines of blood blooming into rusty petals in the stainless steel basin. They're not deep, they never are. They don't even hurt any more. They did to begin with.

I remember very clearly the moment I first met Jack. Dark hair, those flashing blue eyes. When I looked at him full in the face I had to look away; I had the sensation of falling, and I didn't want to fall. Not then, not now, not ever.

I was holding an empty polystyrene cup of coffee, clutching it hard between my fingers. I hadn't wanted to come that day, and it turned out neither had he. I'd forced myself – he'd had a friend drive him. It was my friend Lisa who'd recommended Albion Road to me, but when she'd first suggested it, I'd gone mad. I shouldn't have done, really. She was only trying to do the right thing. We were good friends for a while, Lisa and I. We grew up together – she was one of the very few people who knew me from when I was young, knew about

152

my parents and how hard it all was. I liked her, I suppose. When Harry was little she was still there, looking after him for me sometimes, a friend when I needed one. But then the accident on the stairs happened, we moved to Ashdon and I had Sophie and Finn. Lisa and I grew apart. Plus, she didn't approve of Jack, of our relationship. She's the only person I ever thought might actually be able to see through us. And I didn't want any reminders of my past hanging around. Not after what happened at the old house. How close Jack and I came to falling apart.

Often, I think about what would have happened that day – if I'd been firmer with Lisa, told her I wasn't going; if I'd followed advice and kept myself to myself, focused on the task at hand; if when, at the end of our third session, Jack had scribbled his phone number on a piece of ripped off polystyrene cup, I'd never called him – whether I'd be where I am now. Trapped by the choices I have already made. In a life I've built and cannot escape.

Sandra Davies insists on dropping Finn and Sophie back to the door. Harry is already home, slumped in front of the television, his dark hair hanging over his face.

'Can I get you a snack?' I ask him, nerves sprinkling my stomach, but he shakes his head, his thumbs and eyes glued to his iPhone. I'm relieved the police haven't come near him again, but I can't stop thinking about how close a call it all was. I don't want them speaking to my son again. The bruise on my arm has faded to yellow now, so that's something.

Jack has taken himself up to our bedroom without speaking, the door slamming shut behind him. I took him a tea, left it on the bedside in a china mug with the NHS logo on it. He'll appreciate the gesture, at some point. In the old days, he used to bring me flowers afterwards, kiss my hands, fall at my feet, beg me. He doesn't really bother now. I leant down over him while he slept, or pretended to, brought my lips right up close to his ear.

'Thank you so much for having the kids, Sandra,' I say to her now, wincing slightly as Finn barrels into me, his little head butting my stomach like a tiny, hornless bull. 'Was everything alright?'

'Fine, no trouble at all, pair of little angels,' Sandra says, smiling at me as Sophie rushes past into the house, dropping her red reading folder onto the floor as she goes. She hovers there, on the doorstep, her eyes darting from side to side, until something inside me gives in and I say what I know she's been waiting for: 'Would you like to come in for a quick drink?'

'Ooh,' she says, as though the thought has only just occurred to her, 'well, Monday night, don't mind if I do! But only one mind!' Here, she looks slightly reproachful, as though I am accustomed to pouring white wine down her throat by the bucket-load at any opportune moment. Which, I suppose, I am. Jack won't come down for hours now; at least if Sandra's here I'm not drinking alone.

I extend my arm, widening the door a little and she hustles inside, removing her coat as she does so. I take it from her and hang it up on the peg where it nestles amongst the others: Harry's hoodie, Jack's big blue duffel coat, the children's assortment of brightly coloured anoraks, my cashmere scarves in shades of pastel. Our perfect little life. Suddenly,

I think of Clare's trainers on the Edwards' shoe rack that morning, the rush of hope I'd felt when I thought she'd come home safely.

'Is Jack in?' Sandra says, peering around slightly as if he might pop out of a cupboard. I see her eyes go to his coat.

'He's upstairs,' I say quickly, 'bit of a migraine, poor thing.'

'Ooh,' she says, although I can see the quick flash of disappointment as it skitters across her face. 'It must be exhausting dealing with patients all day as well. We'll keep our voices down!' She glances inside the house. 'Is that Harry in there?'

I wish everyone would stop treating my husband as if he's some sort of God. If only they knew.

I usher her into the kitchen so I can see through the beamed archway into the living room, where Sophie and Finn have seated themselves in front of the television with Harry, eyes fixed on the screen. A wave of irritation flashes over me; I need to put them to bed, I don't want them staring at the screen all night while Sandra witters on. Bringing up the children properly is all I've got space left to care about right now – it's important.

But Sandra is already plonking herself down at the marble counter, easing a Birkenstock shoe off to reveal coral-painted toenails. For goodness' sake. It isn't even summer! She runs her fingers over the surface like she always does, sighing a little, and I know she's jealous of my home, of my life. Good. She cranes her neck slightly, so that she can see through the window into the Edwards' house. So *that's* why she was so keen to come in.

'What can I get you?' I say, even though I can almost feel the tang of alcohol on my tongue already. I move to the fridge, pull out the bottle of white that's been sitting there since yesterday. There's still three-quarters left. I silently congratulate myself.

She takes a deep sigh, her elbows settling themselves on the counter. The new vase of lilies beside her shudders slightly; a deep pink petal releases tiny yellow buds. I usually buy flowers once a week from the market in Saffron Walden, just after I've had my nails done or been to the shops. It's part of my routine. The little things I cling onto. I suppose it's about control. The ones I buy for myself are nicer than any Jack brings me – prettier, more expensive. I've got good taste.

'Let's have a glass,' Sandra says. 'Have you heard what's been happening up at the school?'

I shake my head, turn away from her, busy myself with the glasses and the wine so that she can't see my face. I've put on a jumper, thicker to cover my arms, but the material still chafes against them as I twist the wine open. Screw top: Walker's finest.

'Apparently Madeline Shaw's been in, whipping them all up again, meanwhile Nathan's on the bloody road moving his cone up and down like nothing's happened.' More sighing. 'I'm so worried about Natasha.' She glances over at the kids. 'I wonder how much they take in.' Rather than reply, I pass her a glass of wine – filled to the white line, no ice, but it doesn't really matter. Putting my own glass down, I look over to the partitioned living room that leads off the kitchen, watching the children's heads, resolutely focused on the screen. Harry, normally fairly interactive with his younger siblings, has moved away from the sofa onto the armchair by the window, still studiously fixated by his phone. Finn is wiggling his toes off the end of the sofa; Sophie is absently fiddling with strands of her hair, no doubt trying to do a plait. Her hair's too curly, really, but she persists nonetheless. My fingers twitch; I want to go over and help her, but Sandra's looking at me expectantly.

'OK, Soph?' I call out, and she jerks her head up, nods at me happily. 'Not long 'til bedtime,' I say warningly, wondering if Jack really has gone to sleep upstairs.

'Ooh, what're they watching? My Natasha's always got her nose buried in a book these days,' Sandra says, and my fingers curl in on themselves. Ignoring the question and the implied dig, I take a seat opposite her, swallow a large gulp of wine. It does need ice.

'I'm not sure how much good the police are doing, Janey,' Sandra says. I don't like her saying my nickname like that – it's what Jack used to call me before everything went wrong. Another sip of wine; I feel it smoothing my edges, softening the grind of Sandra's voice. I know she looked after the children, I know I should be grateful. But the town feels like it's closing in on me: the women, the gossip, the exhaustion of trying to hide beneath the façade of my marriage. I just want out. But of course I can't have out, can I? I look down into my wine, imagine myself drinking more and more until everything else stops.

'Jane?'

'Sorry,' I say, shaking my head slightly, trying to focus. 'No, I agree. D'you think it'll just drag on, be one of those things that never gets solved? Like a cold case, I mean? Harry listened to a podcast about those. The media picks up cases the police decide to write off.'

She looks shocked. 'Write off? They can't write it off, not so soon, not while there's a murderer out there, wandering the streets. I won't stand for it – the town won't!' I might be imagining it, but she even sits up a little straighter on her chair. 'Ashdon is a beautiful town, Jane – we shouldn't have to live like this! And what if he's still out there – this man – this, this murderer.' She lowers her voice, inclines her head towards me. I stare into her irises, brown flecked with black.

'What about our *girls*, Jane? They could be in danger! We all could!' A glance at the window. 'He obviously targeted next door – what if it's you next?'

I glance over at the children but they look oblivious. Still, I don't want Sophie having bad dreams again so I reluctantly inch my stool closer to Sandra's.

'I really do think,' I say, hoping to calm her down so she doesn't rouse Jack, 'that it was probably an isolated incident – after all, wouldn't whoever it was have struck again if it wasn't?' Another sip of wine, a glance at the bottle. 'It could even have been an accident,' I continue, the thought suddenly occurring to me, but Sandra scoffs at me, shakes her head.

'It wasn't an accident, Janey. The police said so, you know they did. There was nothing she could've tripped on, plus her phone was gone. Definitely on purpose. Poor girl.' She shudders.

'Then why Clare?' I push, trying to keep my voice down for the children even though I can feel it rising slightly, becoming what Jack would call 'shrill'. 'Why *hasn't* he targeted someone else?'

She does pause on that. 'Maybe he's biding this time,' she says then, her left hand scrolling its way around the base of her wine glass, wiping away the mist that has formed on the glass.

The wine is going to my head; I haven't eaten anything yet. You'd think after all these years I'd be used to it, but sometimes it still hits me.

'Have you seen Rachel lately?' Sandra asks me, and I close my eyes for a second, see the woman splashing across my dark eyelids: gaunt, broken, alone.

'No,' I say, 'I haven't actually. I keep thinking we—' I stop.

'We ought to go round?' Sandra finishes my sentence and I nod.

'Mmm,' I say non-committally and she jumps in.

'I thought that too. With food or something? But the truth is, Janey,' she leans forward again; this time I can smell the wine on her breath. 'I don't like going next door – because of Ian.'

'You don't like him?' I ask, taking another sip of my drink, and Sandra shakes her head.

'I don't like the way he came into this town, took over that family,' she says. 'I liked Mark, he was a nice guy.' Her words are slurred slightly now, her edges blurred.

'I didn't know him well,' I say, picturing his face: blond hair, thin. Smaller than Ian by quite some way.

Sandra nods, presses her lips together. 'He's where all the money comes from,' she says, gesturing at the window where the Edwards house sits. 'He left Clare a bloody fortune.'

'Did he?' I ask, surprised, and she nods, raises her eyebrows.

'Yep,' she said, 'when he died. She was meant to inherit it all on her twenty-first, Rachel said.' She takes a gulp of wine, hiccups. 'But who d'you think's got all that cash now?'

I stare at her.

'*Ian*,' she hisses, leaning even closer to me. 'And rumour

has it, his business hasn't been doing so well. A cash injection right about now could be quite convenient, don't you think? And if Clare's no longer there to inherit it…' She raises her eyebrows, smiles at me. She loves being the bearer of bad news, I know she does.

'Sandra,' I say, 'is that really true?'

'Word on the street,' she says. 'Shall we have another bottle of wine?'

Chapter Twenty-Four

Clare

Monday 4th February, 12.00 p.m.

The queue for lunch snakes all the way down the corridor. I'm standing with Lauren, my stomach rumbling with hunger, when Harry Goodwin walks past with a packet of chips. The Year Twelves get food and then take it round the back of the sports hall so that they can smoke. You can smell it on their clothes, but no one ever does anything. He winks at me when he sees me, then stops in front of us. My stomach clenches, but Lauren's on high alert; I can feel how tense her body is next to mine, the way she's arching her back, pushing her boobs out.

'Alright Clarey?'

My eyes dart around, checking if anyone's watching.

'Hi Harry,' Lauren says, smiling at him in the way that I know she thinks is sexy. I've seen her practising, when she thinks I'm not looking.

'We were just getting food, Harry,' I say, as politely as I can, then to my relief the queue in front of us shifts forward a bit and we can move away. I can feel his eyes on my back as I turn, and although I know it's just a laugh, just a game to him, I feel a little cold shiver of unease run through me when I turn back and see his blue eyes still boring into me.

'You lucky thing,' Lauren says, 'he's gorgeous, Clare.' She nudges me in the ribs. 'God knows what he sees in you.' She grins to show me that she's only joking.

I just shrug. I don't tell her about how frightened I was when he grabbed me by the shoulders this morning, or about the look on his little sister Sophie's face and how it made me feel. There are a lot of things I don't tell people; it's easy now.

'His dad's not bad either,' Lauren sighs, and I laugh, glad to break the weird tension between us.

'Lauren, he's a hundred years old.' I make a vomiting action with my two fingers.

'And a doctor! Loaded.' She grins at me. 'I bet he's dying to get away from his uptight wife. What is it your mum calls her? Little Miss Perfect.'

Chapter Twenty-Five

DS Madeline Shaw

Tuesday 12th February

Ian Edwards is fifty-five, slightly balding – although he'd never admit it – and takes the 6.41 a.m. train into London Liverpool Street, Monday to Friday. Fond of mowing the grass, likes a pint or five in the Rose and Crown, always has a good word to say about the armed forces, and a bad word to say about his wife's ex-husband (deceased).

On the night they told Clare's parents, Ian was very protective of Rachel, constantly with an arm around her, or a hand clamped over hers, wedding bands clashing together. He did most of the talking. There were lots of photos of him in the Edwards' house, which was slightly odd – almost more than there were of Clare, and certainly more than there were of Rachel's ex, Mark. But other than that, anyone looking would say he was devastated, they both were, he wanted to find Clare's killer and strangle him with both hands. Gave the police a DNA sample straight away, and the photograph of Clare that is now dominating the front pages. Compliant, helpful, wanting to do anything he could to help. Your standard dad reaction.

Except he's not her dad.

He's a relative newcomer to Ashdon, used to live full-time in the city, now has his own business in the City. Newcomers always get people talking, and Mark was well liked by the sounds of it. Madeline made the mistake of mentioning him to Ruby Walker and she proceeded to detail his funeral (in St Mary's, the local church, full to the brim of mourners) and then warmed to her main topic – the stages of his cancer. She has never known anyone quite so turned on by illness as that woman.

What Owen had to say about Ian Edwards was not shocking, exactly, but certainly surprising. They have had to let him and his dad go; Daniel Jones insisted on there being a lawyer present if the police were to question his son again. Madeline watched Owen's hunched form slope off to his dad's car, trying to picture it – Clare's legs wrapped around him, their bodies entwined. Owen angry with her, fed up of being a secret. His big hands pushing her, down onto the ground. No mother, absent father. Too much time on his own. She might even have been about to call it off with him, and he got desperate. It could be true. It could be false.

An abandoned newspaper catches Madeline's eye on the way to the station on Tuesday morning. *Chelmsford Police at a loss in Golden Girl death*. They will have to hold a press conference soon if this keeps up. If only they could find Clare's mobile phone. Taking it suggests evidence, suggests something more personal between attacker and victim. But Clare had no known enemies. She was only sixteen. And the necklace. Madeline has seen photos of her wearing it, one taken on her birthday, the day she was given it, and one a week or so later, a candid shot snapped by her mother. In it, Clare is sitting at the kitchen table in their house, her head bent over school work, a fancy-looking fountain pen in her hand. You can see the glimmer of the necklace against the collar of her stripy blue T-shirt. She isn't looking at the camera, but her expression is annoyed, as though she didn't want the picture to be taken at all. As though someone in the house might have upset her. It was only four days before she died.

Inside the station, the DCI is on the phone. Ben Moore is in Madeline's usual seat, checking ANPR records for the road into the town. Lorna, tapping away at her computer, waves.

Quickly, Madeline fills her in on the interview with Owen. She frowns.

'The boyfriend, huh. Can we get a search of his house for the phone or the necklace?'

'We can try, but his father was getting pretty worked up towards the end. I don't think they'll speak to us again without a lawyer. I'm going to speak to Ian Edwards this morning and if that gets us no further, we can issue a warrant to the Joneses. Could you start getting things in place?'

She nods. 'Will do. The DNA results should be in today – hopefully we'll get something from the body, or from her clothing. Oh, and Alex called. Wants you to know they've tested the cotton fibres at the scene, they're a match for the scarf Clare had on. He thinks it might've come off her in the struggle, been pulled at at some stage.'

'Shaw?' The DCI is in front of her, raking a hand through his hair. Madeline follows him into his office, feeling suddenly inexperienced, as if she is twenty years younger and fucking up on her first case. Disappointment courses through her; the fibres could have been something else, a lead. They are hardly any further on than when they started.

'As you know, Shaw,' DCI Sturgeon begins when she has barely sat down, 'the papers are feeling less than fond of us, and we aren't really in a position to put more resources on the buttercup case.' The word buttercup sounds strange in Rob's mouth – at odds with his gruff voice and beard. She wishes he wouldn't call it that, it trivialises Clare somehow, but the word has caught on.

'I understand that, sir, but new information has come to light – I've got the transcript of Owen Jones's interview from yesterday, and he's made some allegations against Ian Edwards—'

'The stepfather?' At this, the DCI seems to sit up a little.

'Yep.' She places both hands on the table in an attempt at authority. 'I think we need to speak to Ian again, and I think we need evidence, evidence that's more than the word of a wronged boyfriend of Clare's but that might support his theory. Think about it – Owen would have known Clare better than most. They'd been together since last summer, and you know what young love can be like – intense, consuming. She'd have told him stuff, opened up. If he thinks there's something we're missing with Ian Edwards, I need permission to bring him back in.'

'Boss?'

There's a knock on the office door, and Lorna's face appears around the side. Her face is tight, her smile pinched.

'I picked up your phone, Madeline. The results from the lab are back in for the buttercup case – finally – it's the DNA from the body. Thought you'd both like to see.'

Chapter Twenty-Six

Jane

Tuesday 12th February

Tuesday dawns – the night of the PTA meeting. I'm dreading it. I dress carefully, a navy blue blouse covered in little white swallows; dark, wide-fitting trousers. Hair back in a bun. So different to how I used to be, before I married Jack. So much more expensive, too.

I didn't sleep well. I thought a lot about what Sandra said about Ian. Jack was asleep by the time I came up, my mind foggy from the wine I'd had with Sandra. We drank a bottle and a half, in the end. No ice. Harry came into the kitchen when we were about a bottle down, but my memory of him is fuzzy, unsure.

'Aren't you looking grown up, Harry!' Sandra said to him, her voice high and grating, and he flinched away from her, the moment awkward.

'Where's Dad?' he asked me, his eyes piercing into mine.

'Dad's asleep, got a migraine,' I told him, trying not to slur my words, and he nodded, looked at me with that concerned gaze, the one I saw when he confronted me about the spread-sheet from the surgery.

'Sleep well, darling,' I said to his retreating back, turning back to Sandra and the wine. It was gone 1.00 a.m. when she left; I slid into the sheets next to Jack as quietly as I could, wincing as my arms brushed the cotton sheets. He was out cold, lost in oblivion.

We had a terrible row before he left for work this morning – Finn started crying halfway through and I rushed to him, my heartbeat throbbing violently in my ears.

'It's all right,' I told him, 'it's all going to be all right.'

Except it's not, is it? Not unless I do something.

I can't bear the thought of the children finding out what Jack is. I have spent so long trying to cover for him, to distract them, cushion them, give them the very best life. I buy them beautiful, high-quality outfits from the shops in Saffron Walden. I am scrupulous about their school work. I am determined to raise my children in the way I wish I had been – attentive, caring, privileged. But sometimes, Jack and his temper make that hard.

I paint foundation onto my face, covering up the splotches of red. Last night I dreamt of Clare, of the curtains next door, of Rachel Edwards' beautiful face shattering into little pieces, like fruit splitting under a knife.

'Mummy, why was Daddy upset this morning?' Sophie asks as I tie up Finn's shoelaces, and I stop, my hands frozen still.

'Daddy's fine, darling,' I tell her, but she doesn't answer me, puts her little head down and looks at the floor.

After I've dropped them off at school, I get the chicken from the freezer, set it on the counter to defrost. I have to keep to the routine. Routine is the only thing keeping me sane at the moment. I bake casseroles on Mondays, shepherd's pie on Wednesdays, steamed fish on Fridays. The children begged for chips at the weekend and despite myself I capitulated, running down to Walker's shop and grabbing a pack from the tiny little frozen section at the back, and another bottle of white on the way to the till. I could almost sense Ruby's disapproval, but I was wearing a nice shirt and lots of mascara so I raised my eyes up to hers, readily met the challenge. She knows we're an important part of this town. She won't push it too far.

I know I'm drinking too much – all the signs are there, the way they used to be. But there is no one to watch out for me any more. I want to ask Jack about his late-night conversation with Ian Edwards in the garden, what they were talking about. Instead, I go round the house, checking on the shard of glass wrapped up by the matches, the knife in the paperbacks. I look at his side of the bed; the tidy pile of papers on the bedside table, the half-drunk glass of water. His reading glasses, folded neatly. When no one is looking, I slug wine straight from the bottle, my head buried in the fridge, hidden from view. I tell myself it's okay. The women in the town – well, none of them think twice about having a bit of liquid lunch, of softening the edges of the drudgery of wifehood. If only that's what it was. Diane's voice echoes in my head. *A dependence on alcohol is often the gateway into much more troubling addictions…'* Not now, Diane. I push her away, force myself to be present in the kitchen.

My eyes prick as I stare into the cupboards, wondering what I can put with the chicken. I reach my hand in and it comes back sticky and red. For a moment, I panic, but it's just jam, leaking onto the cupboard surface, the lid unfastened from where I made the children's packed lunches at 7.00 a.m. Jack thinks I make the jam myself but of course I never do; I just peel the label off and stick on a home-made one, stolen from the shop at work. I'm so tired already; Sophie has started having nightmares, quite regularly now. I can feel the exhaustion settling over me every morning, having sat up with her for an hour or so during the night, the little bunny lamp casting its glow in the bedroom, bouncing off the balloon curtains, my hand to her forehead, stroking and soothing to take away the bad dreams. On Friday I brought her home one of the dreamcatchers that Karen at the shop makes, twisted threads forming a rounded net, interlinked with tiny brown feathers and orange beads. We hung it together above the window in the bedroom, and I whispered in her ear that it will take the horrors away. Often when I come into her room she is twisted up in the bedsheets, sweat coating her small limbs, making little mewling noises that strike right into my heart. Sometimes, I think of poor Clare. Did she cry, did she want her mother when she took her last breath? Jack never wants to discuss anything like that.

Occasionally, Jack goes in to comfort Sophie, and I listen carefully, my heart pounding in the other bedroom as he murmurs to her, his deep voice carrying back to me. Finn meanwhile sleeps soundly, his forehead unfurrowed. He is too young to understand the ins and outs of this town, of the way Clare's death has changed everybody; changed the school, changed the house next door, changed the parents, changed us. Our marriage. How aware are my children of that?

Later that day. The butterflies that have been in my stomach since this morning have galvanised, and as I walk to the school for the meeting, I feel them flutter at my throat and have to force myself to take deep breaths; in for three, out for five, the way Diane used to teach us back in London. It's a little while since I've faced them all together like this; somehow, the women are worse in a pack. I didn't go to the last meeting; Jack and I had had a particularly brutal row and I didn't think I could. I spent most of the evening holding an ice pack to a bruise instead. I got told off, of course, by which I mean messages from the other mothers – Sandra's passive-aggressive text, *So sorry to have missed you tonight! Lots sorted though – nothing for you to worry about!* Tricia's faux-concerned phone call, *We heard you weren't feeling well, is everything alright?* I often wonder how concerned any of us really are about each other, deep down – who would be there in a true moment of need? Who would help me if I knocked on their door and told them the truth about Jack?

I think that exact thought as I look around the faces tonight. We're in the big room of the secondary school, all of us sat on too-small plastic chairs that don't quite cover our middle-aged backsides. Andrea Marsons is holding court at the front of the room, dressed in her usual slacks and cardigan. It's hard to imagine her cardigan-less; I screw up my eyes slightly, try to picture her in the summer – I must've seen her thousands of times over the last couple of years – but an image of her in short sleeves just won't come to mind.

It's too cold in here – the window is open, unnecessarily, but no doubt someone will be in danger of a hot flush (a pleasure that hasn't yet hit me) and I pull my scarf a little tighter around my neck. I feel as if I'm on display, on show, as if all the eyes in the room can see straight through me, into the jumble that is Jack and I, me and Jack. Sandra smiles at me across the table, her bright pink lipstick slightly running into the skin at the corners of her mouth; Tricia taps her pen on her brand new notebook to my right, like a child on the first day of term. Moleskin, black. Only the best for the PTA. I have to sit on my hands to stop myself from rolling my eyes. Andrea is shuffling papers, looking more harassed than she usually does, and I take the opportunity to continue my sweep of the room. Donna, Helen, Kelly, who always looks a bit rough. Most of these women have been to my house, drunk my wine, held the hands of my children and I theirs.

Andrea's clearing her throat. I switch my eyes over to her, move a hand to my collarbone, underneath my scarf, but my fingers touch a scratch and I adjust my position at the last moment, tuck a strand of dark hair behind my ear instead.

'Thanks for coming, everyone,' she says, frowning slightly as she looks at something on the paper in front of her. I haven't got anything in front of me except a chipped mug full of tea, and I know that when I get to the bottom there will be soft white flakes of limescale, courtesy of the school kettle. It's not an overly appealing thought. The taste of it reminds me of my mother, of cups of weak tea because we re-used the teabags, of huddling around the oven to keep warm. The old embarrassment floods my face but nobody can see, nobody can tell. I know that now, but sometimes, my body forgets. I'm not who I used to be. I'm Jane Goodwin, the doctor's wife. And that's how it has to stay, no matter what he does.

I can see Tricia neatly writing the date in the top-right corner of a brand new page in her notebook, underlining it laboriously in wet black ink. I imagine her mind – orderly, underlined, everything in its place. Not like mine. Not like Jack's.

'There are a few things on the agenda for us to discuss today,' the headteacher says, clearing her throat again. It looks to me as though she is tired; there are bags underneath her eyes that could even rival mine, and if I look really closely it almost looks as though one cheekbone could be twitching. I feel a pang of sympathy – the bags under my own eyes are covered in Chanel foundation, a product which I somehow feel is not sitting in pride of place in her own make-up bag. Like I said, I'm the doctor's wife. I have to look smart.

'First up, and I may as well start with the obvious, is the ongoing investigation into the Clare Edwards case. As some of you already know, I called in a police presence,' (I catch Sandra nudging Helen and rolling her eyes – we all know that 'police presence' just means Madeline Shaw) 'last week and the students responded well to DS Shaw's presentation. She reminded the children about safety, the importance of communication and the importance too of refraining from gossip, from the spreading of false information.'

Something in Andrea's tone feels like a warning, as though suddenly we too are the pupils, as though her words are directed just as much at us as they were at the kids. I don't blame her – some of the women in this room could give the *Daily Mail* sidebar a run for its money. They probably have, in their time.

'This was a useful morning,' Andrea continues. 'However, we of course remain disappointed that the investigation has not yet been resolved. I think I speak for everyone in this room when I say I have absolutely no wish for this case to be closed without resolution; however, as the PTA of the school we do have a duty to decide when to begin the more formal healing process.' She pauses, looks down briefly at her paper. Thank God Rachel Edwards never became a member of the PTA. Also, Andrea looks quite pretty when she puts her mind to it.

'Having spoken to several other teachers, we would like to put forward tonight the idea of a memorial garden for Clare, which would be planted to the left of the school, just in front of the sports field. If everyone is in agreement, we will speak to the Edwards family and of course gain their consent. My wish is that they will be involved in the process, as much as they would like.'

I can see Tricia scribbling away unnecessarily in her notebook, dotting a defiant question mark after the words 'memorial garden'.

'The garden will hopefully be called "Clare's Garden", and will be used as a space to remember her, honour her memory and – we hope – will also become very much a part of the school as the primary pupils will be encouraged to use a part of it to learn – growing vegetables and the like.'

I can see Sandra raising her eyebrows at this – she was moaning the other day that Natasha never gets taught anything at the primary. Privately, I think this is more to do with Natasha than it is with the school; Sophie never seems to have any problems. I didn't say that, of course, but she brought home some cress last week, so she's obviously learning something, even if it is only basic science. It's sitting on the windowsill at home; in fact, I think I've forgotten to water it.

'So,' Andrea is looking around the room expectantly, 'does anyone have any thoughts on this?' It's obvious she's only looking for reassurance, and I'm about to give it when Kelly pipes up. She's wearing far too much eyeliner for a PTA meeting; the dark flicks outline her eyes like a cat's.

'I don't mean to be the voice of doom here,' she says, quite loudly I think, 'but are we sure this is a good idea? I mean—' she looks around the room as if for support, but if I'm honest Kelly isn't particularly popular so no one says anything yet, 'I mean, we're talking about a *murder*. It's not as if that poor girl died in a car crash or something. There's somebody out there who could attack again, who might love the attention a garden would create. I watched a TV show about a man like that. On the BBC.'

She says BBC as though the branding makes her sentence believable, and there were noticeable winces around 'that poor girl'.

Next to me, Tricia opens her mouth. 'What is it you're suggesting here, Kelly? That we *forget* about Clare? I personally think a memorial is a lovely idea. Although,' she looks down at her notebook, 'I'm not quite sure a garden is the best way to go – what about something a bit more permanent? A statue, or something? Stone? Something with a touch more class?'

'I can't think of anything more morbid than a *statue*,' Sandra says, which is actually along the lines of what I was thinking; the notion of walking past an immortalised Clare every day might be too much to bear. Concrete features blaze into my mind and I feel suddenly sick, take a sip of my lime-scale tea in spite of myself.

'Statues aren't *morbid*, Sandra,' Tricia says, and I can hear a little edge of annoyance creeping into her voice, an edge I've heard before when she's had a couple of Sauvignons round mine. 'Statues are things to be *revered*, respected – and crucially, they last a lifetime.'

Given the subject, lifetime was a poor choice of word and I do think *revered* is taking it a step too far. I can tell Andrea agrees because she's pursed her lips, the way she always does when she's not convinced.

'Any other thoughts?' she asks hopefully.

'I like the idea of a garden, it feels right somehow. What Clare would have wanted,' I hear myself offering, and the headteacher flashes me a smile, as does Donna across the room. I can feel Tricia bristling a bit, but she won't cross me. I don't think any of them will. They never really do.

The minute I say I like the garden idea, it's like a light switches on in the room and Sandra jumps in, saying what a lovely thought it is. They're all always so desperate to ingratiate themselves with me, and with Jack. I've heard them talking about him, giggling about how good-looking he is. Well, he is better-looking than most of their husbands, but nothing comes without a price.

Andrea gets us to do a show of hands in favour of the garden and all bar Kelly vote yes.

'I really think a fundraiser would be a good idea too though,' Tricia is saying now, looking up from her posh notebook. 'It'll cheer everyone up, the kids can dress up—'

'Can we dress up too?' Donna Philips interjects, grinning naughtily, and there is a titter of laughter that circles around the room. I don't laugh, but I smile, a tight little smile that doesn't show my teeth. The thought makes me shudder – all that flesh on show. They'd see every little hurt.

'Well,' Andrea says, clearly trying to change the subject,

'as always, we'll be having the annual Easter concert on the Thursday evening before the school holiday, and that usually raises a little bit of money—'

'But that's not until March! Don't you think this year we ought to do something special? Something to really bring the community together?' Tricia asks, warming to her theme. 'We could give the money to charity, set up a foundation for Clare.' She looks at me. 'As well as the garden, of course.' I stare back at her. Tricia's voice rises. 'Or the money could *fund* the garden?'

Clare, Clare, Clare. She is almost like a presence at the table. What must her family be going through now, while we sit and talk about dress-up and money and gardens? None of it will bring her back.

'The concert might remind people of a funeral,' Sandra Davies is saying, lowering her voice as though funeral is now a dirty word. 'You know, with it being in the church and everything…'

'Where else would we hold it?' Kelly snorts, and I'm inclined to agree. The Easter concert is always in St Mary's. It's actually one of my favourite nights of the year – the children dress up in white shirts and black bottoms, the choir sings beautifully at the front by the altar, surrounded by tealights, and Jack and I stand on best behaviour with all the other parents. It's lovely.

'The Easter concert needs to stay where it is,' Andrea says firmly. 'We can discuss the possibility of an extra fundraiser but it would require quite a lot of planning, and timings are tight now—'

'A Valentine's fair!' Tricia sparks up, and there's a little ripple of excitement around the room.

Valentine's Day. It's this week – we're not doing anything. I remember last year and an unfamiliar panicky feeling builds inside me, as though the women are rising up and over me, a tidal wave that I can no longer control. I'd made Jack dinner; it had gone wrong.

'Andrea,' Tricia is saying, one hand stretched out slightly towards the headteacher, nails shining in the harsh overhead school lights, 'we all know you've had an awful lot to handle at the school recently. If you'd like, I'd be more than happy stepping up and taking ownership of this one. The girls can help me! Can't you, ladies?'

Assenting nods. Smiles. The protest sticks in my throat.

Chapter Twenty-Seven

Clare

Monday 4th February, 1.00 p.m.

I'm walking back from lunch to afternoon registration with Lauren when someone in the corridor bumps into me, hard. I drop my bag, and my things scatter out across the floor – my books, a pair of knickers, my things for tonight. Shit. Quickly, I gather everything back up, not wanting the girls to see. My heart is thudding.

'You okay?' *Lauren's staring down at me; her attention caught by a group of boys walking the other way. It must have been one of them that hit me.* 'Sorry, let me help you.'

She bends down and picks up the last of my books. 'Here you go.'

'Thanks,' *I say, my breathing coming fast, and she looks at me more closely.*

'What happened?'

I look up and down the corridor, but it's thinned out now, everyone's in registration. I'm overreacting, like I always do. That wasn't violence, that was an accident.

'I don't know,' I say, checking that my phone's still in my pocket, 'I didn't see.'

'Come on, hurry up,' she says, linking me by the arm, 'we'll be late.'

My arm throbs; I bet it'll bruise.

Chapter Twenty-Eight

DS Madeline Shaw

Tuesday 12th February

Clare's covered in her stepfather's DNA. They tested her coat, a little blue puffer jacket she had on when she was found. The DCI swabbed Ian and Rachel right at the start of the investigation, but Ian's is the only print that shows up on the jacket. Nothing from Owen.

'What d'you think?' Madeline asks Rob, and he sighs, makes a clucking sound with his tongue. Superintendent Wilcox has given him a grilling already this morning on the phone, threatened to take him off the case if there isn't any progress soon. They're empty words, probably, but even so.

'Could be innocent, I suppose,' the DCI says. 'They live together, after all. But it proves he touched her, innocent or not. And it proves Nathan Warren probably didn't.'

'It's on her neck, too,' Lorna says, pointing out the area with the tip of her pen. Clare's collarbone, the dip in her neck. Madeline thinks of fingers pushing, anger rising.

'Would he have given her a hug?' she asks, and Lorna makes a face.

'Well, doesn't sound like they were close, from what Owen said, does it? But it's possible.'

The DCI nods. 'My problem is that there's no other prints on her though, not on the jacket. And she was wearing it when she died, unless they undressed and dressed her, which looks unlikely and would have lead to prints on the clothing.'

'Gloves?' Lorna asks, and I frown, thinking of the cotton fibres that forensics found.

The DCI looks at his watch. 'Bring Ian in again anyway, see how he reacts when we confront him with this. We need to speak to him without his wife being there.'

Ian Edwards arrives at the station in a suit with his trademark rucksack on, unruffled, wedding ring glinting gold on his left hand. Looks a bit on the small side, as if it's digging into the flesh. He tells them Rachel wanted to come with him, but he explained to her that it was all routine, part of the process.

'It is, isn't it?' he asks, and for the first moment there is a glimpse of vulnerability in his burly features. Rather than reply, Madeline leads him into interview room two and switches on the tape.

'Can you remind us of your movements on the day of February 4th, 2018?'

He loosens his tie a bit. It's bright red, too jovial for the occasion. It feels like an insult, somehow. She wonders if he plans on going into the office directly after this, where he will tell them he has been. Doctors? A dentist appointment that overran? Has he even had much time off after his stepdaughter's death?

'Of course,' he says, leaning forward a little in the hard plastic seat, 'it's not a day I'm likely to forget. I was working – I work in London, as an engineer, as you know by now, and I came home a bit earlier than normal because I wanted to spend some time with Rachel and I'd been doing overtime the week before. So I got the three o'clock train out of Liverpool Street instead of my usual one.'

'Which is?'

'The 6.31 p.m. Goes direct.'

'So you got the three o'clock train back from work,' she repeats. The police already know this – the CCTV at Liverpool Street confirms it. Madeline has watched his shadowy figure moving down the platform, getting onto the train. This particular part of his story is true, but that doesn't mean the rest is. 'What time did this put you back home in Ashdon?'

He clears his throat. 'I park my car at Audley End Station, the next town along – we have a permit for everyday use. So I picked it up at about quarter past four, drove back into Ashdon. Rachel was at home, we were going to go out for dinner.' He pauses.

'You drove straight back to Ashdon?' Madeline asks. She is thinking about the CCTV, the possible pocket of time between Ian leaving Audley End and arriving back home.

He shifts a bit in his seat. 'Probably, yes. Sometimes I take a longer route home but I didn't stop anywhere, I went straight back to Rachel. Like I said, I wanted to take her for dinner.'

'Where were you planning to go?'

'Um, we hadn't decided for sure. Maybe Riduccio's in Saffron Walden, it's meant to be nice.' He scratches the back of his neck. 'I've told you guys all of this before.'

'Had you made reservations?' she says, ignoring him. 'Isn't Riduccio's notoriously difficult to get into?'

The gamble pays off; he shifts slightly in his seat, back-tracks.

'Well yes, of course, we hadn't quite thought. The other option was to try the new place that's opened up just outside the town. Towards Audley End.'

'Paula's Italian?'

'Yeah, that's the place. Anyway, like I said, we didn't have a concrete plan as such. We might even have cooked something together.' He sighs, runs a hand through his thinning hair. 'But then Clare didn't come back from school. We weren't too worried, not at first, we thought she might be with a friend or doing some after-school activity – she was a good sport, was Clare, always getting involved with things, studying hard, so popular. Smart brain on her – was considering finance, when she was older.'

Madeline knows from speaking to her that this isn't strictly true – Clare was interested in the police. But is his statement a downright lie, or just something that he's led himself to believe? How well does he know his stepdaughter at all?

'So when was it that you *did* begin to worry about the whereabouts of your stepdaughter?'

Ian frowns, rising to the deliberately judgemental emphasis on *did*.

'I told you all of this last week.' He sighs. 'It got to five-ish, I guess, and we were beginning to feel a little bit concerned. She's usually home by four thirty, you see, and she's always let us know if there's a delay – she knows her mum gets anxious. We couldn't get hold of her on the mobile, but she did often keep it on silent so that in itself wasn't particularly unusual.'

Madeline nods. Clare's mobile is still missing.

'We kept trying though,' he says. 'I went out at about half five, started looking for her. Walked up to the school, it's not far.' He pauses briefly, runs a hand through his hair. 'I thought she might have stopped to talk to someone on the high street, or had a fall – anything. God. I never imagined…' His voice falters. *He never imagined this.*

Madeline knows the route from the Edwards' house to the school well, has walked it many times now. The main route, anyway. But Clare didn't take the main route along the road; she took the back way, through Sorrow's Meadow – which could have been towards Owen Jones' house. And Ian Edwards had already been out walking at the point the pathologist thinks Clare was killed. *Somewhere between five and seven p.m., give or take.* The policewoman frowns. It's plausible, but they cannot be sure.

'Anyway, obviously I couldn't find her. Rachel started ringing around, trying Clare's friends – the ones we knew of. None of the mothers had seen her, she wasn't at anyone's house. I was mainly focused on calming Rachel down; I was convinced there'd be a reasonable explanation for it, that Clare was a big girl and had probably just gone off somewhere of her own free will. She wanted to call the police – call you guys – straight away but I thought we should hold off. God,' he puts his head in his hands, just briefly. 'I can't tell you how much I regret that now.'

Madeline keeps quiet, lets him talk.

'Rachel went next door, to the Goodwins, and I called you when we hadn't heard from her by seven forty-five.'

The team must have listened to the recording of that phone call upwards of ten times now. *My daughter hasn't come home from school.*

'What did you do after the emergency call?' She checks

the time on the recording. They've been in here for seventeen minutes so far.

Ian sighs. 'I told Rachel to wait inside by the landline in case there was any news. Then I went back out, in the car this time – it was dark as anything by then.'

Early February – it was darkening already by quarter to four. Makes everything worse, of course.

'And then she called me on my mobile,' Ian continues, closing his eyes for just a second as though remembering. Madeline watches him closely. Is it grief, or did that call mark the beginning of a desperate double life for him? Did he come back from work early on purpose, with the intention of intercepting Clare on her way back from school? Had he found out about her and Owen? She cannot imagine that he likes being disobeyed.

'After we found out, well, it's all a bit of a blur,' he says. 'I've been looking after Rachel, of course, and we have the family liaison officer,' he nods at me, 'Theresa's great. Rachel's on Valium, you know. Valium and wine.' He meets her eyes. 'It's a nightmare.'

Everything he has said matches the statement the police took on the night she died. Madeline watches his face; the look of relief is fleeting but palpable. He thinks it's over; his whole body shifts slightly in the chair, and she can almost see his fingers itching to undo his bright red tie, whip out his iPhone, get back to his life. But they are not done yet.

'As you know, Mr Edwards, Clare's body and possessions were tested for DNA samples,' Madeline says, and he nods, sits up a little straighter in his chair.

'And?' he asks, 'have you found anything?'

She is watching him closely, now. His pupils are dark pinpricks.

'Mr Edwards, can you think of a reason why your DNA would have been found all over your stepdaughter's jacket?'

For a moment, he looks nonplussed. Either it's genuine or he's buying time.

'We lived together,' he says eventually. 'We were – we were close. It could be anything – I probably hung her coat up for her, brushed past her at home. Gave her a hug.' He stops for a second. 'In fact I did give her a hug, to say sorry. I know I did. That doesn't mean anything, detective – surely you can see that?'

'To say sorry for what?'

His mouth is open, wrong-footed. He didn't mean to tell her that.

'Well – we'd had a bit of a to-do,' he says slowly, waving a hand in the air as if it doesn't matter, as if it's nothing. 'Just about her exams and stuff. The night before. So I wanted to apologise, the morning she – the morning she went missing. I think I gave her a hug.'

Madeline waits, says nothing.

'Why are you focusing on me when whoever killed Clare is still out there?' he says, his voice rising on the final words, and she can sense it; the anger in the room. 'I've been very compliant, detective, I've done everything you've asked. But when you start accusing me, I have to ask – don't you think your resources would be better spent looking for whoever did this to our girl, don't you think that would be a better idea than trying to plant some sort of blame on me?'

His cheeks are flushed now, and she can sense his annoyance.

He didn't want to lose control in this room. He didn't want to lose his temper.

But he has.

Madeline takes a sip of water, glances at the tape.

'We appreciate your compliance, Mr Edwards.' She keeps her voice steady and even, watching as he inhales through his nose, tries to calm himself down.

'I didn't mean to snap—' he begins, but she holds up a hand, signalling that there's no need. Cutting him off.

'One more question, Ian,' Madeline says, almost casually, her eyes on his face. 'What is your relationship with a boy named Owen Jones?'

Chapter Twenty-Nine

Jane

Wednesday 13th February

Ian Edwards came back in a police car last night, just as it was getting dark. I saw it all through the upstairs window. He walked up their drive, his shoulders slumped. So they're onto him, then. The journos still hanging about were on him like a pack of wolves the minute he stepped out of the car; microphones in his face, all of them snapping at his heels. Rachel came out to meet him. I was shocked at her appearance. She looked like a ghost, completely pale, as if all the energy has been washed out of her. I still haven't taken her over that lasagne. Bad Jane. The flowers are still there in their front garden; no one has moved anything. I noticed some candles have been added to the mix too. It's becoming like a shrine. We'd never be able to sell ours now, even if we wanted to, not with all that next door.

Jack saw the car pull up too, and I seized my moment. 'What were you talking to Ian about in the garden, last week?' I asked him, and he glanced up at me, surprised.

'I saw you,' I say, 'down at the bottom of the garden.'

'Jane,' he says, 'the man's lost his daughter. I was comforting him.'

'She's not his daughter,' I said.

We didn't speak again until the morning, with the kids.

It's not as if there's nothing to distract me; all anyone in this town can talk about now is the Valentine's fair. Ever since the PTA meeting, it's like the women have gone into overdrive, trying to get everything ready for this Saturday. And I'm sorry if that sounds sexist but it *is* the women – they badger me about it when I'm dropping Sophie and Finn at the school gates, they corner me in Walker's newsagents, they ring me up and send me messages asking about a tombola and whether I think Jack's surgery will support it with some flyers in the waiting room.

'Yes,' I say, without bothering to ask Jack, because that is the fastest way I can think of to get Tricia off the phone. I don't want to bother Jack with something like that – he'll think it's ridiculous, trivial.

I saw DS Shaw on my way home from the school run yesterday. She looked as though she might've been coming from next door. My plan was to nod and smile, but she slowed down when she got near to me, so I had to stop too.

'Jane,' she said, 'how are you doing?'

'Hello,' I replied, tugging the sleeves of my coat down a little bit further over my hands. I need new gloves; my hands are freezing. 'How's the investigation going?'

She pressed her lips together; they looked cold and chapped, and I wondered fleetingly about lending her some of my Elizabeth Arden. Jack buys me pots of the stuff, he likes me to look presentable. An image of my bruised ribs comes to mind. Well, presentable in public, anyway.

'We're making headway,' Madeline told me, but I wasn't sure if I believed her.

'Is everything alright with you, Jane?' she asked me, and I knew she was thinking about the bruise on my arm, my slip-up. My son.

'Fine,' I said quickly, 'we're glad Harry was helpful to you.'

'And things are going well at home?'

I panicked at that, thinking of the way she'd side-eyed Harry, the quick movement of her eyes down to my bruised arm. I had to distract her.

'You do know,' I said, 'about the money.'

'The money?'

Emboldened, I took a few more steps towards her, closing the gap between us. 'Yes,' I said, 'I meant to tell you before. The money Clare was set to inherit from Mark. He left it to her when he died.' I paused. 'I suppose that would go to Rachel, now. And Ian, of course.' I wait a beat. 'I thought you might be interested. The whole town wants to help, you know. Anything we can do.'

She stared at me for a second. 'How much money?' she said at last, and I shrugged.

'I suppose you'd have to ask him.'

I watched her as she walked away, striding down along the River Bourne that runs parallel to the main road, bisecting the town like a vein. I can't imagine she's worrying too much about me and my family now.

Last night after the PTA meeting, I drank an entire bottle of wine to myself after the children went to sleep. Finn woke up crying and I stumbled sloppily to his room, smoothed his forehead, felt guilty about my alcohol-fumed breath on his face. Jack went out for a drive after we saw Ian and came home late, very late. I thought of him sitting alone in his car, his head against the steering wheel, and I forced myself to lie still when he came into our bedroom. The wine was making my head spin; I squeezed my eyes shut tightly, as tight as they would go. Images of the PTA girls danced before my eyes; they were holding yellow ribbons, twisting them around like maypole dancers, chanting endlessly about the Valentine's fair. I heard Jack taking off his shoes, loosening his tie. Silk against cotton, the whispering sound I know so well. When we used to go to Albion Road, I would look forward to seeing his ties – would spend the week in between wondering what pattern he'd wear in the next session. My favourite was the yellow one with little red party hats on. I don't think he has that any more.

I know he saw the wine bottle by the sink. I should have hidden it. I should have tucked the corkscrew under my pillow. Shame covered me like an extra duvet; my heart quickened as I felt the weight of him sink down onto the bed.

There was a pause, as if he too was holding himself still.

'Jane?' he said quietly, and even without seeing his face I could tell that he had been crying, and I know that I should've been crying too but I couldn't. I've tried that before. Instead I pictured his face: the redness of his eyes, the strange way his dark hair would be sticking on end after he's spent hours running his hand through it, over and over again. When Finn and Sophie cry, they look like themselves, but when Jack cries, he becomes changed, a different person entirely. Harry never cries. I haven't seen him shed a tear in years.

I kept my eyes shut.

In the morning, he is up and has left the house before me. *Happy Valentine's Day*, I whisper to myself. There are no flowers, no breakfast in bed. No sex.

Sophie brings me in a card, kisses me sloppily on the cheek. It's all I can do not to cry.

'I love you, Mummy,' she whispers in my ear, and I clutch her tightly to me and tell her that I love her too, more than anything in the whole wide world. It's true. I'd do anything for my family.

After breakfast, I need to go into the shop and see Karen but I put it off, dawdle on the way back from taking the children to school, pretend to be on the phone when Tricia catches my eye. The fictional person on the other end says something funny and I laugh, mouth an apology at her and walk away before she has the chance to get too close.

I make it to the shop around eleven. Karen smiles at me, but there is something odd in it, something I don't like. I pull my sleeves close to my wrists, tugging them down around my hands. We're making a stack of prints that Karen wants to turn into greeting cards, so rather than chat to her I concentrate on the work, try to lose myself in the methodical stamping of pink and red ink onto paper. They're Valentine's cards, of course. She wants to sell them this afternoon, ready for the panic buy before this evening.

'I bet Jack has got you something special, hasn't he?' Karen coos, and I just nod, half laugh.

'You're so lucky to have a man like that,' she says wistfully, and suddenly, I don't know what comes over me but I think about what Jack told me that night, the finality with which he said it, how he's done nothing to make up for it since, and I feel this big bubble of desperation rise up in me.

'Actually,' I say, 'we've been having a few problems lately. Jack and I.'

The air in the little room seems to stop moving. I can't believe I've actually said it. I never say it. I never let on.

Karen's holding a pen in one hand; it hovers between us. Her wrists are thin.

'Really?'

Now is the moment, I think to myself, the moment to undo it, laugh it off, pretend it was a joke. But I don't. Instead I look down at the table, and watch as a tear splashes down onto it, a perfect pearl of sorrow. It feels almost like it's come from someone else, but it's my own eyes that are wet.

'Really.'

We've never been huggers, Karen and I, we don't have that sort of relationship, but within a few seconds she is by my side, her slender arm around my shoulders.

I bite down hard on the inside of my cheek. The ulcer I made last week has only just healed but my teeth re-open the wound and I taste iron in my mouth.

'All couples go through rough patches, Jane,' Karen is saying to me, her voice soft and soothing, and I am nodding along, embarrassed by the way the tears will be streaking my cheeks, erasing the carefully applied make-up, destroying the image I try so hard to cultivate, every single day.

'Jack seems like a lovely man,' Karen continues, and I know then that it's pointless, that this town is well and truly under the Goodwin spell.

She continues to rub my arm ineffectually for a few minutes.

Eventually, I manage to gasp out that I am fine, that it really is nothing to worry about. But I see the look in her eyes when she pulls away from me, and it fills my stomach with butterflies.

At half past one, Karen announces she's going out to get some fresh air.

'Can I get you anything, Jane?' she asks me and even though I am quite hungry I shake my head mutely. She gives me a funny look, and I know she's pitying me. I hold my breath until the shop door closes behind her, then I reach under the table, pinch my thigh through the thick fabric of my trousers. I hold it until I can bear it no longer, then release. It helps, but only a little bit.

That afternoon, as I'm walking home from the shop, I see Rachel Edwards. I'm horrified, and then, stupidly, slightly jealous when I see how thin she has become, how gaunt. Her coat hangs off her, her bones jut out beneath the folds of beige material. She hasn't seen me yet, so I turn, my mind racing, and start walking aimlessly the other way, back in the direction of the school. I know I'm a coward, but the thought of seeing grief up close like that terrifies me. It's still an hour to pick-up time, but seeing her now would push me over the edge. I can just about cope with it all if I don't see her poor mother. Seeing her reminds me of how much I too could lose, if this thing between Jack and I blows up. I can't risk losing my babies. I can't run away. She's a living reminder of what might happen.

But it's too late. As I'm walking, I feel it: a hand on my arm, feather-light, barely there. Her wedding ring glints at me.

'Jane?'

Her voice is soft. I've always thought of Rachel Edwards as being the timid sort, especially when Mark was alive, but in the last year or two since Ian's been on the scene she's seemed a lot louder, more confident, on the few interactions we've had. Now though, she is almost unrecognisable; her face is bare of make-up (she always used to wear a lot) and her skin looks gossamer-thin, shadows beneath her eyes. Immediately, I feel as if I am going to be sick but I feign surprise, reach up a hand and find hers, grip it between my own. Her skin is rough and coarse, her nails bitten right down. My shiny pink shellac glares up at me, my skin smooth with the expensive moisturiser I order once a month from L'Occitane.

'Rachel! How are you?' The words sound false, even to my ears.

She just looks at me, and to my absolute horror I see that tears are pooling up in her blue eyes, threatening to spill over onto her pale cheeks. My mind is whirling and a part of me is breaking for her, this woman who has lost everything, but another part of me is aware that we're in a public place and more than that, we're in a small town where even the trees have eyes so I move closer to her, shielding her from the main road, putting a comforting arm firmly around her shoulders.

'There, there,' I murmur, as though she is Sophie in the throes of a nightmare, and she walks with me as if injured, leaning heavily on my arm. Her body weighs almost nothing.

We're only two minutes from our houses and Rachel is sobbing now, noisy, undignified sobs that soak the shoulder of my cashmere-lined jacket. I wonder about walking her to her door, but I don't particularly want to see Ian, or see inside their house – I don't want to feel the full weight of what has happened, the hole Clare has left.

I fix my eyes on the little roundel next to our front door, the badger shining at me in the light. I hate that roundel. I hate the name Badger Sett. When we first moved here on that boiling hot day in August, Jack laughed at the sign.

'Badgers are one of the most vicious animals in the UK,' he'd said, and I'd smiled, kissing him right there on the step, feeling the tension of the day seep out of him as he giggled. It was funny, then. It isn't remotely funny now.

I glance at the Edwards' house. The front door is shut, disclosing nothing, but there's a small pile up of packages just inside the porch. Well-wishers, I suppose. Or worse.

'Let's get you inside, Rachel,' I say gently, and I fish my keys from my handbag and, ignoring the house next door, we fumble our way into my house, tears still flowing down her face.

Once inside she quietens a bit, whispers a thank you. I fetch a box of tissues, the nice kind that none of us ever actually use, and flick the switch on the white chrome kettle to make her a cup of tea. The wine on the side winks at me. We'd probably both prefer it.

'I'm sorry,' she says suddenly, 'I'm sorry to be here like this, you must think…'

'I don't think anything,' I say, getting two mugs down from the cupboard, my fingers just missing the one with all the hand-drawn pupils' faces on that the school produced last year. 'I just want to make sure you're alright, or as alright as can be under the circumstances.'

I get the milk out, still with my back to her. The carton is cold against my hand but I'm buying time, thinking how best to deal with the situation. I select full-fat for her and skimmed for me; she looks as though she could do with it.

'How are you coping?' I say carefully, finishing off our teas, giving them both a stir and setting down the mugs on the counter. Steam rises into the air and Rachel cups her hands around her drink, as though comforted by its warmth. I can feel the waves of grief almost pulsating from her body.

'I'm not, really,' she says at last, and when she speaks her voice sounds odd, as though it has been deadened, all the life taken out of it. 'I miss her so much, every day.' She looks down at the tea. 'I used to think I'd been through the worst part of my life, I thought it was all in the past, but the loss of a child – nothing prepares you for that, Jane. Nothing.' She pauses. 'Ian's got me on Valium.'

I think of Sophie and Finn, tucked up tight in their beds, bobbling along next to me on the walk to school, chattering away at the dinner table. Of Harry, tapping away at his iPhone, ruffling his little brother's hair. The thought of losing them, of having them taken away from me, is unbearable. If she only knew how many times I'd pictured it. How close it has come.

'No,' I say softly. 'No, I don't suppose it does.'

Another sip of tea, her teeth clanking slightly against the china as the last ebb of tearful tremors pass through her body. I think about what she's said – *I thought I'd been through the worst part of my life.* She must mean when Mark died, I suppose.

'And the worst thing now,' she says, shaking her head from side to side as though she can't quite believe it, 'is that people are turning on Ian. Have you heard? The police are after him, asking him more questions, taking advice from this bloody town full of gossips who don't know any better.' Her voice at least sounds a tiny bit more alive now, there is a hint of anger in what she's saying.

'Gossip can be incredibly cruel,' I say to Rachel, 'but the police know what they're doing. They know better than to listen to idle speculation – it's not enough to get anyone convicted.' As I'm saying the words, I'm wondering whether they really are true, but for Rachel's sake she needs them to be so I press on regardless. I feel a splash of guilt for telling Madeline what Sandra said, but still, I was only passing on information.

'I know it's hard,' I say, 'and I can't even pretend to know what you're going through, but I think the best thing that you and Ian can do now is focus on healing, on taking the time for yourselves to be together and get through this.' I pause, watching her. 'That's better than stirring things up, Rachel, isn't it? I hate to see you so upset.'

She's nodding, twisting her wedding band round and around her finger; plain silver, not like mine. The gesture is making me feel anxious; I look away.

'I wish I could just see her,' she whispers, and I lean forward slightly to hear. 'Just see her one more time.' She puts a hand to her face. 'We'd been arguing so much, in the weeks before she – you know. I wish I could take back every cross word I ever said to her. Ian does too – he's a good man, Jane. You know that, don't you?'

I feel my stomach tighten. 'Of course I do,' I say, 'of course.'

'I feel so guilty, Jane,' she says, and this time the words are so quiet that I think I might have misheard. 'So guilty, every single day. It never goes away. It never will.'

'I can't imagine,' I say, taking a too-large sip of tea, and she starts to cry again, the tears sliding down her cheeks like a leak that can't be fixed.

Chapter Thirty

Clare

Monday 4th February, 2.00 p.m.

My arm hurts a bit from where that guy knocked into me in the corridor, but it's two o'clock and tonight is getting so close now that I don't care! I message Owen throughout the afternoon – it's only DT, Mrs Thomas never notices us being on our phones. We're meant to be making wooden wind chimes, but mine's rubbish.

I haven't even seen him today – some days, we spot each other in the corridors or the canteen, and I get a rush of excitement inside when our eyes connect. I wouldn't have that if it wasn't all a secret.

Lauren would never understand why I like Owen – he's geeky, I suppose, although I don't like using that word. He's not in the popular crowd, he'd never be friends with someone like Harry Goodwin, even though they're in the same year, Year Twelve, and he isn't the sort of boy who gets invited to the cool parties.

But the main reason why I haven't told anyone is because I don't want Mum and Ian to know. Whenever I'm with him, I tell them I'm at Lauren's, and his dad is away a lot of the time so then we get his place to ourselves. His mum's dead.

It's been a bit harder during the winter, but when we met in July, we spent a lot of time outside – we'd go places, sit in Sorrow's Meadow in the buttercups, drink cider together in the sunshine. But we've been together just over six months now, and I want things to be more serious. That's why I'm so excited about tonight, and what I've got planned. Lauren thinks I've already done it – she has – but she's wrong. I want it to be special. Really special.

Chapter Thirty-One

Jane

Friday 15th February

We're supposed to be having book club tonight. I've already bulk-bought the crisps, and I thought I might make my own guacamole because Sandra did last time and I don't want comparisons as to who's the more committed. My hands are shaking as I type out the group text.

I'm so sorry, I write, *I'll have to cancel this evening. Finn isn't well – we think it's something he ate. Do go ahead without me if you can find another host! P.S. loved the Zadie Smith. Lots to think about!*

I hit send before I can think about it too much. The antiseptic hurts as I place the cotton wool pad against my cheek, but I don't want the cut to get infected. I should never have brought everything up again with Jack – riled him, pushed it too far. Now I've waded my way through Zadie Smith for nothing. Idly, I wonder if I'll ever learn, learn not to walk into his traps, learn to anticipate the triggers. *Don't bring up the night of Clare's death. Don't make him apologise for what he said.* Perhaps I ought to write it down and stick it on the fridge, hidden amongst the school timetables and children's drawings.

It's always been the same between Jack and I. The cause and effect. I push him too far, he lashes out. But all I'm ever trying to do is make him love me, make us go back to how we were at the start.

I find it so hard to let things go.

The messages ping back. *Oh Jane, such a shame! Can't Jack watch the kids? You come to mine?*

Jane! I was looking forward to your guac! Zadie overrated in my view.

Don't worry Jane! So tricky when kids get ill at that age. It's all down to diet – though I'm sure you know that already ☺ – let me know if you need any tips.

I put the phone down on the side, all their little judgements locked inside it. Finn is fine, of course. But I can't let them see me with a face like this. It'll have calmed down by tomorrow.

'Jane?' My husband enters the room. He sees me with the cotton wool to my face, and I watch as his expression tightens, his teeth grit. *No apology flowers this time,* I think. We're a little too far past that.

Upstairs, I run my hand over my paperbacks, my fingers finding *Wolf Hall*. Inside, the knife is slim and sharp to the touch. It will get better soon, I think, it has to get better soon.

At about midnight, he comes into the bedroom. I can tell he's been drinking; his movements are wobbly, slightly out of sync. I'm already in bed, the covers pulled tight over me, the curtains closed. I don't want to think about the Edwards family tonight.

I can feel the weight of him as he sits down, the mattress sinking slightly under the pressure of his body, the body that I know so well.

'I didn't mean to do it, Jane,' he says. 'You know I never meant to do it.'

I stiffen, my cheek throbbing. 'It doesn't matter,' I say to him, and I feel the shaking, the way his body collapses in on itself. I know he feels guilty now. I can sense it.

Good.

But he still won't talk about the things he said that night.

Chapter Thirty-Two

Jane

Saturday 16th February

The PTA mothers got what they wanted.

It's a nice day, at least; the crisp wintery air is warmer than usual and the sky is a cloudless, azure blue. I must be grateful for that. I put on a brighter than normal pink blouse underneath my coat, trying to get into the spirit of things, then head towards the secondary school with Sophie for nine a.m. I woke up early, spent the best part of forty-five minutes tending to my face, making sure the cut was covered by the expensive make-up I keep in the drawer. It's still visible, of course, but with all the powder it looks like a thin grey line.

Jack isn't here yet, he's with Finn and Harry at home. He said he was tired from a long shift at the surgery yesterday, but he's obviously hungover. Guilt will do that to you, I suppose.

Finn didn't sleep well either, so I said they could have a lie-in and join us a bit later, though I doubt Harry will want to come. He normally has football practice on a Saturday morning, but they've cancelled it today for the fair. He'll probably sleep late, appear around lunchtime, the smell of teenage boy emanating from his pores. Jack didn't say goodbye to me, turned his head the other way as I left the bedroom. I didn't bother taking him tea. Not this time.

We're using the sports hall – even Sandra agreed that an outdoor fete in February was pushing it a bit. They've been setting things up at lightning speed all week, behaving like dogs on heat: organising the raffle, which has turned into a competition between the mums to see who can donate the best gift; painting giant red hearts in the primary school; setting up lots of wooden tables covered with frilly white cloths.

Tricia Jenkins has been busy-bodying around like nobody's business, whipping the town up into a kind of frenzy over what is essentially a small fete. A small fete to distract from a dead teenager. Lovely.

Personally, I think a garden on its own would have been perfectly fine. More than fine.

'Morning Jane!' Tricia herself is sailing towards me, wearing a top that is bizarrely low cut for a community occasion, one that exposes her slightly crepey, fake-tanned chest. Her husband Hugh is trailing dutifully behind, carrying what looks like a hamper.

'Last-minute raffle idea!' Tricia is saying, although I doubt it was last minute at all judging from the size of it. 'I thought it'd really cheer people up – it's got champagne, chocolates, special herbal tea, the works! A perfect V day gift for someone special!'

'Sounds nice,' I say, forcing a smile and wondering what exactly herbal tea has got to do with it all. Not to mention champagne. It's bordering on inappropriate at a fundraiser for a dead girl. Plus, I can't *stand* the words *V Day*. Sophie tugs at my arm and I stroke her hair, feeling its softness under my fingers.

We haven't got long until everyone starts to arrive; for some reason we went for a ten a.m. start. People are already here, coming in dribs and drabs; several of the mums have volunteered to run stalls. Funny how you hardly ever get the dads putting themselves forward for these things. The people start to swarm around the hall: the stifling, all-white crowds of Ashdon. So different from all the variety of London. So different from my past. I swallow. We're bag-checking on the entrance to the sports hall – Tricia's idea, of course.

'Safety must come first,' she announced to us all seriously, 'and you never know what might happen. Better safe than sorry, don't you think?'

'Of course,' I said. It was an hour until any of them even noticed my face.

'An accident with Soph,' I said, 'some slightly overzealous playtime.' Laugh, smile, wince.

'We were so sorry to not see you at book club,' Sandra said, 'it wasn't the same without you.'

I looked at her, then down at the ground. 'I'm sorry,' I said, 'Finn is much better now.'

Anyway, nods all round to the bag checks. So now we have two of the PTA at a little table at the double doors, asking everybody to open their bags as if we're at an airport, not a fundraiser. We're getting people to put any big bags and coats in one of the school classrooms; Kelly Richards is taking them all through, looking very self-important. I know why they're anxious, of course, but honestly, what do they think is going to happen at a school fair? It's hardly likely that anyone's got a machete in their handbag.

I decide to hold court with Sophie over by the raffle stand;

it's the most central point, should anyone need me. But perhaps they won't need me at all.

'Jane!' I was wrong. Sandra is accosting me, wearing a tight dress covered in bright pink flowers; she must be absolutely freezing. I look closer and I'm right; her arms are goose-pimpled. She starts talking to me about numbers and crowd control, as if we're running Glastonbury rather than the town fete. 'Is Jack not here?' she says, casting her eyes around hopefully, and I force a smile and say he's coming in a bit. Her husband Roger is over by the doors, talking to one of the teachers. I've seen them together before.

To get away from her, I go and set up the tea stall with Danielle from the doctor's surgery, losing myself in the methodical actions of laying out the cups and saucers, setting out the glasses of weak squash and even weaker tea. Sophie knocks over a glass of squash and I scrabble around for a tea towel to soak it up. Parochial, parochial. As we fill the glasses, Danni and I chat. Her sing-song voice goes up and down, up and down. She's so young, really. Easy to talk to.

'Good turnout,' I say to her, and she nods, looks around the room. I wonder if she's looking for my husband.

'D'you think Rachel and Ian Edwards will come?' she asks, pouring another glass of squash absent-mindedly. 'I don't know what I'd do, if I was them.'

'No,' I say, 'I can't even imagine. I haven't seen them yet.' I smile at her, place my hand on her arm. 'Steady with the squash.'

More people are arriving, and the babble of chatter fills the air, but this day feels all wrong to me. As though we are making a mockery of Clare, of her memory, as though we are glossing over the fact that there might be a murderer wandering around – we'll all be too busy eating Candy Hearts to notice.

Danni's disappeared suddenly, leaving me with the tea stall, and I look through the open doors of the hall, out to the school playing field. Someone has attached heart-shaped bunting to the trees that line the edge of the grass; the bright flags flap in the breeze. Despite the hot air blasting out from the sports hall vents I feel chilly, as though I'm behind a cloud.

As I'm finishing up the teas, there's a sudden shout from across the hall and I look up, my head snapping too quickly on my neck so that I get a pain, shooting down my tendons and into the top of my collarbone. Wincing, I squint across the crowd of people, trying to see what the commotion is for.

It doesn't take me long.

Nathan Warren is standing in the corner near the bric-a-brac table, manned by one of the teachers – Emma Garrett, who looks as though she might be about to cry. Nathan is standing, helpless, dressed in the same neon jacket he always wears, pulled over a stained black jumper and baggy blue jeans. On his feet are boots: large, workmen's boots.

'You're not welcome here!'

The shout is male; I don't recognise it at first. Hurriedly, and ignoring the increasing pain in my neck, I move closer, gripping Sophie's hand, abandoning the tea stall to the clutches of Lindsay Stevens. It's Daniel Jones. It's Owen's dad.

He is standing two feet away from Nathan, his feet set apart, a completely different man to the somewhat meek, dis-interested guy who sometimes shows up at parents' evenings. As I approach, I see the anger writ large across his face; a vein in his forehead is throbbing and his fists are tightly clenched. A little crowd has started to gather. Somewhere, the wail of a baby starts up: high, piercing, shattering the air. Sophie's grip is vicelike on mine. There are lots of kids here. This should not be happening.

I look around to see if Jack has appeared, or if any of the teachers are nearby – it's quite a big hall, and not everyone has noticed what's going on. Miss Marsden, Head of Reception, has both hands to her mouth, eyes wide as she stares at the scene unfolding before us. Anna Cartwright who coaches the hockey team is standing with both arms held out in front of a group of Year Sevens – a bit over the top, granted, but her heart's in the right place. We need someone who can step in. I see Mr Carter the PE teacher on the other side of the hall, supervising the children as they enthusiastically kick slightly deflated footballs into a makeshift board, 5 points for a big hole, 10 for a small. I should call him over.

Nathan is still standing, mute, and I feel a flash of fear.

A couple of other parents are beginning to form a little circle around Daniel. I can't see Owen anywhere and my neck is hurting too much to swivel around. Doesn't Nathan know that coming here wasn't wise, after everything? Personally, I've always thought it unlikely that they'll blame him for Clare's death – he doesn't look like he has it in him. He's simple, that's all. But there's no denying it; he's an easy target. Suddenly, I feel sick.

Sophie's fingers are clenched so hard against mine that I'm worried they might break. My ring presses into my skin. I have a sudden, rare desire to have Jack with me, to not be alone as Daniel Jones shouts at Nathan Warren.

Sophie is scared, I can feel it and I know I ought to pull her away, I know that we're standing too close to two grown men, one of whom has his fists clenched, but somehow I can't, I can't tear my gaze from Nathan's face. Kelly Richards has abandoned her position as bag-checker and pushed her way closer to Daniel.

'You might think you can get away with it, but you can't,' she hisses, and there are murmurs of assent from the other parents as Nathan stands there by the bric-a-brac, blinking. His hands are held behind his back and his face looks impassive, blank.

'Go home!' Daniel says, clearly gaining confidence from his supporters. He takes a step forward, towards Nathan. 'Did you know my son's been hauled over hot coals because of you? Because of what you did?'

Nathan moves, one quick movement, stepping closer to the bric-a-brac stall. As I watch, his large fingers land on a pile of cheap beaded necklaces, gathered in a makeshift display at the end of the table, and he grabs for them like a child, lifts them up for the crowd to see. Sophie used to do that when she was a baby; grasp at shiny objects like a small, loud magpie. I was forever finding my jewellery in with her soft toys, my coins tucked into her pram. I used to panic that she'd swallow something, choke to death while I was looking the other way.

'Pretty lady,' Nathan says, and his voice is desperate, pleading, as though he's trying to explain something but none of us are listening. Beside me, I feel Sophie tugging at my hand, her little fingers growing slippery with sweat.

Kelly is shaking her head.

'It's disgusting,' she says, 'people like you coming here,

being close to our girls. I don't care what the police say. It's obvious to anyone with half a brain that you're guilty as sin. It's not as if it's the first time you've followed a girl home, is it?'

There is a sort of hissing noise from the little crowd, more whispers on the breeze.

A hand reaches out, touches my arm and I gasp involuntarily, release Sophie's hand. She buries her head in the folds of my skirt and I turn to see Sandra at my side, her face undeniably one of joy at the hideous drama in front of us.

'Sandra,' I say, but at that moment Mr Carter appears, stepping quickly between the two men and holding out his hands, as if that ever really stopped anyone.

My heart is thundering in my ears and as the PE teacher starts trying to disperse the small crowd, I can't look away from Nathan's face, and as I stare, he shifts his gaze from Daniel Jones and stares straight back at me. Fear goes through me, cold and deep, and I am the first to break the spell, turning away from him as he shuffles off, out of the open sports hall door, away from the fair. I watch his back retreat, and my breathing doesn't fully slow until he is completely out of sight. *Pretty lady*. The words make me think of Rachel. The beautiful ice queen next door.

Sweat coats the back of my neck and the cut on my face itches. It's hot now, the sports hall is full; those who were not here for the incident with Nathan are swiftly being filed in, I can hear the murmurs, Chinese whispers on the wind. Sophie cries a little bit after Nathan leaves, then makes a quick recovery when I give her a chocolate bar from my handbag, wrapped in extra tin foil so as not to spoil the lining. She starts to drag me around the stalls, pleading with me to buy her a giant chocolate bunny holding a bright red heart between its paws. I'm just deliberating, on the verge of giving in, when hands slide themselves around my waist and Jack's breath is in my ear.

'Think of the E numbers in that,' he whispers, then kisses the side of my neck, too passionately for a school fete on a Saturday afternoon, especially when he wasn't even speaking to me this morning. Something inside me stirs, replacing the rod of fear that lodged itself when I saw Nathan. What is he trying to prove? When I look at him, his eyes are dead. Completely at odds with the show of affection. The performance for the crowds. For a moment, I remember how we used to be, back at the very beginning; tearing each other's clothes off, legs touching underneath the table. Secret glances on Albion Road. In amongst the crowd and the noise and the heat, I am overwhelmed by the need to cry.

'Made you jump?' Jack says, and I swallow hard, shake my head and look around. A couple of the mothers are looking at us, their eyes flickering over Jack and I, their faces almost unreadable. I can read them only because I am used to it – the look of jealousy. *The green-eyed monster.* I push the phrase out of my head as quickly as it came. It's what my mother used to say when I complained to her about the holes in my shoes, the rips in my coat. She'd tell me I mustn't covet the belongings of those more fortunate than myself. That the green-eyed monster would get me if I did. Along with God, of course. My family were quite big on God too. Diane used to say it made me repressed.

'Where's Finn?' I say, looking back towards my husband.

He sees the way the women look at him, I know he does. He must do.

Jack nods in the direction of the football nets, and I see Finn's familiar figure clad in his favourite football shirt, kicking a ball towards the makeshift nets. 'He wore his footy T-shirt specially. Harry's at home, didn't fancy a fair, surprisingly.'

He seems remarkably chirpy today and I pause, wrong-footed. I stare again at his eyes – this time, they glimmer at me and I remember the old attraction, the desperate sense of urgency I felt, that need to be with him, part of him, owned by him. It's still there, just about, but now it makes me feel afraid. I think of last night, him sitting on the end of our bed.

'Do you want to go find your brother, Soph?' Jack asks her, pointing over at Finn, who is now standing next to Mr Carter, watching another boy take shots – the first of which misses.

'Can I have the rabbit?' Not one to be deterred, my daughter. I suppose she must get that from me. Instinctively, my hand goes to my handbag, the reassuring solidity of the gold lock.

'Maybe, if you're good,' Jack says teasingly and I force a smile. Sophie runs off; I watch her spindly legs in their white cotton socks make their way towards the football nets. We are left alone, save for the bunny.

'So,' Jack says, and I feel it again, the glint of fear, the horrible sense of unease.

'Nathan Warren was here earlier,' I say in a low voice, and as I say his name I feel sweat begin to prickle again at the back of my neck, dampening my pink blouse. Jack opens his mouth but a tannoy begins to boom across the hall, the headteacher's voice infiltrating our conversation. They're announcing the raffle.

'I'm just going to check on our tickets,' I say, and I slip a hand into my bag, angling my body slightly away from Jack's.

The purple tickets are flimsy in my fingers; I grip them tightly to try to stop my hands shaking. I don't want Jack to notice. The numbers are read out; the hall is quieter now, everyone consulting their tickets. My eyes circle the crowd: I see Sandra with Natasha, and Sophie standing with Finn by Mr Carter. Quickly, I beckon the kids over; we should be keeping our children close. What am I thinking letting them run off away from me?

Jack has been accosted by one of the other teachers, all of whom love him – do they really think their doe eyes and hair flicks aren't obvious? They're obvious to everybody, not just to me.

And then I see them. Rachel and Ian are standing, their bodies huddled together, near the corner of the hall where the arts and crafts table is. The primary school children have all made bunches of papier-mâché roses, displayed neatly along with their names – Sophie's is good, Finn's less so. I see Rachel's dark head, bowed slightly as the raffle numbers continue, punctuated by the odd yelp of joy from a winner and the inevitable moans of disappointment from everyone else. As if anyone could really be seriously distraught at not getting their hands on a box of Milk Tray and warm Prosecco. Small-town life at it's very best.

Sophie pulls the raffle tickets from my hand and she and Finn pore over them. I can't even remember what numbers we have.

'Number 434, pink!' Andrea calls, but her voice sounds

strange. Behind us, there is a little cry and a small child I don't immediately recognise comes forward, face flaming at the attention, clutching her winning ticket between her hands. Sophie makes a loud huffing noise.

'Daisy. She doesn't deserve to win, Mummy. Her bunch of roses wasn't very good.'

As the girl turns back towards us, I look again – she's Lindsay Stevens' daughter. Getting-a-divorce-Lindsay. I look for her, and see her standing watching her daughter, alone in the crowd. I never did bake her that cake that I promised.

Rachel and Ian have moved closer now; I catch heads turning slightly towards them, looking away quickly as though they have seen something they shouldn't. Nobody wants to look grief in the face, do they. Least of all me. Rachel is still horribly, terrifyingly thin. But still beautiful. Pretty.

'And the final ticket, number 85, green!' Andrea says into the speaker, and again there's a rallying cry from somewhere across the field.

'Well!' I say, 'that's that then! Who fancies something to eat?'

'Me! Me!' both the children squeal and Jack's attention is diverted back to us, like water rerouting. I feel his eyes on me, and my stomach tightens at the thought of the rest of the day spent playing happy families. Suddenly, I have to get away.

'Will you take the children?' I ask him. 'Just nipping to the ladies.'

I leave them before he can reply, heading vaguely in the direction of the corridor leading away from the sports hall, where a bright pink handwritten sign advertises the toilets. There is a buzzing sound in my head, growing louder and louder. Somewhere, music has started to play, a strange, piped music that drills through my mind, forcing me to squeeze my eyes shut against the brightness of the day. The sunshine feels inappropriate. All of this feels inappropriate. I want everything to stop now.

Chapter Thirty-Three

Clare

Monday 4th February, 3.00 p.m.

We've got a free period this afternoon – we're meant to use it for exam prep. Lauren spends most of it giggling with Andy Miles and his stupid friends, but I tell them I'll see them afterwards and go instead to the girls' bathroom. There's no one else inside and I find a cubicle at the end, lock the door behind me and sit down. I take a deep breath and pull out my phone, googling everything again even though I've read all the info so many times. But I feel stupidly nervous now. I don't know why.

The most common pill is called Microgynon – that's the one Lauren's older sister has, I think. I read through all the side-effects again, heart thumping. It'll be fine, I'm just being overanxious. I force myself to think about how many people take the pill; the chance of something bad happening is so small that it's not worth thinking about. Besides, I can't back out now. I've already got the doctor's appointment – it's at four thirty, straight after school. The girls don't know where I'm going – I don't want them to know that I didn't lose my virginity last year, that I've been bluffing for months. They'll take the piss.

Instead of worrying, I try to focus on how happy Owen is going to be. I know he's been wanting to sleep together for months now – he's never forceful or anything, he knows I'd hate that, but I've always been too nervous. I know it's silly but I hate the thought of condoms – they showed us them in that cringe PSHE class once – all rubbery and slimy. I don't like the thought of the latex on my skin. Besides, everyone says this way is better – for the girl and for the guy. He'll be so excited. I have to take them for a week before they kick in, so I can't actually sleep with him tonight, not the whole way, but I've got it all planned. I'll show him the packet tonight, so that there's no going back, and I'll stay overnight, get used to the idea of sleeping in the same bed. We've never spent the whole night together before – it's such a big step for me, not that I'd ever admit that to anyone else. It feels like I'll be leaving the old Clare behind, watching her disappear – shy, scared little Clare – and stepping into my new, adult self. Then, this time next week – I shiver with anticipation, or nerves – next week we'll do it, the whole way, at his dad's house. It's going to be perfect.

I remember the moment it all began with Owen, at an after-school football game on the fields next to the school. It was last July, and the weather was really hot and sunny. The boys were playing a friendly. I was sitting on the sides with the girls, drinking lemonade – Lauren had snuck some vodka into hers, but I didn't really want any. She and a couple of the other girls in our year had got a bit giddy and sloped off by themselves, thinking a walk would sober them up, so I'd pulled out my book, sat by myself for a bit. Owen was subbed in the second half, and he plonked himself down next to me.

He'd been sweating slightly, his forehead glistening, red strands stuck fast to his skin as if they had been pasted on. There had been a smell, too, that unmistakeably outdoors smell of football boots and muddy legs and clothes that need to go straight into the wash. A male smell. A smell that frightened me.

'What you reading?'

I was surprised, had assumed he'd only sat next to me because I was quite close to the pitch and he wanted to concentrate on the rest of the game. My body tensed, as it always did when members of the opposite sex got too close. I'd reluctantly turned over my book so a sweaty Owen could see the front cover: Of Mice and Men *by John Steinbeck. He'd leaned a little closer to me and my stomach had clenched, my heartbeat quickened.*

'It's on our reading list,' I'd said, regretting the words instantly. Why did I have to sound like I was telling him off?

He'd nodded. 'Sure, we did it too, last year. I liked it. Do you?'

His eyes had flicked from the book back to the game, but there was something about his face that showed he was listening for what I said next, alert to my presence even if he was pretending not to be.

'Umm…' I hadn't quite made up my mind yet; I didn't like the George character much, the way he was mean to Lenny. But I didn't like the thought of Lenny's big, too-strong hands either; they frightened me, though I'd never put that in an essay. 'It's good so far,' I said, keeping my voice light, and Owen had turned back to me, smiled.

'Come back to me when you finish it. That ending!' He let

out a long, low whistle, a whistle that in my head, immediately cast him as much older than his sixteen years – here was a sophisticated guy, a reader, a guy who could whistle. One who might be different.

'Are you going back on?' I'd asked him, nodding awkwardly at the pitch, and Owen had looked directly at me, grinned, shook his head.

'Nah. Think I'm better off here.'

I gave him my number, and we spent the best part of a week texting from the last school bell to midnight every night, ignoring each other at school, until on the Friday evening he'd tapped me on the shoulder as I was standing at my locker, fumbling with my books.

'Hey, Clare.'

This time he wasn't sweaty and he didn't have that outdoors smell. Still, I felt the old familiar fear wrap itself around me, but Owen smiled and his smile was so gentle and I wanted so badly to be free of the past, to prove to myself that I could be different now, that I texted Mum saying I was going to Lauren's and instead we went for a walk, up through Sorrow's Meadow at the back of the town. Owen produced some cider from his rucksack which he must have been carrying around all day and we sat there in the blaze of yellow, talking and laughing and taking sips from the sweet, fizzy cans. I'd felt an odd feeling come over me when we stood to leave. It was the first time I had gone more than five minutes without thinking about my father.

Since that day in Sorrow's Meadow, we have seen each other in secret as much as we can. I often go to Owen's when his dad's away, choosing the easiness of his empty house over *my own home, where Mum and Ian watch my every move, and the house is filled with bad memories. Some nights, the knives come out: I'm wasting my time with my friends, my GCSEs need to come first. They suspect a boy, sometimes, and say that boys my age are only interested in one thing. That, and football. I've tried to argue, to tell them that that's not true, but Mum defers to Ian every time and Ian is not one to be proved wrong. The idea of it makes me shudder.*

Chapter Thirty-Four

Jane

Monday 18th February

Jack's home early from work on Monday night. Dinner is already on the table; the children are silent, still tired from Saturday's fair. We saw Nathan on the way home from school; someone had broken his cone, smashed the top of it so that the orange shards poked up into the air. They look violent, angry. He didn't smile at us like he normally does, but I smiled at him, looked at my watch. Then I grabbed the children's hands, hurried them along.

'How was work?' I ask Jack, to break the strange tension that is gathered in our kitchen, but he shrugs at me, won't meet my eye. I almost laugh to myself, imagining if the PTA girls could see us now. The loving husband who kissed my neck at the fair is nowhere to be seen.

Finn isn't eating his food.

'Eat up, please, Finn,' I say briskly, tapping the end of my knife on the tablecloth beside his plate. The silver glints in the overhead lights of the kitchen.

'Not hungry,' he says sullenly, and I pause, a little surprised. Of the three children, Finn is the sunniest – my easy boy, my golden-headed child. Sophie was always the most difficult baby – screaming through the night, throwing things on the floor as soon as I gave them to her. She's calmer now, but still there are the moments of defiance, the strops that won't stop. Harry was somewhere in between.

'What's the matter?' I ask Finn, more brusquely than I'd intended, but I didn't sleep well and I just want them all to co-operate. Just for once. After everything I've done for this family, is that too much of an ask?

'Nothing,' he mutters, pushing the casserole I've cooked around his plate, the metal of his fork scraping unpleasantly against the ceramic.

I look over at Jack. He's hardly eaten anything either, and he isn't helping with Finn. A bubble of panic starts to form in my chest, blurring the corners of my vision. Is this how it's always going to be from now on? Are things ever going to get better?

'Mummy?' Sophie says, and I try to smile at her, but my chest feels tight and her voice sounds tinny to my ears.

I try to speak but this time, nothing comes out – a roaring noise fills my head and the next thing I know Jack is at my side, an arm around my shoulders and a hand on the back of my neck, pushing my head down between my knees.

'Deep breaths,' he is saying, and for a moment I am back in the hospital, having just had Sophie, and he is holding my hand and smiling and everything is as it should be, without any mistakes, without any anger. Tears prick my eyes even as I feel my heartbeat slowing. I force myself to breathe deeply, in for five, out for three, the way they taught us back on Albion Road. I was never very good at it. Jack was better than me.

I'm never good enough.

'Kids, Mummy's feeling a bit poorly, so why don't you take your plates into the living room and you can watch some TV?' Jack is saying, his voice above my head, and I distantly hear the sounds of the children scurrying away, perked up at the thought of ITV on tap.

'Come on,' he says to me after a few minutes, and slowly, reluctantly, I follow him up the stairs to our bedroom, one hand on the bannister as though I am an old lady.

'You're alright,' Jack says as soon as I'm lying on our bed, little beads of sweat dotting my brow. 'Just a panic attack.'

He's frowning at me, and I feel a surge of anger. As he comes closer, my body tenses out of habit and he almost laughs, the left corner of his mouth crinkling up in that familiar way.

'I'm not going to hurt you, Jane,' he says, 'I think we've done enough of that, don't you?' At that I feel the tears begin to come, seeping out of the sides of my eyes onto our big white bed. Gently, he gets up and closes the curtains even though it is still light outside; it's early evening, just after six. The heavy blue drapes block the sounds of the outside world and I feel my body relaxing into the bed. If only I could stay here, like this, keep the doors and windows shut, keep my little family inside for ever. In here, no one can break us, any more than we have already broken ourselves.

When I close my eyes, the bright bunting of the Valentine's fair dances behind my eyelids, stops me from falling asleep.

Chapter Thirty-Five

DS Madeline Shaw

Tuesday 19th February

She is drifting between wake and sleep when there's a hammering noise, loud and relentless. It jolts her awake, and she starts, reaching out a hand to grab her phone. It's nearly one a.m. Sleep is elusive at the best of times, but she could do without someone at the front door in the middle of the night.

Madeline takes the stairs two at a time, reaching the door just as the knocking starts up again. She hears a voice: female, crying. Quickly, she yanks the door open.

Rachel Edwards stumbles forwards into the little hallway, her face a mess. Tears are streaking down her cheeks and her hair looks matted, as though she has been running her hands through it over and over again. She's wearing what looks like a dressing gown underneath a dark purple jacket, its buttons all done up wrong.

Quickly, Madeline steps outside to see if there's anyone behind her, but the street looks deserted, the street lamps glowing eerily in the light, casting white moon shapes onto the empty pavement. She looks from side to side. The nearest house is owned by the Bishops, a young couple with a four-month-old baby who moved in just before Clare died. They're probably biding their time until the little one is old enough before moving again. The town can't have made a great first impression on them, can it? On the other side of Madeline live Donna Phillips and her family: she's a PTA member, friends with Sandra Davies, Jane Goodwin, Tricia Jenkins and that lot. She doesn't want anyone seeing Rachel standing outside her door like this, it'll be round the town in no time, so she makes a split decision: she closes the door behind them both.

Still sobbing a little, Rachel goes ahead of her, walks shakily over to the sofa as Madeline guides her into the house.

Quickly, she runs into the kitchen and fills Rachel a glass of water, places it down on the coffee table in front of her.

'Are you alright, Mrs Edwards?' Madeline sits down beside her. It is odd having her here, in her personal space; she ought perhaps to take her to the station, but she senses the other woman is in no fit state to be carted to Chelmsford at this time of night.

'I can't sleep for thinking about it,' Rachel says suddenly, her voice bursting out into the room, louder than Madeline has heard her speak before.

'For thinking about what?' she prompts, hoping that this isn't just a night of insomnia, that this is something more, that this might even be the breakthrough they so desperately need.

Rachel starts pulling at the skin around her fingernails, tearing little white strips of skin away from the bone. Madeline wants to reach out a hand, tell her to stop it, but instead she forces herself to wait. Rachel has come here to say something. If pushed, she might lose her nerve.

'Rachel, if there's anything you want to tell me about the night Clare died, please, you're doing the right thing by coming here,' Madeline says at last. The other woman doesn't look at her. She's afraid. Instead, she hangs her head so that her chin rests against the top of her coat, her hair dangling down with a strange slithering sound as it brushes the material.

'I shouldn't be here,' she whispers, but Madeline shakes her head, feels a sudden desperation grip her. She's so close to speaking.

'Is this about Clare?' Madeline says carefully, watching Rachel closely. Rachel nods her head, straight up and down, like a puppet on a string. *Whose string*, Madeline wonders.

'Does this have anything to do with your husband, Mrs Edwards?' Madeline asks, and at the mention of him she breaks down again, the sobs echoing through the tiny room. Reaching inside the pocket of her coat, she slowly draws out an object – and when Madeline sees what she's holding, it is clear why she was so afraid to come.

It's Clare's mobile phone. An iPhone 6, clad in gold casing, one of the corners slightly dented. They had the parents describe it over and over in the station, did everything they could to try to track the device's last known movements. But it all stopped dead in Sorrow's Meadow.

She's still gripping the phone tightly, as if she doesn't want to let it go, as if she knows that when she does, there won't be any going back. Madeline is watching her fingers clutch the hard plastic and her mind is racing with possibilities, combing back through everything in the last fortnight: the false starts, the endless interviews, Clare's blonde hair fanned out against the dark, muddy ground. There were reports of an argument that morning. An argument between Clare and her mother. Rachel felt guilty, she said that herself on tape.

Guilty for being cross with her daughter, for chastising her about her exams.

What, then, is Rachel guilty of now?

'I found it in his things,' Rachel says. Her whole body is shaking slightly.

'Whose things?' Madeline's voice is careful, but Rachel just shakes her head, presses a hand to her mouth.

'You found Clare's mobile in Ian's belongings?' the policewoman asks, wanting to be crystal clear, and Rachel nods, looks up to meet the other woman's eyes for the first time. Madeline can see how much this is costing her, this admission, can sense the guilt she feels in coming here, the sense of betrayal.

'Rachel, I'm going to need to ask you to come down to the station to make a statement,' Madeline says gently. Rachel isn't going to want to, but if what she's suggesting is true, it is far too serious to be alleged in this cramped little house.

She begins to shake her head, her body tense.

'He didn't do it,' she whispers, 'he can't have done. He loved her.'

Her hands go to her mouth, as though she wants to press the words back inside her.

'When did you find the phone, Rachel?' Madeline asks, and she lets out a little moan.

'Mrs Edwards, you do need to comply with my questions,' the policewoman tells her firmly. 'Concealing evidence is a chargeable offence, as I think you might already be aware of.'

Rachel sits up straighter, takes a deep breath. Madeline can see the resolve in her tighten at her words.

'I found it a couple of hours ago,' she says. One of her fists is clenching the sofa cushion, her fingers twisting around the patterned material. 'I was looking for my phone charger, we share a little battery pack one that we take if we go out.' She takes a deep, shuddery breath. 'Things have been weird between us since Saturday – we came back from the Valentine's fair and it – it was horrible, being around everyone, we shouldn't have gone. We haven't talked properly since – I don't know, it feels like there's this big gap between us.' She looks at Madeline, almost pleadingly.

'So this evening, Ian suggested we went out for a drive, anywhere, just anywhere away from here, so that we could talk in the car. We've always talked on long drives, you know, something about being in that small space together...' Her voice breaks, and Madeline thinks briefly about how terrible it must be for her, trapped in Ashdon, surrounded by the memories of her daughter. 'So I looked for the battery pack,' Rachel continues shakily. 'I always want to keep my phone charged in case – in case there's any news.' She looks at Madeline. 'I'm frightened of not being contactable. Ever since Clare.'

'Go on.'

'I was looking in his backpack,' she says, 'the one he always carries. I wasn't expecting to find anything, like I said I was just looking for the charger, but I felt the shape of the phone and pulled it out, thinking he'd forgotten his. We all have the same one – had the same one.' She runs her fingers over the gold casing of Clare's phone, as though it's her daughter's hand.

'I've been going crazy, I couldn't bring myself to ask him, I just took the phone and hid it in my handbag. Went out for the drive. I tried to work up the courage to ask him about it while we were out but I just – I couldn't. I've been trying to think of a reason, an explanation, but I know she had her phone with her that day because she texted me from it, and Ian was at work. The only way it could be in his bag is if, if…'

Her voice tails off and Madeline steadily gets to her feet, goes to a drawer in the kitchen and pulls out a spare carrier bag, which she places over her right hand. Returning to Rachel, she reaches out a hand, open-palmed, the bag covering her skin. As Rachel places the phone inside it, something seems to change within the small room – a heightening of nerves, a charge.

'I charged it up just now,' Rachel says, 'looked through the messages. The code is her birthday.' She shakes her head, as though in disbelief. 'I didn't even know she had a boyfriend,' she whispers. 'What kind of mother am I, Madeline? What kind of person doesn't know their own daughter?'

The DCI is ecstatic, even when Madeline rings him at two a.m. and tells him to meet her at the station. Using Clare's code, they unlock the phone, and find it all – the messages from Owen, the calls and texts, intense and often, pages and pages worth.

The texts fly between them on the day of the murder, but the last exchange makes Madeline's breath catch in her throat.

You know I said I had a surprise for you?
I like surprises.
You'll love this one. I'm on my way over now. See you soon. I love you.
Call me when you're outside. Xxx

A surprise for him – she's hinted at it all day but never says what it is. Rachel shakes her head when they ask if she knows what it is.

'We never even knew,' she said. 'Why would she keep that a secret, Madeline? Why wouldn't she tell me? I'm her *mother*.'

'That's something we're hoping to find out,' Madeline says, and she accompanies Rachel back to her house to collect Ian's backpack, give her the opportunity to shower and change while Ian is safely on the early train into London. Back to his business, Madeline thinks.

They searched the house directly after Clare was found, but there was nothing. No phone. The SIM card and battery are now intact, but there hasn't been a reading for it since the night Clare died. Not until tonight, when Rachel charged it up.

'It's possible he's been keeping it on his person, or at work,' the DCI says. 'Got sloppy, now that a bit of time's passed. Thought he was in the clear. It showed up on the system a few hours ago, look, must've been when she turned it on. Bloody Ben says he was asleep.'

'Why would he put the SIM back in?' Madeline asks. Ian must've disconnected the SIM in order for it not to show up on the masts. But from what Rachel says, the phone was complete in his bag. Dead, but not taken apart.

The DCI goes through everything again with Rachel down at the station, recording the whole thing on tape. She looks better now she's out of her dressing gown but anyone can see she's terrified – her still-beautiful face is white under the harsh station lights and she's biting her lips, shredding the skin with her teeth. The station smells as it always does, of stale coffee and body spray. Too many officers without time to go home and shower.

'I'm going to walk you through what's going to happen next, Mrs Edwards,' Rob tells her after she's told him everything, and she nods quickly, clearly hanging on his every word.

'We will be bringing your husband back into the station, in light of the new information you have given us. He will be further questioned, in the hope that, for his sake, he can explain his reasons for possessing and concealing your daughter's mobile phone. If your husband cannot produce a reasonable explanation for this, we may need to arrest him, and if further evidence comes to light, he will then be formally charged.'

A pause. She's looking down now, at the table top, her eyes hooded. Exhaustion is writ large on her features. She looks so fragile. So alone.

'Have you ever worried about your husband harming your daughter before, prior to this incident, Mrs Edwards?' Rob asks, and she blanches, flicks her eyes up at us again.

'They— they argued, sometimes,' she says, her voice little more than a whisper, 'but I don't know, I don't think I'm a very good judge. I misread people. I know I do.'

Madeline frowns. 'What do you mean by that, Rachel?'

She can see Rachel's pulse beating in her neck, the fragility of her throat as she swallows.

'I just mean – I don't trust myself,' she says, and when she looks up again, her blue eyes are filled with salty tears. Madeline can feel Rob's impatience beside her; he won't like this, he'll just want the facts. Carefully, she stands, fetches Rachel a tissue from the box they keep on the cabinet in the corner.

'Sorry,' she says, 'it's all just been so much to take in.'

'Of course it has,' Rob says, nodding while she dabs the tissue to her eyes, blows her nose, the sound too loud in the small interview room.

'These arguments,' he says, 'were they about anything specific? Did you notice an increase in tensions between them in the run-up to February the fourth?'

'Your husband told us there'd been an argument the day before Clare died, Mrs Edwards,' Madeline says bluntly, and she blanches.

'Yes,' she says, 'yes, but it was just about exams. We were too hard on her, I know we were.' She puts a hand to her forehead, as though tending a sick child. 'Sorry, I'm trying to think, to remember – they argued a bit about silly things, mostly, her school work, how often she saw her friends. He wanted her to do well – well, we both did. I think it's partly the army training, you know, he's very big on discipline. But I never saw him – I never saw him hurt her. He wasn't like that, I never thought he had a violent bone in his body.'

Rob nods. 'And prior to you finding your daughter's phone in his belongings, you had no reason to suspect your husband of involvement in Clare's death? There was nothing that you noticed – any strange behaviour, perhaps, any feelings of guilt?'

Rachel seems to struggle with this, balling the crumpled tissue up in one hand, her fingers tightening into a fist. 'I don't know,' she says. 'I didn't think so, but yes, we both felt guilty. I still do.' She presses her lips together, as though keeping her words in check. 'I feel guilty for everything – waiting too long to call the police on the night it happened. For being too strict with her about her exams. For every single argument, every cross word. Every time I let her out of my sight. Every time she lied to me about Owen – why couldn't she just tell me? Was I really such a terrible mother?'

'You're not a terrible mother, Rachel,' Madeline says. At this, Rachel buries her head in her hands, her voice muffled.

'I am,' she says, the words indistinct, 'I am a terrible mother, detective. You don't know.'

A loud sob escapes her and Madeline brings the whole box of tissues over to the table. Rachel's hand shakes as she lifts her head and plucks another from the box, takes a deep breath as if trying to pull herself together.

'But in terms of thinking he was involved – no, I never thought that, I never would have believed it of him.' A pause. 'But like I say – I don't trust myself, detectives. That's why I had to tell you. I had to let you know.'

Her hands clasp and unclasp on the table.

'You have been very helpful in this investigation, Mrs Edwards,' Rob says, attempting a smile. 'I am aware that this new information has been a great shock to you, but our job is to protect you and rest assured, you will be protected from your husband.'

At this, a strange flicker crosses her face, there for a second, then gone. When she looks at Rachel Edwards, Madeline can't help but get the sense that there is something she's not telling them, some piece of the jigsaw that hasn't yet fallen into place. *I am a terrible mother, detective. You don't know.* What makes her so convinced?

'I'm frightened, detectives,' she says suddenly, as though

trying to push the attention back onto Ian, 'I'm frightened of what he might do.'

'We need more.'

The DCI slams his hand down on the table. Lorna's out the front with Rachel Edwards, arranging somewhere for her to go for the rest of the day. The best thing for the police would be if she went home, listened up to see if Ian confessed to anything, but they would be putting her in danger, and on top of that, they can't trust her. Madeline has seen it before – couples helping each other out, right at the last minute, just when you think they'll do the right thing. That's the thing about making mistakes early on in your career – you'll do anything you can to avoid making them twice.

'The CPS will need more to charge,' Rob says, running a hand through his hair. 'A witness, a weapon – anything. We're so close.' He starts muttering to himself under his breath.

'We agreed that the perpetrator may not have had a weapon,' Madeline reminds him. The wound on the back of Clare's head looked as though it could have been inflicted by someone slamming her into the ground, into the base of the tree stump where she was discovered. Christina confirmed it. The DCI ignores Madeline.

She hovers, then when the DCI still doesn't reply, Madeline goes back out into the station, her head throbbing, feeling in her pockets for change for the vending machine in reception. Rachel's words are still thrumming through her head. Is it just the guilt of a mother who's lost a child? Or could it be more than that? Frustration eats at her. They are close, she can feel it.

Madeline is about to select a Twix when she sees him.

Nathan Warren, standing just outside the glassy front doors, his hands in the pockets of his trousers, no coat even though it's cold out today. For a moment, he is frozen behind the glass, standing totally still, and the next thing she knows he is inside, three feet away from her. He is paused, alert as though he is about to say something, but something is holding him back.

'Nathan?'

It is all the prompt he needs. At once, he is speaking so fast that she cannot properly understand what he's saying, but she hears the word 'Clare' and her heart starts to race.

'Nathan, whoa, whoa, slow down, will you. Slow down.'

The officer on the front desk opens his mouth, about to speak, but she holds up a hand.

'It's alright,' she says, 'I'll handle this.'

Nathan's brown eyes are staring at her, and she puts a hand on his arm, leads him carefully through the double doors into the station. He keeps glancing back over his shoulder, as if he's worried someone will come after him, as if he's not alone.

'Lorna!' Madeline calls out as they enter the briefing room. 'Get Rob for me, will you? Something's come up.'

Chapter Thirty-Six

DS Madeline Shaw

Tuesday 19th February

Nathan speaks slowly now that they are inside the interview room. His eyes are fixed on Madeline's. He states his name for the tape, and she fills in with the date and time then sits back in her seat. She catches a glimpse of his boots underneath the table, solid black army ones, then looks up to meet his eye.

'Nathan, could you please repeat what you told me in the lobby again, for the purpose of the tape?'

'I saw him,' Nathan says. His voice is clear, with none of the mumbling they saw in his original interviews, back when they were questioning him. 'I saw Ian kill Clare Edwards in Sorrow's Meadow. The buttercup field.'

The DCI takes a sharp breath, the sound loud in the room. Madeline nods, watching Nathan.

'Can you tell us why you did not come forward with this information before?'

'I was frightened,' he says in his funny, childlike way, and he looks at the door again, as if expecting it to spring open at any time.

'Frightened of who? Or of what?'

His brown eyes stare into hers. 'I was frightened of Ian.'

'And can you describe for us your movements on that day, February fourth? What did you do in the field?'

His eyes are still locked on hers: unblinking, still. There is a pause. Madeline holds tight. The DCI coughs.

'I was walking,' he says, 'I walk that way a lot. I was walking and I saw the girl, I saw her lying on the floor. There was a man standing over her, that bad man, Ian. He was crying. He knelt down next to her and I saw him hurt her, I saw him hurt her head on the ground.' He looks away. 'There was blood, red blood, lots of blood.'

She looks to the side window of the room, where Lorna is watching.

'And what did you do when you saw this, Nathan?' Madeline asks. He takes a deep breath, nods as if knowing that this will be her next question.

'I waited,' he says, 'I waited until the bad man was gone, and then I went to see if the girl was okay. Not okay though. Not okay.'

'No,' she says, 'she wasn't okay, was she? And then what did you do, Nathan?'

He looks confused. 'Told you,' he says, 'I told the police. Did the right thing.'

Madeline thinks back to the day they got the call up at Chelmsford. Nathan's panicked voice, reporting the body. The call from the Edwards reporting her missing, *She hasn't come home from school.*

'But you didn't tell us straight away, did you Nathan? You waited. What were you waiting for?'

He swallows, looks down at the chipped table. Someone has scratched on it, *fuck you all*.

'I was scared,' he says eventually, 'I didn't want to get in trouble.'

As he says the words, Madeline feels a great sense of failure, a sadness heavy on her shoulders. Because he's right, isn't he – the first thing they did was suspect him, try to pin this on him because of who he is. Because he's an easy target. Because they wanted it sorted so that they didn't look bad in the press. Because they'd listened to gossip from years ago that wasn't even founded on fact.

Madeline pulls out a folder from beneath the desk, opens it and places it in front of him on the table. His eyes widen as he sees the row of faces staring up at them.

'Nathan, can you tell me which, if any, of these people you saw in Sorrow's Meadow that night?'

His finger lands on the printout of Ian's face before she has finished speaking, the doughy skin covering the little photograph.

'Nathan, did this man ever threaten you in the time between the discovery of Clare's body and you coming here to see me today?'

A pause, followed by a nod.

The DCI leans forward.

'Nathan,' he says, 'it's important you cooperate with us now. What were your interactions with this man?'

Immediately, his eyes look panicked, and Madeline feels a wave of sympathy for him, this poor, lonely man who has been through the wringer, outcast by the town, scrutinised by the police for a crime he seemingly didn't commit.

'At the fair,' he mumbles, 'the school fair. He said you'd think I did it. You'd think it was me if I told you it was him.'

The silence in the room is heavy, shameful. Even Rob looks uncomfortable.

'It's alright, Nathan,' Madeline says, in a voice as gentle as she can muster, 'you're not in any trouble now. And you've done the right thing. It's always better to tell the truth.'

He says nothing, looks at the door again.

'I'm going to need you to sign a formal witness statement, Nathan,' she says, 'which corroborates the story you've just told me. Does that sound okay? DS Campbell will sort that out with you.'

He nods.

'Thank you for coming in to see me, Nathan. You did the right thing.'

Madeline watches as Lorna talks Nathan through the witness statement, the DCI at her side. He nudges her in the ribs.

'I'm sorry,' he says, and her jaw almost falls open in shock. It is the first time he's apologised to her since she joined the Chelmsford force.

'What for?'

He winces. 'You know what for. For trying to put it on Nathan, force this into being something it's not. You were right not to let me.'

'Christ,' she says, 'this is a turn up for the books.'

He looks away, half smiling. 'Do you want to give our Ian a ring, then? Or shall we pay a visit?'

Madeline swallows, looks behind him at the wall, where Clare's picture gazes back at her, frozen in time. She pictures

Rachel's face, the gold mobile phone in the palm of her hand. Ian smiling at them from across the interview table, the brightness of his jubilant tie. An 'I've got away with it' tie.

'I think a visit,' Madeline says. 'He's due one.'

Chapter Thirty-Seven

Jane

Wednesday 20th February

In the morning, I wake up from a heavy sleep full of distorted dreams to find six new messages on my mobile. Immediately, my heart jumps; thoughts of the children flash into my mind, lying mangled in the road or face down in the playground, blood seeping around them. I scrabble to sit up, the soft sheets suffocating me. Jack has left already, and there is a note propped up on the lamp by the bed saying he's taken the kids to school, didn't want to wake me. I've slept in. A rarity.

Picking up my phone, I see the names flash up – Sandra, Tricia, Donna. I've a missed call from Jack's office too. My heart skips a beat. But it isn't the children. It's the girls.

They've arrested Ian! Hubby saw the police outside the house early this morning. You can't say we didn't warn them... Sx

Rachel's nowhere to be seen – we ought to pop round. Bake something. What do you bake in this situation? 'Sorry your husband's a murderer' biscuits...? T xx

Missed you at school Jane, have you heard the news? Donna.

PS. Saw Jack earlier with the kids, lucky you having a lie-in! Sx

I'm thinking maybe a cake. Or a lasagne. Something to last her a while. Doubt she'll feel like cooking. D'you know if she's vege? Did she eat the last one you took round? T xx

I always thought there was something weird about Ian. Think he came onto me once, at a sports day. How inappropriate! I probably had a close call. Anyway, talk soon. Donna.

I lie back against the pillows, my heart thumping so hard that I have to put a hand to my chest, press down against the bones of my ribcage. I can feel every one of them, thin and hard under my fingers. Thank God I'm not at the school gates – I imagine the women's faces, like vultures, crowding towards each other, the news travelling like wildfire from one end of the town to the other. Poor Rachel. Poor, poor Rachel.

There's a text from Harry, too. *Are you alright, Mum?*

I wonder again how much my son knows about his parents. *Of course, darling,* I reply, *everything's fine here.*

I picture Ian's face at the Easter fair, the way he towered above Rachel. His gruff voice, military background. His concern over his stepdaughter; his hatred of Mark. Arrested. Murder. He'll be tried. Unless he pleads guilty. In which case, he'll be sentenced quickly. Over and done with.

Christ.

I turn over, push my phone away from me and bury my head into the pillows, my pulse beating through my ears. My phone beeps again but I don't even look at the screen. A few seconds later, it begins to ring but I ignore it.

The warm cotton soothes me for once and I force myself to close my eyes, feel the brush of the duvet against my cheek. In my head, I begin reciting the menu I'll make for the children this week – casserole on Monday, chicken on Tuesday, shepherd's pie on Wednesday, carbonara on Thursday, steamed fish on Friday. I have to just keep going. I can do it. There's no reason why I can't. Repeat, repeat, and repeat. That is my only option.

Unless, of course, I tell the truth.

Chapter Thirty-Eight

Clare

Monday 4th February, 4.10 p.m.

The final bell rings and I move fast, slipping my biology textbook into my bag and walking quickly ahead of Lauren, claiming I have to get home early tonight for dinner.

'See you tomorrow!' she says, giving me a little hug, and I blow a kiss in her direction. As I slip out of the gate, I see Harry Goodwin looking at me, then catch sight of Lauren looking at him. God, I wish he'd just switch his attentions over to her. It'd make her so happy. And get him off my back.

I feel weird as I walk towards Low Road Surgery, my hat pulled down over my hair. It's the same practice I've been going to since I was a little girl – I think I can even remember early visits, clutching onto Mum's hand, terrified at the prospect of the sliding doors and the sterile seats and the smiling man with his stethoscope and needles and thermometers. Mum was always fully made up, long-sleeved, nervously dodging questions. Still, there was always a red lollipop at the end. The building looks more modern than most of the houses in Ashdon – they did a big refurbishment two years ago. Set back from the road, it shines in the weak wintery sunlight, a neat box hedgerow surrounding the stone path leading to the door. Once inside, I am suddenly and irrationally nervous, as though out of nowhere Ian or Mum might appear, bearing down on me in anger, dragging me from the surgery, stopping my adulthood firmly in its tracks.

Approaching reception, I clear my throat and carefully, quietly announce my name in a soft voice to the lady on reception, who has long, manicured nails painted a silvery grey and a little name badge with 'Danielle' written on it in a round, cursive font. She writes it down without even looking up at me, her attention on an iPhone beside her that keeps flashing up with WhatsApp and Bumble notifications. The receptionist taps her nails onto a form on the desk and I scribble my signature, then the silver nails whisk the form away. Instinctively, I close my fingers together, making a fist to hide my own nails, which by contrast are bitten, bare, childish. Once tonight is over I'll paint them, perhaps even do something with my hair, which is long and blonde and boring.

'Take a seat, won't be long,' the woman announces casually, then picks up the phone and begins chatting to someone who is presumably a friend rather than a patient, judging by the bouts of sing-song laughter that permeate the waiting room. I sit, keeping my hat on over my blonde hair, gingerly parking myself with my back to Danielle next to the pile of glossy magazines, which, disappointingly, date back to 2014. I've barely flicked open the cover of a slightly decaying Elle when I hear him – Dr Goodwin – saying my name, smiling at me invitingly. I stand and walk towards him. The door closes behind me.

Chapter Thirty-Nine

Jane

Wednesday 20th February

As I'm making the shepherd's pie for our dinner, I think about my second option. The truth. Truth is a slippery thing, isn't it? But I am tired – yesterday's panic attack hovers on the edge of my consciousness. I am terrified that it will happen again, the longer I keep this up, this charade that has become my life. The narrative I have spun for myself. For my audience.

I stop stirring for a moment, leave the pan of vegetables bubbling on the hob of the Aga. Slowly, I walk over to the window, pull back the curtain to let in a dribble of light from outside. The truth inside me builds. There is nobody here to listen.

The truth is that Jack and I met at anger management class.

There is no easy way to say that, no form of sugar-coating it – believe me, I've tried. I thought that class was going to save me, and for a while it did. But then Jack Goodwin walked in, and my whole world changed.

Jack is a beautiful man. Dark hair, strong jaw, blue eyes. I didn't think I'd ever seen anyone quite so attractive in my whole life. I barely spoke to anyone else in that class; I don't think he did either. Even after everything that has happened,

I can't bring myself to wish those first few weeks away. They were the most exciting time of my life.

When I first walked through that door, got out of my car on that freezing November evening to begin what I thought was the road to recovery, I felt as if I was doing the right thing. Now? The lines between right and wrong have become horribly, frighteningly blurred.

I walk back to the Aga. The pot of food is bubbling, threatening to boil over. I pour a glass of red wine from the bottle by my side, feel the sharp sweetness of it on my tongue. I want to drink all night, drink all this truth away.

The sessions were held on Tuesday evenings, 7–9.45 p.m. on Albion Road near East Finchley underground station. I usually ate before, grabbing a sandwich from the little Tesco Metro after work at the ad agency, then got the tube to Albion Road, my eyes darting round the carriage, irrationally paranoid that an unsuspecting colleague would be behind me, somehow see where I was going.

The room was always cold, with dusty fan heaters whizzing out hot air to try to take the edge off. It was icy, that November; my shoes skidded a little on the glazed over puddles outside the centre. My hands were red from the cold in the time it took to walk the short distance from the tube station; I blew on them on the walk up the stairs. Outside the door on that first night, I hesitated, as no doubt everybody does. Psyching myself up to go inside. Face the strangers. Face up to it all. I almost turned around – I'm not ashamed to admit that. But then the look on my friend Lisa's face flashed through my mind, the shock, and I knew I had to. I opened the door, and went in.

There was a circle of chairs, with faded green cushioned seats, and the coffee machine in the corner with a stack of polystyrene cups and three big jugs of water – still, no sparkling. The place could've done with a lick of paint, but still, I wasn't interested in good aesthetics. Not back then.

It was uncomfortable, at first. I wasn't in control – none of us were. The woman leading the group was called Diane; she had shoulder-length red hair, a dark suit that looked like it belonged in court rather than a badly lit hall. The website advertised it as a 'quiet, leafy area in N2' but we didn't get to see much of the leaves. I arrived in the dark and left in the dark. Maybe it was better that way.

We had to introduce ourselves. Diane went around the circle, asking us all to say a few lines about why we were here and what we wanted to get out of the sessions. She told us our anger was an energy to be harnessed, something we had to take control of.

'Anger is a natural emotion,' she said, 'and one we all experience. I'm guessing there are a lot of you in here that feel like the anger is controlling you, am I right? What we need to do, our aim in these sessions, is to make you feel as though you're the one in charge. Your emotions, your life. Your choice.'

There were twelve of us in the initial session, and I remember glancing around the room, wondering whether these people were the same as me, whether they struggled with the same things I did. How they'd all come to be here – if they'd admitted it to themselves, been forced into it by a loved one, recommended by a colleague. One woman stepped forward and told us her family had performed an intervention, cornered her one night when she wasn't expecting it.

'Everyone was in on it – my mother, my aunt, both my sons,' she told us, shaking her head as if she couldn't quite believe it. She said it as though it was humiliating, but part of me felt a pang of something like jealousy – I didn't have anyone who loved me enough to actually drag me here. Not by then. My family had moved away, and I'd done as much as I could to distance myself from them. I'd taken myself, on Lisa's advice.

Just as it got to my turn, the door opened and a man walked in – a puffy winter coat, smart shoes, nose red from the cold. He took his place in our circle silently, smoothly, without making a fuss.

When it came to my turn I said my name was Rebecca. I didn't want them to know my real name; it would have made it all worse somehow. I told them all the basics: that I was in advertising, had been struggling with anger since my teens. I brushed over my father, told the room that we didn't get on, that he made me feel small, that he pushed me around, that we hadn't spoken for almost eight years to the day. I could sense the nods, some sympathetic, some knowing, some perhaps a little dismissive. Poor little girl with her daddy issues. What made me special? Nothing, except the fact that I'd put myself through university, cut all ties with my father as soon as I possibly could and never looked back. I could feel him looking at me as I talked, his dark eyes on my face. It made my cheeks feel hot.

We all said the word 'anger' out loud so many times that it started to become strange in my mouth, the consonants and vowels losing their meaning. Our eyes met, just briefly after

I'd finished speaking, and it felt as though we were sharing a secret.

Even though it was hard, I forced myself to stay, to keep my feet on the ground even though they wanted to head for the door. If I'd done that, things might be different now.

I take another sip of wine, stir the food. It'll be done soon.

'Often,' Diane was saying, 'our anger comes from ourselves. We create stories that aren't real, we have disproportionate reactions to small things. There is always something else, something underneath, and that's what I want us to work on over the next few weeks. Understanding that, and working on ways to be *ourselves* – but in different, new ways. Not negative ways, or positive ways, but *different* ways.'

The man in the smart shoes liked coffee – the two of us found ourselves standing by the machine at the end of the first session, after Diane had told us that we'd all done a great job, that she'd see us next week.

'One for the road?' he asked me, and I smiled at him, a half smile.

'I'd better have water,' I said, then leaned in close to him, lowered my voice to a whisper. 'I'm Jane. Coffee addict. Nice to meet you.'

He stared at me for a moment.

'I thought – Rebecca?' he said, awkwardly, and I shook my head.

'I didn't want to use my real name here. Thought it'd help, you know? A confidence thing. But you looked like you could handle the truth.'

He stopped for a second, staring at me, and I wondered if I'd got it wrong. Then he filled up my cup for me, handed it back with a smile. 'Nice to meet you, Jane. Go on, have a coffee. Our secret.'

I smiled, and took it from him. I've always been good at keeping secrets. That was the first of many.

The memories rush back to me now, standing by the Aga, they come at me thick and fast. I think of the bruise I gave Jack the other night, the way he scratched at my arms, trying to fight me off without hurting me.

You see, Jack will tell you he hasn't had an anger problem in years. That he defends, not attacks.

It's safe to say he's better at controlling his temper than I am.

Chapter Forty

Clare

Monday 4th February, 4.30 p.m.

*T*he inside of Dr Goodwin's room smells of antiseptic. It reminds me of when my dad would hit my mum. She'd try to hide it, but I always knew – she had a whole drawer in the bathroom dedicated to repairing herself: plasters, wipes, Savlon. A wardrobe full of long-sleeved tops. A box full of heavy-duty make-up: thick foundation, concealer to dab on the bruises. The other kids used to tell me that my mum wore too much make up, 'like a Barbie doll,' they said.

I was the only one who knew why.

I hated the looks the other women used to give her, hated the judgements people made. My mum's so beautiful. None of them knew the truth. They still don't. Mum says it's better that way, that we should 'preserve Dad's memory'. Just after he died, after we'd gone home from the packed church at St Mary's, Mum had pushed her face up close to mine, held me tightly by the shoulders. It hurt, just a tiny bit.

'It's our secret, Clare,' she'd said, 'we have to keep the secret for your Daddy.' I can still remember Mum's hot breath on my face, the wine from the wake, how tight my body felt in my black velvet dress, like a spring ready to uncoil. Some days, I feel so angry with Mum, so angry at her for making me stay true to a promise to protect a man who caused us nothing but pain. But I've kept my promise, haven't I? I've kept my secret. Not even Owen knows why men can make me feel so afraid, why I want to join the police when I'm older. He thinks it's all to do with Ian, but he's wrong.

The antiseptic smell feels like it's growing stronger. I twist my fingers together impatiently as Dr Goodwin taps away at his computer. Glancing around the room, I see a framed photograph on the desk – there's a picture of his youngest kids, smiling out at me, ice cream around their mouths. Harry isn't in it.

'Clare!' he says, spinning around on his chair to face me. 'How nice to see you. What can I do for you?'

I take a deep breath. Be confident.

'I'd like to go on the contraceptive pill, please. If that's okay.'

Immediately, I'm annoyed with herself. If that's okay. He doesn't get to decide, does he? I touch my necklace – I'm sixteen now, I love my boyfriend – of course it is okay! Dad's face flashes through my mind, his voice loud in my ears. Spittle flecking my cheeks. Somewhere across the room, my mother is crying. I squeeze my eyes shut, blocking out the memories of my father that surface whenever I feel uneasy, unsure of myself. It's all in the past now. He is dead. It is over.

'Are you alright?' Dr Goodwin is staring at me, concern on his face. I give myself a little shake.

'Sorry! Yes, I'm fine. So. Is that okay?'

'Should be fine, yes,' he says, still looking a little confused by my behaviour. 'Now, I just need to ask you a couple of questions, Clare, and I'm going to need to check your blood pressure as well, then we can discuss the different options available to you. Sound good?'

I nod, take a deep breath. That antiseptic smell again. I wish he'd open a window. As I stand to have my blood pressure tested, I feel my phone vibrate against my thigh. It'll be Owen, no doubt, asking again what the surprise is. Briefly, I wonder if he will be nervous next week, about what is going to happen between us. Lauren always says that the pressure is on the boy, but I hate it when she says things like that. It's part of the reason I haven't told them – sex should be between me and Owen, private, special. Maybe I am old-fashioned, a square, all the names they'd tease me with if they knew, but I don't care. I love Owen. I trust him. It has taken me a long time to trust any man after Dad, but I do trust him. The same cannot be said yet for Ian, but I'm trying. I know I'm jumpy around him, but I can't help it – Dad trained me well. Ian is a big man and his presence in our small house still puts me on edge. No matter how he seems, I know things could change at any time – tempers could flare, snap, break. I've seen it happen before.

'Do you want to have a seat again?' Dr Goodwin has removed the blood pressure cuff from my arm.

'Now, there are a couple of different contraceptive pills we can start you on,' he says. 'The most common is known as Microgynon, so we can kick off with that one, although we always advise people to come back if they feel it's not working for them – everyone's body can react differently, you see. Have you ever been on any kind of contraception before?'

I shake my head, and he pulls out a green prescription pad, starts scribbling. My phone vibrates again but I resist *the urge to look at it, try to concentrate instead on what the doctor is saying.*

'And are you sexually active now, Clare?'

I shake my head again. He is good-looking, I realise as I lean closer to see what he's writing, and as I lean forward he looks up at me, meets my gaze. Another smile.

Chapter Forty-One

DS Madeline Shaw

Friday 22nd February

Ian still hasn't confessed. He has drafted in a lawyer, an expensive one, so now they sit opposite Madeline as the woman discreetly writes notes, frowns occasionally, whispers things to Ian Edwards that go against everything Madeline believes.

She has always hated defence lawyers. Defending the lawless, the liars, the morally bankrupt. Cashing in on beating the system. It drives her mad.

This one's called Annabel. Annabel McQuirter. Long blonde hair like Clare's. Madeline wonders how she felt when she saw the photographs, the photos of Clare lying in the woods, of the blood on the back of her head? She wonders how she feels listening to Ian and knowing that he's lying, that he must be lying. He tells them he's no idea how the phone got into his bag, that it must be a plant.

'Who would do that?' Madeline says, and he comes up blank, time and time again.

Nathan Warren is lying, he says, possibly to throw suspicion away from himself. He's a simpleton, a fool, his word can't be trusted. Madeline winces at the words, the prejudice they convey.

'That's for a court to decide,' she told him, and he clenched his teeth, made an animalistic sound – half fury, half pain. It's been two days since they arrested him, and he hasn't budged an inch.

'Why did you want to hurt your stepdaughter, Ian? Were you interested in the money her father left to her?' Madeline asks him, over and over again, but eventually he stops speaking, says no comment to everything on the advice of his lawyer. At one point, Madeline thinks she sees tears in his eyes, of frustration, or grief, or panic – she isn't sure.

'Maybe he wanted Rachel to himself,' Lorna says, sighing. 'Clare's in the way, they don't get on, she starts causing problems between the two of them. And he doesn't like that.'

'Or he has issues bringing up Mark Lawler's child,' the DCI says. 'We had a case like that a few years ago. Men get funny about things like that. Territorial.'

Madeline raises her eyebrows at him.

'Not me,' he says, 'just – you know – some men.'

Lorna snorts. 'If he won't confess now, let's see how he is in a week or two,' she says. 'I think the CPS will take this one on, based on what we have.'

Madeline looks back at him, listening to his lawyer, his fists clenched on the table. 'We'd better send support for Rachel,' she says, 'I don't think she'll bail him now.'

They had warned Rachel, of course, she knew it was coming, but still – when the police came to the house on Wednesday morning she just started crying, and when the DCI barrelled past to get to Ian they could all still hear her sobs echoing around the house. Ian was upstairs, it was around six a.m., just before he'd normally leave to get the train. He didn't come easily – he was grappling with them, shouting his head off.

'This is a fucking disgrace!' he said as the DCI read him his rights, and Madeline felt the flecks of spittle land on her face, her arms. It only made Rob grip him harder, snap the cuffs over his wrists more quickly.

When they took him away Rachel stood in the porch of their house, her body stock-still behind the neat green lawn and the ornamental bird bath. As they put him in the car she stared at them, the tears streaming down her face, and then she opened her mouth and let out this sound. A terrible, piercing scream. Lights began to flick on in the neighbouring houses, curtains began to twitch next door.

Ian shouted more then, and he'd already shouted a lot. Out in the open, Madeline could easily see it – the streak of aggression. Maybe he did want Rachel all to himself. Maybe bringing up another man's daughter got the better of him after all. Maybe Clare saw something she shouldn't have. Maybe he just needed an outlet, and she got in the way.

'I'll send Theresa over to Rachel,' Rob says. 'You're right. I don't trust her to be on her own.'

Chapter Forty-Two

Jane

Friday 22nd February

The first time I hit Jack, he cried. Horrible, drawn-out sobs that went right through me. I held an ice pack to the bruise, sat up all night with him. He brought me flowers the next day, said it didn't matter, that he understood. He doesn't do that anymore.

In the old days, I suppose we were both as bad as each other, but I'm the one in control now. Ever since Clare was killed, I've been in control. Jack doesn't dare.

He's too scared I'll tell the police what he did.

It began to unravel on the morning Clare Edwards died.

It was early, before the children were even up. February fourth – the sky didn't even get light until seven thirty. He brought me tea in bed, the teabag left in, just the way I've always liked it. He sat on the edge of the bed and reached out to touch my hair, but I flinched away.

'Jane,' he'd said quietly, 'I think we should go back to counselling. We don't need to tell anyone. We don't need to tell the kids. We can go separately, once a week or something. Just for starters. I've been looking it up – there's a group in Saffron Walden, it's not that far, or we could even get back in touch with Diane—'

I'd reached out and grabbed his wrist, angry at once. It was already sore and he flinched at the movement. He's used to me now; you'd think the flinching would stop. I hadn't slept well, I was hungover, angry at the suggestion.

'What are you saying, Jack? You think I'm not good enough anymore? Not good for the kids? You knew the deal when you married me, you knew this wasn't going to be an easy ride.' I pause. 'You've always known what this relationship is.'

I knew I wasn't being fair but I couldn't help it. Our fights had been getting worse. The PTA mothers were driving me mad. All of it was getting to me. I felt guilty for being a bad mother. I felt panicked.

'I'm not saying anything of the kind, Jane. You're a wonderful mother to the children. You know that. This is between you and I. It always has been.'

I was silent for a moment, my head laid back against the white pillows of our bed. The room was shadowy, half lit by the lamp at my side.

'I don't want to talk about this now,' I said finally. 'I have to get the children ready for school, and then I need to go to the shop, see Karen. Sandra will be round later, wanting something else from me. Can't you see I have a life to uphold, Jack? I can't let this – this ugliness rear its head. Not again. I've worked so hard to get away from it.' I smooth out the duvet, flatten the bumps out with my hands. 'I work hard at this life every day.'

'But that's what I'm saying!' he'd said to me, frustrated. 'I'm worried about you – about us. I want to deal with it, nip it in the bud. Like we did before. Remember?'

He put his face close to mine, tried to kiss my cheek. 'Remember when we had Sophie, Jane? How happy we were?'

I didn't want to look at him, I looked past him to our wardrobe, the door half open, his shirts hanging next to my neatly ironed blouses. I do remember, of course I do – we were giddy, high on each other, determined to get better, stop the fighting, stop kidding ourselves the things we did together were passionate, normal. They weren't. But the seed in my stomach changed things, for a while. We wanted Sophie, we were smug, pleased with ourselves – we'd come out of anger management with marriage and a baby. Doesn't get better than that, does it?

I met his eyes, dark into light. Shook the memories away.

'You should go,' I said. 'You don't want to be late for work.'

'Come meet me tonight,' he said to me, 'after work. We'll walk home from the surgery together, through the meadow, like we used to. We can talk.'

I just stared at him, repeated my words. 'You should go.'

He stared at me, his eyes sad. 'Janey,' he said, 'I don't know who you are any more.'

I didn't like that at all.

Chapter Forty-Three

Clare

Monday 4th February, 4.50 p.m.

*O*utside the surgery, I call Owen as I wait for my pill packet, which will be ready at the little window in a few minutes. My stomach is churning anxiously. Dr Goodwin was nice, but what if this somehow gets back to Mum? To Ian?

When he answers, Owen's voice is urgent, excited. It makes me want to laugh, stops the butterflies galvanising.

'Where are you? I waited for you after school.'

'Sorry,' I say, but my voice sounds giddy and I can't keep the excitement from spilling out. 'I'm coming round.'

'To mine?'

I giggle, high on the fact that it all went well, that I've actually done it.

'Yes, to yours, silly. I've got a surprise for you. I said I had.'

'How long will you be?'

'Not long, fifteen probably.'

I turn away as an elderly lady shuffles out of the surgery; I don't want anyone to see me here.

'Okay. I've just got home. My dad's out,' Owen says, and I can hear the sound of the acoustics changing around him, know he will have just let himself into the Jones's big detached house at the end of Little Dip Road.

'See you soon, then,' I say, 'I'm going to take a shortcut through Sorrow's Meadow. Love you.'

'We should do another cider session there when it gets warmer,' Owen says and I nod happily, forgetting that he can't see me.

'Yes,' I say, 'yes please. I'd like that.'

I collect the pills at the counter from the pharmacist. It's growing dark outside now, but if I walk quickly I can be at Owen's in less than fifteen minutes. As I fiddle with my headphones, untangling the wires, someone calls out a goodbye and I see Dr Goodwin striding away, finished for the day. I think of the photo on his desk, the smiling faces of his children. His beautiful wife. Not all families have to be like mine, do they? Maybe some day Owen and I will have a family, start again, make our own story. Maybe that will help me erase my parents. I imagine their story diluting over time, the memory of my father getting dimmer and dimmer until one day, in the future, he will be a faded shadow that nobody can remember any more. The thought makes me smile, just a little bit.

My breath mists the air as I begin to walk. I should be listening to the audio book of 1984, which is on our exam programme for the summer, but I've downloaded a new comedy podcast and the temptation is too strong. I text Owen once more telling him I'm on my way, then press play and wriggle on my gloves, purple mittens that are surprisingly warm. My phone vibrates with another text – it's Mum. Shit. I forgot to tell her that I'm 'staying at Lauren's', but I can't be bothered taking my mittens off now to use the touchscreen. I'll text her from Owen's. Easier that way.

I tuck my phone and hands into my pockets as I turn the corner off the main road, through the little footpath that leads down to Sorrow's Meadow. The buttercups aren't in bloom now, but in the summer I love it here, everyone does – the bright blaze of gold lighting up the town like a cheerful yellow blanket. There's a crunch beneath my feet – the beginnings of frost. This Christmas had been colder than usual, but I don't mind the winter; I like the cosiness of it, like being able to curl up with a book in front of the fire without anyone pressurising me to stop being boring and come out. Not that there are many places to go out around here – we go to the local pub sometimes, but a few months ago the barman got stricter. Owen reckons he might have had a visit from the police – which would be random, there are never police out here in the countryside. Besides, Ashdon hardly needs them. The most common crime here is usually some Year Eights stealing sweets from Walker's corner shop.

As I make my way through the field, I hear raised voices, penetrating the canned laughter of my headphones. Briefly, I stop, pull out an earphone in case I'm wrong and it's just something on the podcast, but no, there is definitely the sound of shouting, coming from the scrub of woodland at the far end of the meadow, just in front of the wooden stile that leads back down to the high street and Owen's house. It's only a small patch of trees; in the summer the younger children play here, making dens amongst the branches, shading themselves from the sunshine that lights up the field. There are no children now. I didn't think there was anyone here at all.

Frowning, I remove my other earphone and squint into the gloom. The darkness is falling fast now but I can just about make out two figures, standing in front of the first row of trees. A male voice is raised, the syllables darting towards me. I can't make out quite what's being said, but then I hear the words 'the children'.

I take off a mitten and press the home button on my iPhone, illuminating the screen. It's just gone five. Could be kids from school, of course, but school got out nearly an hour ago and no one really hangs out up here in the winter. It's too cold. Too dark. Besides, the shadows look tall, and the voice is deep. Older.

I stand still for a moment, the happy glow that surrounded me as I walked away from the doctor's beginning to fade. I want to see Owen, want to get home, but if there is something going on by the woods, I don't want to just ignore it. I think of Madeline Shaw, smiling earnestly at me on that morning at school, when I told her I wanted to join the police. 'You have to be ready to step in,' she'd said to me, 'put yourself in situations that others won't.'

It's probably nothing, I tell myself, probably just my old paranoia creeping up on me. I read too many books. Have too many bad memories. That's all. But I ought to just check. What if it's someone my age, what if she needs help?

Keeping my phone in my bare hand, I move forwards. The only way out of the field now is past the wood and over the stile – otherwise I'll have to go all the way back, out the way I came, back past the doctor's, the long way round to Owen's.

Then I hear it: a woman's voice, clearer than the man's. Vaguely familiar, but I can't work out who it is.

'We are good parents!' the woman is saying, the sound quite clear now, carrying through the darkness, and is it my imagination or does she sound scared? I'm reminded, for a moment, of my mother, see her cowering in my mind's eye, shielding her head from my father's fists. I picture Mum standing, calm in front of the bathroom mirror, dabbing beige concealer over a blossoming purple bruise, painting red lipstick over a cracked mouth. Cotton wool buds in the bathroom bin, tinged with blood. Dad crying, apologising, doing the same thing two days later. Flowers dying in their cellophane on the kitchen table. Me in my room, fingers in my ears, blowing bubbles with my own saliva to block out the noise.

The cancer diagnosis. Tears as Dad's condition worsened. I used to watch him from a half-closed bedroom door as Mum stroked his forehead, held a straw to his lips. Gently, gently. Far more gentle than he ever was with her. Did she forgive him? Or was she frightened, right until the end, even at the point where Dad was dying, weak and ill, unable to lash out at anyone even if he'd wanted to? Does that fear still trap her, prevent her from speaking out about what happened? It is a thought that keeps me wide awake at night. I don't want anyone else to become my mother. I'm sure about that.

The man speaks again and this time I force myself to be brave. I move forward, towards the trees, shine the light of my phone forwards into the dusk. One of the figures turns and I see suddenly the handsome face of Dr Goodwin, but his expression is different to how it was in the bright lights of the surgery. It is strained. Angry.

Beside him is a woman, who I recognise now as his wife, the woman next door. His beautiful wife, mother of the smiling *children in the photograph. Jane. Harry's mum. Her face is calmer than his but her jumper is pulled slightly off one shoulder, as though someone has yanked at it violently. The pale white jut of skin glows in the odd shine of my iPhone. She sees me looking and pulls it up, zips her big coat up over it. Hiding herself.*

'Are you alright?' I ask. The words are out before I can stop myself, before I can think too much and lose my nerve. I step forwards, closer to the couple. I'm only a few feet away.

Chapter Forty-Four

DS Madeline Shaw

Saturday 23rd February

The DCI wants to press charges – it's either that or they let Ian out. They applied last night to have an extension – Madeline was convinced he was going to crack, admit it all, but time's up now, and he hasn't.

The press is baying for blood. The town is baying for blood.

Owen Jones walks around like a shell of himself, his shoulders hunched, his slightly-too-big jacket flapping around him. Madeline saw him yesterday on her way back to the town; she was driving slowly, exhausted from a day of questioning, worried she might fall asleep at the wheel.

Owen was walking just outside Walker's, a carrier bag in his hand. There was a reporter cornering him, a microphone thrust in his pale young face.

'Get away from him!' Before she could stop herself, Madeline was shouting, pulling over the car and hurrying towards the reporter.

'Do you have any comment you'd like to make about Ian Edwards, detective?' the woman said, whipping around and pushing her horrible angular face up into Madeline's, spittle gleaming at the corners of her mouth. 'I understand he was a former military man. Do you think that has anything to do with why he killed his stepdaughter? Is it true it was financially motivated?'

'We have not yet charged Ian Edwards,' Madeline said, aware of Owen hovering by her side. 'And you'd do well to move out of my way before I'm forced to call for backup.'

'Is it true he was also abusing his wife?' It was as if she hadn't spoken. Exasperated, Madeline rolled her eyes and pushed past, gesturing to Owen to follow her lead. He hurried after her, and they fell into a strange companionable walk, away from the shop, back towards her car.

'I'll run you home,' Madeline had said. 'You're best not to talk to anyone from the press, Owen. They twist things. Vultures, the lot of them. Sniffing round. Wanting to make this into something salacious.'

'I know, ma'am,' he said, and the misery in his voice was such that she stopped and looked at him, really looked at him, right there in the street. There were a couple of other teenagers about, hanging around outside the Rose and Crown on the corner. He didn't seem to notice them at all.

'Are you coping alright, Owen?' she said gently, but he just looked away from her, down at the ground, at the scuffed tarmac pavement that everyone in this town has walked over thousands and thousands of times.

'I just miss her,' he said eventually. 'I miss her every day.'

That was yesterday. And still Ian sits there in the station, his wrists in cuffs, swearing blind that he had nothing to do with it, that he's being set up. Theresa, the family liaison officer, is with Rachel Edwards at the house now, says she's taken down all the photos of Ian from the walls. The words stir something up within Madeline – a memory – looking at the pictures of Clare displayed in frames around the house, realising there were none of Rachel's first husband, Mark. Ian had replaced them all with photos of himself.

He's waiting, head down against his chest, but he looks up at Madeline as she comes in. She stares at him, the hard lines of his face, and pictures again Clare's blonde hair, shiny around her head like a golden, bloodied halo.

She is as sure now as she will ever be.

'Ian Edwards, I am charging you on suspicion of the murder of Clare Edwards. You do not have to say anything, but it may harm your defence if you do not mention, when questioned, something you later rely on in court. Anything you do say may be given in evidence…'

Annabelle McQuirter arrives five minutes later. For his sake, he'd better plead guilty.

'Maddie!' Lorna grabs Madeline as she walks back into the main briefing room. 'Did he confess?'

'Nope, but it'll be a different story once he's seen the inside of a prison.'

She grins grimly. 'Trial date?'

'Not yet. Guessing it could take until Christmas, start of next year even with the CPS faffing about.'

'Something to look forward to, then.'

Chapter Forty-Five

Clare

Monday 4th February, 5.05 p.m.

'Are you sure you're alright?' I say to Jane Goodwin, keeping my eyes focused on hers. Her husband is hovering next to her.

'We're alright,' he says, answering for her.

Jane still hasn't spoken. I don't know what to do.

'Please, Clare, everything's okay,' Dr Goodwin says to me, but I stand still, my feet rooted to the ground. I don't want to leave her.

'What are you doing out here?' I ask, looking between them, trying to hold my nerve.

'We're just talking,' the doctor says, 'we're on our way home.'

The field is still, silent but for our voices.

'My husband's teaching me a lesson,' Jane says, her voice sarcastic, and my eyes widen.

'That isn't true,' Dr Goodwin says, and he takes a step towards her. I can feel my heartbeat thundering in my ears. Part of me wants to turn and run away, run to the warmth of Owen's house, but when I look at Jane Goodwin, all I can see is Mum. I hated the way everyone mourned Dad at the funeral, how they went on and on about what a good man he was, such a pillar of the community, such a good husband and father. He got away with it. And I was too young to do anything. Well, I'm not too young any more.

'I think you should leave your wife alone, Dr Goodwin,' I say, my voice firm and bold in the darkness, surprising even myself, and for a second he turns to me, disbelief in his eyes. Then he turns back to face his wife.

'Jesus,' he says, 'you really have got the whole town under your spell, haven't you, Jane.'

She doesn't speak, I expect she's afraid to, but he laughs then, a horrible, merciless laugh that cuts through the February night like a knife.

'Look,' he says, holding up his hands towards me, 'you've got this all wrong, Clare. I'm not the one doing anything wrong here.' At this, he turns back to Jane again, and there is a flash of something between them, something dark and dangerous.

'You can't handle it, can you,' he says to her, 'me calling you out on your little act.' He steps closer to her. 'One of these days, I'm going to leave you.'

I can't take my eyes off them; I don't know what he's talking about but I know she looks vulnerable, and frightened, and then I see him smile. She steps towards him and suddenly I'm confused; she pulls back her hand as if she's going to slap him in the face, but then his hands come forward and he's pushing her away, his palms pressing on her shoulders, shoving her away from him. She cries out, a sharp little sound that slices into me, and before I can stop myself I rush forward to plant myself between them, stop him doing what my dad did, stop all this before it starts.

There's a rushing sound, a dull thud, and then a wave of pain hits my body all at once. There's an earthy smell, a damp coldness, and I feel a sharp, shocking pain at the back of my head at the same time as a sickening crack pierces the air, echoing horribly through the darkness of the meadow.

For a moment, everything goes still. The world seems to shrink slightly, so that all I can see is the sky, a small lone star twinkling high above me, blackness surrounding me as though the rest of the world has been rubbed out. I'm on the ground. Dr Goodwin pushed me. I feel my eyes closing.

When I open them again, I see a shadowy Jane Goodwin, standing over me, panting, her eyes wide and unfocused. The visions come in snapshots – her face, Jack's face, then blackness again. I can feel him scrabbling around me, on his hands and knees, then his gloved fingers are on my neck, feeling for my pulse. The back of my head feels funny – dull and sticky, as if I've fallen into paint.

I can't hear anything. I want to go to sleep.

Then I hear Jane's voice. 'Jack, get up. Get up, Jack.'

'What are you doing?' he says, but the words sound as if they're coming from deep inside a well, all echoey and strange. 'She's hit her head! Jesus, she's out. Fuck. I didn't mean to push her, I thought you were going to lose your temper – I was trying to protect her, for Christ's sake.' I see a flash, a white light that could be a phone, dazzling me, making my pupils scream against my eyelids.

'We need to get an ambulance out here,' the doctor is saying, 'or there might be someone still at the surgery who can come quicker. Nigel Murphy said he might be staying late.'

'Jack, we need to leave.' Jane's voice is low. I feel rather than see her crouch down next to me, her eyes roaming my face. I want to give her a sign, let her know I'm awake, that I can hear them, but it feels like a huge effort to open my eyes.

'We can't leave her! What are you talking about?' It's the doctor again, but Jane is talking to him, and for a minute, I don't understand what she's saying. I do need help. I want the ambulance. Why won't she let him call one?

'Jack, think. You pushed her over. If it gets out that you've hurt her like this, you'll lose your doctor's licence. They'll run you out of the town.' A pause. 'How would you explain it?'

The pain in my head feels like it's getting a little bit worse. I want to sit up, but I can't.

'Jane, she's got a bad head wound. We can't leave her!'

'Listen to me. We should go home. It isn't serious, Jack, it's just knocked her for six but it's only a bump, she'll be coming round very quickly. I'll speak to her. I'll come back and speak to her and sort it all out, woman to woman, I'll explain to her that you weren't hurting me, that it was an accident. That way no one needs to know. It'll be better if you're not here, she'll be less frightened. Please, Jack. Think of what would happen to us if you're arrested for assault. Of what would happen to you.' There's a pause. 'You pushed her, Jack.'

I feel him crouch down again, feel a gloved hand on my face, my neck. My hair is fluttering a bit in the wind, and I want to push it out of the way, but I can't. It's so cold – the ground is freezing beneath me.

'Shall I cover her with my jacket?' the man says at last.

'No. Come on, let's go. She'll come round any minute and then once she's calmed down I'll speak to her, I'll tell her what happened and make sure she's alright. You go. Please, Jack.

If she comes round now and sees me she'll panic. She might even call the police. I'll fix this.'

'She had an appointment at the surgery, she came to get the pill.' As he says the words I feel myself let out a little moan, and my eyelids flutter, letting in a new shaft of dim light.

'Go, Jack. I'll meet you at home,' Jane says, and then I hear him exhale, the rush of his breath sweeping against my cheek. There's a crunching sound, footsteps on frosty leaves, and then I sense his weight moving away from us, leaving me there on the wet muddy ground, my head throbbing, and Jane Goodwin standing beside me.

Chapter Forty-Six

DS Madeline Shaw

Sunday 3rd March

Clare's funeral is full to the brim. Now that the body has finally been released from the morgue, it's lying in a beautiful oak coffin at the front of St Mary's Church, decorated with yellow flowers. Rachel Edwards sits on a pew at the front, and beside her are, of all people, the mum chums: Tricia Jenkins, in a low-cut black velvet number, Sandra Davies, smiling sympathetically at everyone, and Jane Goodwin, clutching her husband's hand in hers, their children either side of them. Perhaps Ashdon really can put on a show of solidarity sometimes, after all.

Owen Jones stands up, reads out a poem he wrote in English class. The primary school children sing a hymn, all together, and Madeline gets a lump in her throat that grows even bigger at the sight of them all in their little black clothes, hair freshly brushed, shoes shined for the occasion. The DCI doesn't come – there's a new case come in, a rape over in Saffron Walden, so that's where her attention is going to be when today's over, and while they wait for the trial.

'Do you think Ian'll get off?' Lorna keeps asking, and Madeline's response is unchanged.

'I hope not,' she says, 'I really do.' Quite a few people have come forward in the last few days saying they think Ian might have been hitting Rachel – a fact she's never admitted to and one he staunchly denies. The women have latched onto it; Jane Goodwin stopped Madeline in the street.

'Did you know?' she said, her eyes narrowed, watching her from beneath those long black lashes. 'That he was abusive?'

'It's still not something that's been proven,' Madeline said – Rachel's never said so – but Jane put her hand on the detective's arm, her shiny pink nails bright in the daylight.

'She told me,' she said, 'at my house last year. I had a Christmas drinks – we'd had a bit too much wine and she admitted it. I'm so glad it's all out in the open now. I've been ever so worried.'

There was a pause. 'Okay,' Madeline said to her at last, 'thanks for letting me know. We'll deal with it.' Jane smiled at her, her teeth white as snow.

'Thank you, detective. I know you will.'

Madeline watched her walk away, back to that pink house with the fancy front lawn. Badger Sett, it's called. She has seen the women of the town huddled in there of an evening, drinking wine in the large bay windows.

Just as Jane got to the crossing, she turned back. She laughed, gave another smile.

'You should come next time, detective,' she said, her voice warm, like syrup, as though she could read Madeline's thoughts. 'I'll be having the girls round soon. I'd love it if you'd join us.'

Madeline nodded, waved, but to be truthful, she can't think of anything worse. Jane's a funny woman, she thought. But they all are, here. Still, if there's even half a grain of truth in what she told her about him, Madeline hopes Ian Edwards goes down for a very long time.

People tend to, for murder.

Chapter Forty-Seven

Jane

Ten months later

It's cold today: December first. The town is in full preparation mode, same as it is every year, only this year of course, things are different. The tree has been put up at the crossroads by the town sign, and the lights were switched on last night. Jack and I didn't go – Sandra volunteered to take the kids and we let her. That's happening more and more these days. I find it hard to be around other people. God knows what Jack is thinking. Some nights, if the children are elsewhere or in bed, I look out of the window and see him sitting outside our back door, his body freezing against the wood, the cold biting at his ankles and ears.

On other nights, when the children are in with me, he goes out driving. He tells us its work and slips out into the night, sinks into the driver's seat and starts up the engine. I don't know where he goes – I imagine him heading out of town, out to where the anonymous fields rush by and the sky feels huge, where there are no nosy neighbours wondering what he's doing. I imagine him stopping the car in the layby where we used to meet sometimes to talk. It's what I'd do, if I could leave the children. If I could leave at all.

Sometimes when he comes home, he looks like he's been crying. I never say anything anymore, I just let him get on with it. As long as he doesn't confess. The other night when he was getting undressed I saw little purple welts at the tops of his thighs, up high where the children will never see. They are nothing compared to what Ian Edwards must be suffering through in prison. Useless wounds, child's play.

It's been ten months since the arrest, and the inside of my head doesn't feel any easier. The trial is set for the new year; Ruby Walker is telling anyone who'll listen, which is everyone. I thought I would feel a sense of relief when they arrested Ian, but I don't, even now, all these months later. It's not enough. He is awaiting a jury, awaiting a verdict – it isn't over yet. The charges could still be dropped, and until he's sentenced, I can't relax. I do my very best to keep calm and clear-headed, forcing myself to think about everything we stood to lose, watching the children, my family, my family who would have been taken away from us, ripped apart at the seams. We didn't deserve that. We still don't.

I don't see Rachel very often; none of us do. She's holed up inside the house, and the curtains are drawn more often than not. Occasionally, I'll see a glimpse of her in the back garden, standing outside, looking up at the sky. She is thinner than ever. I did catch her late one afternoon, as I was hanging the little lights in the tree outside the front, some new red ones the children clamoured for last week. She had a big winter coat on, clumpy brown boots.

'Rachel,' I said, 'how are you?'

She had her head down, her arms wrapped around herself as if to keep out the cold.

'I've been visiting Ian,' she told me. 'They don't exactly celebrate Christmas in there.'

'No,' I said, 'I can't imagine they do. But let me know if you ever want to pop round to ours, we've far too many mince pies to go round.' I was trying to be nice but perhaps it came out wrong. She looked like she was going to cry. I put my hand on her arm, tried to give it a rub, but her coat was so thick that I could barely feel anything. Eventually I let her shuffle away from me, busied myself with rearranging the wreath I'd bought for our front door.

It's not that I want poor Rachel to be unhappy; of course I don't. But I have to protect my husband, our family.

'Perhaps she'll leave the town,' Sandra hisses at me one night over a glass of mulled wine. 'I mean, what's left for her here?' She shakes her head sadly. 'All those memories. If it were me, I'd up sticks and go. Start again.'

I think about what Sandra said later that night, lying awake with the moonlight spilling into the room. Jack doesn't sleep very much, pacing around downstairs long into the evening, so I'm left with my thoughts more often than not. I imagine a For Sale sign up next to the bird bath, movers coming and carting away Rachel's belongings. A new family next door; a couple, perhaps, children. People I could be friends with. A woman who would sit out in the back garden with me, nod along admiringly when I showed her the wisteria that climbs up our back wall, the pretty garden furniture that sits around the chimera on the large flagged patio. A friend as well as a neighbour – someone who might pop round for dinner, exclaim at the shine of my kitchen, run a hand over the beautiful silver candlesticks when she thinks I'm not looking.

We'd laugh together about the goings-on at the school, the lascivious husbands in the town, the children. She'd join our book club, maybe even the PTA. We'd swap recipes, babysitter numbers; shoes, at a push.

I let myself imagine that, just for five minutes. What it might have been like. What it could be like in the future.

Jack doesn't trust me. I can tell by the way he slopes around the house, coming home from the surgery late, avoiding my eyes as we sit at the dinner table, focusing his attention on the children as if he thinks I won't notice what he's doing. I need to try to talk to him, to rebuild things. Otherwise all this has been for nothing.

'Jack,' I say quietly one night, coming up behind him in the sitting room as the television flickers. I don't think he's even watching it properly. He flinches when I put my hands on his shoulders, actually flinches, as if he can no longer stand the feel of my touch.

'Don't do that,' I say, 'don't flinch away from me when I touch you. I'm your wife, Jack. Your wife.'

When he turns to me, his face looks different, and something about it scares me. He doesn't look like the man I married, the man I fell in love with all those years ago on Albion Road. He looks haggard, beaten down by what he has done. I try not to blame him, but I know he blames himself. We are in this together, 'til death do us part. I see it in my mind's eye; the registry office, our clasped hands.

Slowly, I walk around the sofa and sit down next to him, treating him carefully, as if he is a china ornament, the ones my grandmother used to collect and line up in a neat row above the cooker.

'Jack,' I say, 'I did it for you. For our family.' A pause. 'He won't be in prison for ever. Besides, they're like gyms these days anyway.' I smile, but he ignores me.

It's as if I haven't spoken; he continues to stare at the television. I can see the images reflected in his glassy eyes, the colours fading in and out. A memory comes to me, of us just after we'd first got together. We'd been to the cinema but not seen much of the film. Afterwards, strolling down the high street, we'd passed the entrance to Regent's Canal, a sloping dark tarmac edged by overhanging willow trees.

'Fancy a walk?' Jack had asked me and I'd taken his hand, pulled him down the slope. The water glittered beside us, the usually crowded bank was quiet, as though all the cyclists and runners and dog walkers had cleared the way just for us. I'd stared at the shimmer of the glassy water, at the colours of the boats reflected in the shine, the reds and greens and navys blurring as the water moved.

We'd started walking, not saying much, but the silence hanging between us felt loaded. Prior to Jack, I hadn't felt close to anybody for a very long time. I hadn't felt able to, I suppose.

'Jane,' Jack had said, his voice breaking the strange stillness, his hand suddenly slick in mine. 'Would you be frightened if I told you I loved you?'

My mouth was on his before he had time to be nervous. It was a good job nobody came by the towpath that evening.

'I love you, Jack,' I whisper now, sat beside him on the sofa, and as I say the words, I wonder if they are really true. Do I love this man? We have built a life together, against the advice of counsellors, friends, family. I have lied for him, multiple times, for days and weeks and months. A man is now awaiting trial for a crime he did not commit.

When my husband doesn't reply, I slowly stand, feeling as though my limbs are leaden. Have I always moved this slowly? Or is it all finally catching up with me – the drinking, the guilt, the constant pretence to be something I am not. My past catching up to me. Perhaps I am my father's daughter, after all.

Every part of me wants to go to bed, to strip off my clothes, stand under a hot shower and burn away the day, then slide myself under our crisp white sheets and place my head beneath the pillow. I used to do that a lot when I was single, before I met Jack. Instead, I walk into the kitchen, pour myself a glass of red wine, and open the cutlery drawer. I've already looked here, I know I have, but my fingers run through the same desperate steps – feeling underneath the silver, underneath the mess of our lives that is discarded birthday candles, random nails, Jack's screwdriver that he never uses, a pair of balled up gloves. My nightly ritual, of late. My hand scrabbles against the wooden bottom of the drawer before I slam it in frustration. It's not there. I know it's not there.

'Jane.' Jack is standing in the doorway, his hands either side of the frame. 'Is what you said about Ian hitting Rachel even true?'

I know he wants me to tell him it is, give him that small crumb of peace. It *could* be true, I suppose. But I doubt it. And I've told enough lies. When I don't answer, he eventually goes away.

I finish the rest of the wine, thinking about the idea of a For Sale sign next door. Perhaps then I'd feel free of it all.

Chapter Forty-Eight

Jane

Saturday 7th December

'Mummy, Daddy, can we go now?'

Finn's little hand is tugging at my skirt, insistent and without pause. The action causes the waistband to slip slightly; I feel a loosening around my hips. I've lost weight lately. Not on purpose, and not as much as Rachel Edwards, mind, but it's a nice bonus.

Jack and I have promised the children a trip into Saffron Walden – ostensibly Christmas shopping, but I know all they really want to do is visit Santa's Grotto in the new shopping centre that opened last week. Apparently, every other child in the entire school has already been, which I find a little hard to believe. Still, this is probably one of the last years that Sophie will be young enough to even believe in Father Christmas, so I've agreed to take them. Besides, it gets us out of the house.

'Mu-um! Da-ad!' Finn is annoyed, his little body beginning to rock from side to side in that way that it does when he's at the end of his level of patience. 'I want to go!'

'Sorry, darling,' I say, and try to bring myself back into the day, focus on the task at hand. I'm pulling out the wellies from underneath the stairs and Jack is searching for the children's hats and gloves – the weather has turned and the radio this morning said there might be snow. Last week they came back from the Christmas lights wearing unfamiliar outfits, donated by Sandra ('I didn't want them to get cold – you do know it's winter now?' Cue tinkling laugh). Jack and I had nodded along, apologising profusely. We're losing control of it all, bit by bit.

I pull Finn's little blue boots out of the cupboard and sit him down on the bottom stair, begin the lengthy process of wiggling them onto his little feet. His socks are slipping down and he whines impatiently, but I coax the left foot in, then the right.

'Jack? Can you hurry up?' I call, zipping up Finn's coat and taking him round to the utility room, where Jack is rummaging in the hats and gloves box. We haven't used it since last winter, and the small utility room has developed a fine layer of dust that catches a little in the back of my throat. Finn wants his hat with the fox ears; Jack's put a bright pink bobble hat on Sophie and a pair of gloves that boast sparkling diamanté wrists. She's always had eyes like a magpie.

Jack pulls out an old Arsenal hat and proffers it to Finn, whose little face says it all.

'The *fox* one, Daddy, with the ears! Not that one. That one's stupid.'

He grits his teeth. 'Okay, okay, the fox one. I'll bring it to you.' He glances back at me. 'We'll be in the car in five minutes.'

I'm about to follow Finn as he toddles out to where Sophie is waiting by the stairs, when I see my husband stop still. I turn to face him, and see the glint of something bright, nestled in an old yellow scarf that Sophie discarded last year.

'Mum! I want to go-o-o!' Finn's roar startles us both, and Jack starts, the scarf slipping from his hands and onto the dusty utility room floor. The gold necklace slithers out, separates itself from the material. Both of us stare at it, and I'm about to drop down, scoop it up in my now-trembling hands, when Jack picks it up, quicker than I thought he would, frowning.

My heart is thudding and I don't know if he's realised, I don't know how much time I've got.

'Oh, that's mine,' I say quickly, holding out a hand for it, hoping he doesn't see the way I'm shaking, but my husband takes a step away from me, keeping the necklace clasped tight in his palm.

Frowning, he holds it up to the light. It's pretty, but quite small, with a gold clasp and a heart-shaped locket dangling from the centre. As we both stare at the solid little heart, he shifts his gaze to me.

'I didn't buy this for you.'

I'm about to intervene, to make something up about it being a gift from an old boyfriend, ha ha silly me, when he does it – he prises open the side of the heart.

My whole body begins to shake. I grab Jack's elbow, pinch the skin of it between my fingers, lead him away from the children, into the living room where a long wire of white fairy lights is tangled on the floor. The children are clamouring for a tree already but I've told them we need to wait a bit. Not least because of the mess the needles create. Christmas just means extra housework, another way to trap women.

Jack shakes his arm away from mine, closes the door behind us so that the sound of the children's little chattering is blocked out, and we are alone. He has closed his left fist around the necklace, so that it is hidden from my view.

'Jack, give that back to me,' I tell him, and still he doesn't say anything, he just stretches his fist out towards me and opens his palm.

'Jack, please give me the necklace,' I say again, keeping my voice calm, the glass of red I had earlier with lunch helping.

He still doesn't speak, just looks at me, waiting to see how I'm going to react. I've never been very good at knowing what Jack's thinking. It's something that's always bothered me, right from the moment we met. The Stepford Wives of the town profess to know what their husbands are thinking all the time, clustered around my kitchen table telling me what's inside their partners' heads, but I comfort myself with the fact that most of them are wrong anyway. Sandra's husband Roger's been having an affair with one of the teachers at the primary for about two years – I saw them once when I was collecting Finn from an after-school class. Silly cow's never put two and two together. There are so many things that none of us see.

I look at the necklace. I thought I'd turned this house upside down in my weekly searches, scouring each room for it. The tiny gold letters wink at me from inside the heart, spelling out her name. Clare's sixteenth birthday present. The piece of the puzzle the police couldn't find.

It's quite pretty, actually.

Jack is staring at me as if he's never seen me before.

'It was in with the hats and gloves,' he says, his voice strangely hoarse. 'Why was it there, Jane? Why is her necklace in our house? I never touched it. You know I didn't.' He pauses. 'Did it get stuck in your gloves when you were helping her?'

I look away for a second, trying to think.

'It must have done,' he says, 'it's so delicate, look, you must not have noticed.' His voice takes on an almost pleading tone. 'Is that what happened, Jane? Tell me the truth.'

I can feel my heart beating in my ears, *thrum thrum thrum*.

I've never seen much point in dragging things out. I'm not like Jack. I want this to be finished with; that's why I did what I did at the Valentine's fair, all those months ago now. If we stay in limbo, none of us will move on. And we need to. We deserve to.

'Jane.'

The light in his eyes has changed, darkened.

I know then that it's over. It's time to tell the truth. The whole truth, this time. So help me God.

Chapter Forty-Nine

Jane

Monday 4th February, 5.30 p.m.

Clare is lying on the ground, her neck at a slightly awkward angle. I can hear Jack's footsteps, very faintly, but the frosty grass muffles the sound and they quickly fade to nothing. I think about how long it'll take him to get home, picture him opening our front door, being faced with the house just as I left it. I wonder what he'll do. I bet he has a drink.

There's a soft moaning noise. She's coming round, as we both knew she would. That push wasn't enough to kill her, not really, not unless she was very unfortunate. It is unfortunate. This whole thing is deeply unfortunate. That was what the teachers used to say about me. *An unfortunate child. Unfortunate upbringing, that one.*

Clare's eyelids flutter but she's not fully conscious yet. I can see my breath misting across her face, white clouds forming in the darkness. We don't have much time. I doubt anyone will be out here tonight, but you never know. I was. Jack was. Clare was too.

I went to meet him after work, just like he suggested. I was ready for a walk and talk, a chance to be the old us, just like he'd wanted this morning. We used to come here all the time. With Sophie, and sometimes Finn, and occasionally Jack and I would walk up here of an evening, back when I was first pregnant with Sophie, when she was just a kernel in my stomach. I remember feeling it, even then. The worry that we'd made a mistake. Coming here, to this town in the middle of nowhere. Giving up our lives in London. Committing to each other, to a life we didn't fit into. I could see my future stretching out before me and it made me feel scared. I don't think that feeling has ever really gone away. *You'll love it here,* he said.

'Clare,' I say, my voice quiet but firm. I don't touch her, I don't want to move her yet. She's breathing, shallowly but distinctly, and as I watch her eyes flicker again, open fully this time. We stare at each other in the darkness: her lying, me crouching. The moment seems to still, as if someone's pressed pause on a tape.

'He pushed me,' she says. Her voice has a strange, breathless quality, and I can see it, the surprise in her eyes as she realises what has happened. I didn't think she'd remember quite as quickly. She shifts her body slightly, but I see the pain flit across her face, like a shadow passing over the moon. I study her features, the full lips, the high cheekbones, the blonde hair. She's beautiful, like her mother.

'He didn't mean to push you, Clare,' I say to her, attempting a smile even though my face is freezing cold and my lips feel like ice. 'It was an accident. You got caught in the middle.'

She's frowning at me, and I feel a tiny spark of indignation. I'm trying to help her, I'm trying to explain.

'Is your head alright?' I say, trying a different tactic, but she doesn't reply, just stares at me, as if behind her eyes her mind is whirring and I can't see inside it.

'You and Dr Goodwin,' she says slowly, and now she does move, she shifts her body up onto her elbows so that she is facing me on a level. Her eyes are dark brown, like chestnuts.

'What were you doing?'

'We were just arguing, Clare,' I tell her, trying to make my voice light, casual, but something about it sounds off, even to my ears. I need to stop this conversation from happening, she's too close to me, she's too close to us. Someone could come past – a dog-walker, anyone. Even though it's dark, it's not that late. I think I sense a movement, over to the right-hand side of my vision, but it's just a tiny flash in the darkness and then it is gone. I might have imagined it anyway.

Clare shakes her head, another whip of pain crossing her face.

'No,' she says, 'you were fighting. He lashed out. You were both – you looked like you were going to slap him too.' Another pause. 'Were you?'

I don't say anything.

Clare winces, shifts herself up even further. She looks me in the eye, a hard look, wiser than her years. 'Don't you have children?'

The anger inside me sparks again, begins to ignite. I take a deep breath. I can still save this, I can still save us. I haven't worked so hard all these years for it to come crashing down on the word of some teenager who saw more than she should've.

'Clare,' I say, 'you've had a knock on the head. I don't think you're remembering things clearly. Neither of us lashed out. It's a misunderstanding.'

Tears are beginning to form in her eyes.

'It's not,' she whispers, her voice quiet now. Her face looks very pale. I wonder about the back of her head, how much blood she might be losing as we speak. 'I saw you. I heard you. Your children will too.'

'How dare you,' I say to her, the spark inside me growing into a flame, pushing its way upwards, licking at me, tempting me. 'You don't know what you're talking about.'

'I'll tell,' Clare says, as if I haven't spoken at all. 'I won't let you do this to another child. To your child. You have no idea how much it hurts us.'

I feel sick, suddenly, as she begins to push herself up further, curl her body together as if she's going to stand. I can't understand what she's saying. I can't have her telling anyone. I imagine it – first the rumours, then the questions. Years of hiding what we are. Years of work to keep it from the children. Years of therapy and classes and trying, trying, trying to control this sickness within us both. I've worked for what we have. So has Jack. I've worked to make a success of my life, I've built myself up from nothing, and this privileged blonde girl is about to ruin it all.

I can't let that happen.

Chapter Fifty

Clare

Monday 4th February, 5.35 p.m.

The pain in the back of my head is throbbing but my thoughts are surprisingly clear. When I saw Jack lunging across the field, something strange happened – it wasn't Jack that I saw but Dad, and not Jane Goodwin but Mum. My mouth is dry and tastes a bit metallic, but I don't like the way Jane is speaking to me, pretending I'm a child, a silly child who's had a bump on the head and got things confused. I pretended that for years.

I think she's lying. And I'm not going to pretend any more.

I'm getting ready to stand up even though one of my legs is hurting too, I think I landed on it funny, but suddenly there's a little rush of movement in the cold winter air and Jane is right up close to me, crouching down. There's a funny look in her eyes and I feel a prick of fear.

'Don't—' I say, but before I can carry on speaking, her hands are in my hair. She's pulling at me, yanking my head upwards, and then there is an explosion of pain as she slams my head back down against the stump of the tree trunk. For a moment, I can't see anything at all.

I move my legs, trying to kick her away from me, but my left one's not moving properly, it feels twisted out of shape, and I'm clawing at her arms with my hands but she's wearing a puffy winter coat and I can't grip properly. Her other hand is pulling mine away, gripping onto my coat and scarf to lift me forward again, and it catches on something around my neck, my chain that Mum bought me for my birthday, and the gold metal is pulling against my skin until it breaks, snap, a little sense of relief that vanishes the minute my head connects with the tree stump for the third time. The metallic taste in my mouth is much worse; everything feels woozy and slow, like I'm underwater, except I'm not underwater, I'm here in Sorrow's Meadow and I'm going to see Owen and I don't want this to be happening, I don't want to die like this, not before I see Owen, not before I see Mum.

I don't want to die at all.

Chapter Fifty-One

Jane

Monday 4th February, 5.45 p.m.

When I take my hands off her, I'm breathing too fast, too loudly. She isn't moving. Immediately, I stand, although my legs feel weird and stiff from crouching for so long. For a moment or two, I look down at her, her blonde hair still bright in the darkness, her breath no longer misting the air. I crouch down again, put two gloved fingers to the side of her neck, careful not to get too close, to avoid any part of my body touching hers. My fingers rest there for one beat, two, but there is no flicker, no sign of a pulse. I wait. My body tingles. For a moment, I feel as though she's still watching me, as though someone is gazing through the darkness, a pair of eyes watching my every move, but when I look around the field, I see no one, nothing. Another beat. Her neck is soft, malleable. No pulse. I stand again, drag my eyes away from the awful stillness of her face.

She'll be found immediately. Is it better that way? I glance around for the fiftieth time, checking the dim meadow and the row of trees that edge it. There's no one in sight. I check my body, but there's no skin on show – my coat covers me from neck to knee, my long black boots take care of the rest. My hair is pulled back from my face, encased in a bun. Jack had gloves on too. I've no reason to be out here. Neither of us have.

Her bag is lying next to her, half open on the ground. Carefully, I pull back the other flap, see the paper bag from the surgery, her name written on the side. He'll have written her a prescription. I can't let anyone link him to her. I grab the bag and shove it in my coat pocket, the contraceptive pills rattling against each other inside. My heart is thudding, so loudly that I can barely hear my thoughts. Her mobile's lying on the ground beside her coat pocket, has fallen out in the scuffle. I grab it; it's still slightly warm in my hand, even through my gloves.

Quickly, before I can think about it any longer I turn away from the body on the ground, force myself to walk away in the direction of the stile by which Jack left only ten minutes before. As I walk, I make a plan, rationalise like I always do after I've lost my temper. I've got good at it now.

She would have told the social services, I whisper to myself, I had to do it. I didn't have a choice. My thoughts spill over each other, the anger which flared inside me gone now that its instigator is silent. I think of the children, of Harry's sloping walk, of Sophie and Finn, the way I smooth their hair as they get into bed, the way their little hands fit mine as we walk home from school. Nobody can take me away from them. Really, I had no choice.

I walk quickly across the field, clutching Clare's mobile tight in my gloved hand. I prise the case off, wondering if I ought to throw it away, then see an ID card stuffed in the back, wedged inside the back of the gold case. Clare Edwards. No, best to keep it all together, somewhere safe. As I climb over the stile that leads back down towards our house, I hear a sound and turn, my stomach churning.

I catch sight of him as his torchlight hits me – his brown eyes looking at me from across the meadow. It's Nathan Warren. Thank God it's only him. My mind races – think, Jane, think. I turn back and walk towards him, smiling, shaking my hair loose around my shoulders. It's a risk, but a calculated one.

'Nathan,' I say, 'I need you to do something for me.'

The moment I put my key into the lock, Jack is running, running towards our front door, a half-empty bottle of Jack Daniels still clutched in his hand. I was right about the drinking.

I step inside and catch sight of myself in the hallway mirror; my nose is bright red from the cold.

He stands in front of me, desperation all over his face. Gently, I take his hand, set the bottle of whiskey down on the side, lead him from the hallway into our sitting room, guiding him to our squashy, expensive sofa. There's a pile of Finn's toys on the floor; they look out of place, as if they are from another life. Some Playmobil figures, a little blue truck. Too bright. Too colourful.

'Jack,' I am holding both of his hands now, looking at him. I'm taking slow, deep breaths, the way Diane taught me, knowing how crucial these few moments are. I texted Sandra on my way home, told her I'd pick the children up in ten minutes. That will give him a chance to calm down.

'Is she alright?' he says, and I can tell he can barely get the words out because he's so nervous. 'Did you talk to her, is she going to tell anyone what happened? Did you tell her, did you tell her it was a mistake, that I didn't mean to do it, that it's just how we are and that we'd never hurt the kids, that we're stupid and fucked up and—'

He breaks off into loud, childlike sobs.

'Jack, I have to tell you some bad news,' I say, and I pull him towards me, cradle his head against my chest as though he is one of the children. I'm still wearing my gloves; my soft fingers stroke his forehead. I imagine my husband's panicked mind racing with possibilities – Clare has gone straight to the police. Clare has gone straight to her stepfather. She is in hospital for her head injury. It is much worse than he thought.

But I don't say any of those things. What I say is: 'Jack, Clare is dead.'

At first, he thinks he's misheard me. He sits up, pulls his tear-stained face away from my embrace. The whiskey has made his heartbeat fast and irregular; I can feel it thudding through his body, smell the alcohol on his breath.

'What?' he whispers.

I'm shaking too now, in spite of myself, my body is trembling against his. I take his hand, lock our fingers together. Our wedding rings press against each other, thick through my gloves.

'I'm so sorry, Jack,' I say, 'I waited, I sat with her but she didn't wake up, she didn't come round. I felt her pulse again, three times, I tried everything I could think of to try to bring her round. But she— she was dead. She— I looked at her head and she'd hit it right at the temple, at the side, and then she

302

passed out and it was so cold and... I don't know. Jack, she didn't wake up.'

He's staring at me, his face completely white.

'I'm so sorry, Jack,' I say again. He looks like he might be in shock. He told me about something like this, it happened to one of his colleagues last year – a patient who died, got a blood clot after a knock on the head. Jack said they call them the 'talk and die patients' – the ones who seem fine, then wake up the next morning feeling drowsy and confused, who worsen as the hours go on and the clot inside their brains grows. The unlucky people who hit their head at the wrong angles – the ones who suffer from an epidural hematoma, shocking their loved ones with the suddenness of their death. The pointlessness of it. The terrible waste. I used to worry about it happening to the children, watch them like a hawk whenever we took them to the playground. Of course, that's not quite what's happened here, but it's plausible. Jack knows it is.

'And you left her?' He's found his voice, he's removed his hand from mine. 'We have to go back, Jane. We have to – we have to make this right. We have to do the right thing.'

His voice sounds robotic, and I can only imagine what's going through his head. He thinks he has killed someone, has taken Clare's life. In his temper. His thoughtless action. His pitiful, pathetic attempt to stop me from slapping him, from our stupid argument becoming one of our horrible fights. And in a way, he has.

There is a moaning sound coming from somewhere and it takes a few seconds for me to realise that it's him. It is low, guttural, a wail. My husband puts his fists to his head and start to beat, thumping his skull, yanking at his hair, inflicting tiny doses of pain. He stands suddenly, stumbles into the hallway and towards the door and pulls it open. I feel the blast of cold wind that rushes towards me.

Instantly, I'm at his side.

'No Jack, no. There's nothing we can do. It was an accident, you know it was. An awful, tragic accident. You didn't mean to hurt her. If you tell someone now, do you know what will happen?'

He stops, his hand on the open door. I reach past him, slam it, rip off my gloves and scrunch them into a tight black ball. We are alone in the hallway, face to face.

'They'll take the children away, Jack. They won't let you live here, with us. They might implicate me too. Think of Sophie. Think of Finn and Harry. God knows what will happen to them.'

I see him swallow. 'You won't be implicated,' he whispers, his voice hoarse. 'They'll just take me. I deserve to go. The kids don't deserve to have a father like me.'

I put my arms around him then, sliding them around his waist, just like I did in Sorrow's Meadow, less than an hour ago. I came to surprise him after work, tell him that I'd think about the counselling. But he wasn't in the right mood. He wasn't listening to me. He knew I was angry, deep down. And then he pushed her. He pushed Clare.

'We need you, Jack,' I say. My mouth is pressed against his chest, warm against his still-cold body. 'I need you. The children need you. You can't throw your life away on an accident, on a mistake. You don't deserve to go to jail.'

He's crying, the tears dripping down onto my dark hair.

He's always loved my hair. He's always loved me. That's his problem.

'I can't bear it,' he says, and then my body starts to shake too, so that we are crying together, standing in the hallway, sobbing and sobbing at the mess we have made, the life I have taken.

Chapter Fifty-Two

Jane

Saturday 7th December

'I think you should probably put that back where you found it, Jack,' I say to my husband, reaching out so that my fingers embrace his, folding them in on each other until his palm is closed again, Clare's necklace hidden from sight. I didn't notice it as I walked away from Nathan Warren, leaving him with instructions to call the police, tell them what he'd found. I didn't notice it as I pulled off my coat that night, hung it up on the hook amongst all the others, pulled off my scarf, hat and gloves and balled them up before taking a boiling hot shower.

I noticed the newspaper report.

I remember the day I saw the line about the necklace. It was next to a picture of Rachel's face, beseeching and tearstained. 'We gave Clare the necklace for her sixteenth, two weeks ago. She never would have taken it off.' I remembered seeing it in the moonlight, the bright flash of it against her narrow white neck. But I didn't notice it coming off, catching on my gloves, tailing me home like a tiny talisman of guilt.

For months I thought they might find it, slithered in a coil in Sorrow's Meadow, linking no one and nothing to her death.

For months I scoured the pavement as I walked the kids to school, terrified that it was by the house, had found its way onto our drive, into our car, onto the road just outside our house. I looked everywhere – in our bedroom, in Sophie's things, thinking she might have spotted it and claimed it, unaware of its meaning. I looked in the utility room, checked the gloves I had on, couldn't find it. It is tiny, delicate. I missed it. And now he knows the truth.

'How could you?' Jack says, and his voice is filled with such loathing, such pure, unadulterated hatred that even I am taken aback, just for a second.

I glance at the door. I can't hear the children's voices any more, they must have got bored, gone back upstairs to play. Harry is at football, oblivious.

'How could *I*?'

I'm not scared of my husband; I never have been. I'm scared of what he makes me do.

'You let me believe – Jane, you let me believe I'd killed her! You know how I've been feeling, you know Ian's in jail! And all the time you – you didn't even need to!'

I bristle at that. 'Of course I needed to, Jack. Who do you think would be behind bars now if I hadn't? Me?' I almost laugh, the thought is so ridiculous.

'Jack, if Clare Edwards had stood up and toddled off home, she'd have called the social services on us. She might even have called the police, claimed GBH because you pushed her. That would have started an investigation, they'd have pulled us apart, poked about in our lives like they have in Rachel's. They'd have taken the children. And don't pretend to me any differently, because you already know it's true.'

I step back, wait for his response. I don't know what he's thinking.

'You didn't have to kill her,' he whispers, and that horrible look on his face is still there, one I've never seen before in all the ups and downs of our years together. Revulsion. Hatred. Disgust.

'Don't look at me like that,' I say, and I hear the tiny edge of desperation come into my voice – that thing I've spent so long trying to avoid. I need Jack. I need him on my side. I don't need him ruining everything now, not after I've worked so hard. I can't let that happen.

'I can't live like this, Jane,' he says, shaking his head, opening his hand out again to see the bloody necklace. 'We have to come forward. We have to.'

I move away from him. I'm still holding the Christmas lights in my left hand, the wire cord tight in my grip. The moment stretches. I let it.

'We?'

I'm standing over by the window now. Outside, a car splashes past. The sky is grey – they forecast snow. If he doesn't take them shopping soon, it'll be too late.

'What?' Jack's looking at me but I keep my face turned slightly, my eyes on the road.

'I said, *we* come forward? I don't think it's really a case of that, is it Jack? You were the one that pushed her. You were the one who caused the wound on her head.'

I turn from the window, step closer to him again, lean right up close so that I can see every pore on his face, the familiar, familiar face that I have woken up to every day for the past ten years. I know it as well as I know my own. But he doesn't know me as well as he thought. He doesn't know the half of it.

I tried to do it subtly, to let the police draw their own conclusions. But things weren't moving fast enough – they were slow, stupid. Kept going down the wrong track. And trying to go after Harry; well, that was nothing short of ridiculous.

The records my son found of Clare's doctor's appointment made me the most nervous. After I confronted my husband about it in the car, I saved the recording on my phone – a clip of him reiterating that they were contraceptive pills, of me encouraging him to go to the police. I cut it off at the point where he asked me what sick little game I was playing, asked me why I was getting him to repeat what I already knew. The recording is on my phone, in case I ever need it. You can clearly hear me telling him to come forward, the faux-confusion in my voice.

Little Danielle the secretary, though, now she was a problem. Who'd have thought she'd hold the keys to our lives. Turns out a deposit from our joint account was enough to keep her silence, though. Ten grand is a small price to pay for freedom. In the end, the only record of Clare Edwards visiting Ashdon Surgery was the one I burned in our grate. And funnily enough, Danielle never did see Nathan Warren in the buttercup field after all. Not after we spoke, anyway. The NHS really should pay its employees more, but I can't do much about that. I'm glad I was able to clear him too. He's a sweet man, honestly.

It was Sandra that gave me the idea, although she'll never know it. I guess I have her big mouth to thank, in the end. The money Mark left for Clare was a clincher; the one thing I was missing. Motivation. Ian kills Clare, Ian cashes in.

Even then, the police were reluctant. I practically had to

spoon-feed it to them. If only Ian wasn't such a decent guy; pinning the blame on him was harder than I thought. I've had Clare's mobile in my handbag since February; I thought I'd just get rid of it, but with the way things were going, I had to be proactive. On the day of the Valentine's fair, I slipped into the school and popped it in Ian's rucksack, right where he'd left it in the classroom. Health and safety, and all that. An *opportunity*, if you will. *We create our own opportunities*, Diane used to say.

You really would think that would be enough, wouldn't you? I feel bad about using Nathan one last time, but in the end I had no choice. It's not like those detectives weren't desperate for a break. His witness statement was the final straw, as it were. My get out of jail free card.

My husband is staring at me.

'What do you think the police will do, Jack, when you tell them what you did?'

He meets my eyes now, and I see it, the old fizz of anger that got us here in the first place. This time, it's directed at me.

'I didn't kill her,' he says, through gritted teeth, and I smile at him, reach my free hand up to touch his face. There's stubble on his jaw, that strong jaw that I've always loved, and up close his breath is slightly stale. He doesn't take care of himself properly these days. I've tried to tell him.

'Who do you think the police will believe, Jack?' I ask him, keeping my voice low, quiet, like I used to do when we were in bed. 'A man with a history of violence and a lack of alibi? Or me? A mother of three, pillar of the community, on the committee for Clare's memorial garden?'

His face whitens, only by a fraction.

'What are you talking about, Jane? If the police find out about Albion Road we're both suspicious.'

I look at him, a long look. Then I step towards him. My final card.

'Nice to meet you,' I say, holding out my hand towards his, 'I'm Rebecca.'

It takes a minute. I watch his face, my hand still outstretched towards him, the cogs turning in his brain. I see the memory come to him; the look on his face changes, falls. I let my hand drop to my side and smile at him.

'You remember Rebecca, then. I never told Albion Road my real name, Jack. I'm not on any of their records. I'm not on my therapist's records either. I wanted it all anonymous. I would've thought you'd have done the same.'

He stares at me, uncomprehending. For a doctor, he's slow at times.

'It's confidential,' he says, but even he knows he's talking rubbish now.

'Confidential until police involvement, yes. Same as a doctors' surgery. You know that, Jack.' I leave him, cross to the window again. Carefully, I plug in the lights, watch as the little row of bulbs light up.

'What were you saying about going to the police?' I ask him, and he stares at me, those familiar eyes burning into mine.

'You're insane,' he whispers under his breath, 'you're completely insane.'

I adjust the lights a little, so they twinkle just so. The children will love them. Everyone will be able to see them through the window: the brightest lights in the town.

'I'm not doing this,' Jack says suddenly, and I have to

admit, his words surprise me. I didn't think he had it in him. 'I'm not playing happy families with you anymore. I've lived in hell for months – months of believing I'm a murderer, for fuck's sake, months of you holding this over me, pulling all the strings. This is it, Jane. I'm leaving you. I want a divorce.'

It's not dissimilar to what he said the night Clare died. I wouldn't have it then, and I won't have it now.

I've had my back to him the whole time he's been speaking, but on the final word I turn. His eyes are cold, ice flints in his face, and his whole body is rigid with anger.

'You don't mean that, Jack,' I say calmly, 'you don't know what you're saying.'

He comes towards me, and I back away, my body hitting the window pane, a sickening thud that spreads across my back.

'I've never meant anything more seriously in my life,' he says, and he grabs me by the shoulders, his fingers digging deeper and deeper into my skin. I grit my teeth, holding firm.

'I won't let you, Jack,' I say, 'I won't let you take everything away from me.' My breathing is ragged. 'They'd take you away from your children. Especially when they find out how you paid Danielle Andrews off. I do love a joint account.'

We stand still, frozen together, his grip on my arms still tight. Gradually, I ease myself away from him, keeping my eyes on his face. I see the exact moment that he gives in, resigns himself to me. I'd laugh if I wasn't so tired. Really, he never had a choice.

I know my husband, and I know that the guilt has been eating him alive for the past eleven months, that his sanity has been hanging on by a thread. In some ways, I have done the kindest thing by owning up, by releasing him from his culpability. If I take the blame, he can get on with his life. He won't go to the police for something he didn't do. Not Jack. And if he tries to blame me, I'll turn it back on him. I'll give them dates, places, incidents from our past. All of our fights, spun on their head. I'll tell the girls what he's been 'doing to me', just like I told Karen. Get them to check the records of the hospital, where I was treated for falling down the stairs. I bet the nurses there remember us.

You see, I am nothing if not prepared. A forward planner, if you will. With the necklace missing, this was always a possible outcome. But with the bruises Madeline saw, and the hints I have dropped – the missed book club, the cut on my cheek, self-inflicted with my knife, hidden in the pages of *Wolf Hall* – I think there is just about enough to get them all on my side. Set poor old Ian free, give the ice queen back her man. If it came to it, of course. Plan B, I guess you'd call it.

If Jack leaves me now, I'll point the police in the helpful direction of a certain anger management group on Albion Road. And if all that doesn't work, I'll give them the necklace, covered in his DNA. I haven't even touched it. Then I'll take the pile of twenty pound notes nestled in the cookbooks and leave with the children.

But he won't leave me. He wouldn't dare.

Stalemate. I've always loved a power play, after all. You could say it's what makes me tick.

Chapter Fifty-Three

Jack

Sunday 8th December

It's still dark when I wake up just after 5.55 a.m., slide my feet out of bed onto the cold floor of the spare room. At least she didn't object to me sleeping in here tonight. I've left her alone in the Egyptian cotton sheets, the sheets she bought for herself on my credit card, just after we moved in. She told me it was to make up for the time I pushed her down the stairs. What she doesn't like to think about was that if I hadn't pushed her away, I'd probably be dead. I never meant for her to fall down the stairs, and she knows it. She always has done.

I can still see it sometimes; the look in her eye that day in our old house, the point of the sharp silver kitchen knife in her hand. She was angry with me, particularly angry that day – accusing me of all sorts of things. Telling me I was unfaithful, that I was going to end up leaving her just like her father did. Well, she's right about that. Finally, finally, I am. I reached out to defend myself, and that's when she slipped down the stairs. Or decided to slip. She loves holding that one over me, has done for years now. Her trump card, although now it turns out it's just one of a whole bloody pack. Since the night she came to meet me in the meadow, already spoiling for a fight, she has dangled a dagger above my head, like a lethal icicle about to fall.

There isn't much time. I allow myself a second or two outside the children's bedrooms, fancy that I can hear their breathing through the tightly shut doors. My bag, packed after she went to bed triumphantly, is clutched tight in my right hand, in it only the bare essentials. My phone pulses in my left hand. I'm getting the 05.35 into London Liverpool Street, and from there, I am heading to my sister Katherine's house, the sister who stopped speaking to me the day I married Jane. She told me it was too painful seeing me make such a mistake. I'm sure she'll be happy to hear she was right, although of course, no one will ever know the full extent of it.

For, I too, want what is best for my children. But I can no longer endure my wife.

From Katherine's, I will begin to make plans. I have been mulling them over all night in my head, barely sleeping. I will instruct a solicitor, find out what my options are. Divorce is a certainty, but I need to see the kids. Knowing Jane, joint custody is the most I can hope for at this stage. But I have money, and money will buy me a good lawyer. A great lawyer, who in time, can get me my kids back. Free of Jane, and free of this wretched life.

It comes to me as I silently let myself out of the house, the heavy door closing behind me for the last time. I allow myself one glance towards the Edwards', feel again the wave of sadness that has been with me since that night. This time, though, it is free of the terrible guilt – and the thought makes me almost euphoric. I didn't kill Clare. Whatever my faults – and they are many and deep – I did not cause Clare to take her last breath. My wife did.

I won't tell the police what she has done. I am not a murderer, this I am telling you, but you must see that neither am I a particularly good man. I dealt with my demons as best as I could during those long sessions at Albion Road, but all these months, I have kept silent as another man is accused of Clare's murder. A saint, I am not. But, I console myself – for I feel able to do that now, after all these months of torture – I'm not as bad as my wife.

The train to London is busy, full of commuters yawning, eyes bleary in front of their laptops. The email I tapped out late last night to the surgery sits in my drafts, ready to send; my own laptop hums quietly in my bag. Once at Katherine's, I will send it: my resignation with immediate effect. I will find a new job in London, somewhere large and anonymous, and once Katherine grows sick of me I will find myself a flat, with spare rooms for the children to come and visit. Because she will let them, she will see sense, once she realises I have gone – she has to. She will realise that our partnership, such as it is, can no longer go on. We are ruined, tainted – our marriage died with Clare.

London rises up around me, grey skyscrapers pointing up into the early morning glow. As I gaze at the very tip of the Shard, just visible in the December air, something inside me releases, just a little. Slowly, I disembark and make my way through the barriers, losing myself in the London crowd. I don't look back. Not this time.

Katherine's flat in Bethnal Green is small but warm, the central heating clanks around us. I wake up on my third day of freedom and reach immediately for my phone, desperate for news of the children. But the silence continues. Jane's stalemate. Not even Harry has replied to my texts, and a prickle of true unease begins to snake its way up my spine. For the last forty-eight hours I have allowed myself to believe that Jane will come round, that her initial anger at my disappearance will dissipate, that she will find a relief in the freedom I have given us both. Surely, now, she has no choice.

There is a sound, a knocking at Katherine's door. I am still in my boxers, but my sister has already left for work, so I ease myself out of the spare bed and shrug on jogging bottoms, an old sweatshirt. I must buy some new clothes, I brought barely anything with me and these are beginning to smell.

It takes me ten paces to get to the front door, and when I look back on this day, it is those ten paces I find myself thinking about, for they represent the last of the *before*. The after – well, the after is a life not worth living.

There are two of them, both men. I wish fleetingly that one was a woman, then chide myself for the thought. Neither of them are smiling.

'Jack Goodwin?'

My first, terrible thought is that something has happened to one of the children. Thoughts race through my mind – I should never have left them with her, she is dangerous, that has been proven – but I take a deep breath and force myself to think logically. Jane would never harm our children. Even in her darkest moments, she has never harmed a hair on their heads. They are her world.

'Yes,' I say, 'I'm Dr Jack Goodwin. How can I help you?'

One of them steps forward.

'Jack Goodwin, I am arresting you for the murder of Clare

Edwards, for attempting to evade police capture, and for perverting the course of justice. You do not have to say anything, but it may harm your defence if you do not mention when questioned something which you later rely on in court. Anything you do say may be given in evidence.'

There is the flash of cold metal on my wrists, the sensation of falling.

'This is madness,' I say, the words finding me just in time, and briefly, the officers stop moving. My chest ignites – they are wrong, they've realised their mistake – but then the taller of the two grabs my chin, turns my face abruptly to his. My jaw clicks.

'You can give up now, *Dr* Goodwin.' The word is almost a sneer. 'Your wife told us everything.'

Those words will echo in my head for fifteen years.

Chapter Fifty-Four

Nathan

Four months later

Nathan Warren is a gentle man. He stands on the corner of where Ashdon High Street meets Brook Lane every weekday, not far from the town sign sporting three sheep and an ear of corn. Most days, he has his cone – an orange and white job, on loan from the council after his old one was vandalised. There aren't many cars that come up and down this road, but the ones that do will receive a helpful nod from Nathan, a point of the hand and a cheery smile. He'll put the cone down if they ever need to park, but more often than not, they're just passing through. It is moving towards summer now; there is a new scent in the air, heady and sweet. The flowers in Sorrow's Meadow will be blooming, he knows, but he still doesn't walk there anymore. Nobody does.

Most mornings, he sees Jane Goodwin with her two youngest children, one in each hand. On the way in, she doesn't normally take much notice of Nathan because she's chatting away to one of the other mums or listening to something one of the kids is saying. They're taller now, especially the girl. She's shot right up.

Nathan prefers the way back, when Jane comes past him

alone, the children safely at school. She lives alone with them now, after what happened to her husband. But he's seen a man a few times now, a new man, a bit shorter than Jack was, with sandy blonde hair. He arrives in a sports car, and sometimes Jane comes out to meet him, kisses him on the lips. Nathan doesn't really like that. He likes it when she is on her own, walking – that's when she'll smile at him; their eyes will meet and Nathan will feel it – the hot rush of excitement. It could happen any day now. She could turn to him and speak, they could have a proper conversation, like they did before. He's wanted that for so long. He has always liked Jane. She is so very, very pretty.

He did tell the police that, but they didn't seem very interested. All they ever asked was what he wanted with that younger girl, Clare, the one with the blonde hair. It confused him, confused him a lot. He didn't want anything with Clare – he didn't even know her. He did see Jane with her though, that night over a year ago in Sorrow's Meadow. He'd gone up there for a walk, like he does most evenings – there's not much else to do here. Nathan doesn't like drinking, so the pub is out, and even though his mother told him Ashdon was a friendly town, Nathan doesn't see it that way. He can remember the soft feel of his mother's hand as she died – she'd gripped it tightly, in the house he inherited, and she'd told him to look after the town, to keep himself safe.

'It's a lovely place,' she'd murmured, 'friendly, Nathan. Make the most of it. You'll love it here.'

He'd kept to his word, all these years. But the people of Ashdon are busy, they're not interested in him, and of course that incident at the Valentine's fair hadn't been friendly at all.

Nathan shudders a little at the involuntary memory. That man shouting at him. Shouting about Clare.

The only person who's ever been friendly to him is Jane, ever since that night when she told him what to do.

Jane Goodwin is coming back from the school now; her footsteps are pulling closer to where Nathan is standing. She is on her way home, to the big house. The house next door to hers has a For Sale sign now, the colours bright against the hedgerow. It is taking a long time to sell. He smiles at her, a shy, tentative, but *friendly* smile, and this time, she smiles back, a proper smile. Their eyes meet. He grips the cone awkwardly, a blush starting at his neck. She's so pretty. He remembers how pretty she looked at the Valentine's fair, the way she'd smiled at him as he made his way back home, head down. The touch of her hand as she came up behind him, her cheeks slightly flushed. She must have walked fast.

He'd listened as she'd asked him, asked for the second favour.

'Just a teeny one, Nathan,' she'd said, standing so close to him that he could smell her perfume, the flowery, clean scent that made him feel all tingly inside. He hadn't quite understood at first, but once she'd explained it again, he got it. She'd told him how much he'd be helping her out, asked him to repeat it all back to her, everything he needed to do. Nathan didn't know Ian very well, but he did know Jane. He wanted to help Jane, and he did. She'd tried to do it without implicating anyone, she'd explained to him, she really had tried, but the police wanted a name and he had to be the one to give it to them. It was important. It was his job. But still, he was so relieved when they let Ian go. Turns out he hadn't been the one after all. And now Nathan doesn't need to feel so guilty. He is free.

'Thank you, Nathan,' Jane says now, nodding at the cone, and he stops still, delight rippling through him like the warm chocolate that his mother used to make.

'You're welcome,' he mutters, and she gives a little nod, a quick, brisk nod that could mean anything, but which Nathan takes to mean *thank you*, once again. It is their secret, then. She has acknowledged it, and he will never, never tell. Nathan watches as she walks towards the house, and as he stares, the large, heavy door opens to reveal the sandy-haired man, smiling, his arms open. Jane walks into his embrace, and the door closes behind them. A fresh start, Nathan thinks, and Jane deserves it. She is so pretty, after all. He is glad she got to keep the house. This way, they can share their secret for ever.

Chapter Fifty-Five

Jane

One month later

Fifteen years is a long time – a longer sentence for my husband than even I was expecting, to be honest. But I could hardly stay alone for ever, could I? Besides, Jack left me with no choice. No one believed him when he protested his innocence – not once I spoke to Madeline and her boss, played them the recording of Jack admitting he gave Clare the contraception. I told them how I'd always seen him look at Clare, how I thought the idea of her seeing someone might have pushed him over the edge. *He had these rages, jealous rages,* I told them, touching my arm, reminding Madeline of the day she saw my bruise. *His anger overruled him,* I said sadly, showing them my medical tag from the day I was hospitalised. *He did try to control it,* I explained, giving them the contact details of Albion Road. *But he couldn't in the end. Poor Clare was collateral damage.* They bagged the gold necklace up carefully. I wonder if it'll be returned to Rachel.

Overall, I found DCI Sturgeon the more receptive of the two, if I'm honest – there's something about Madeline that I don't quite trust. Or perhaps it's that she doesn't trust me. But I'll win her round – my offer for a wine night still stands. No one likes to be left out, do they?

The people of Ashdon have been wonderfully support-ive throughout the whole ordeal. One of the mothers even brought me a lasagne the other day – the children and I shared it. The buttercups are coming out in Sorrow's Meadow, now; I might take Sophie up there one day. It's safe now, after all. We'd have the place to ourselves.

Don't look at me like that. If you were me, you'd have done the same. I know you would. It's every man for themselves, in the end. Or every woman, I suppose.

Acknowledgements

Writing this book was such a fun process and I want to thank my wonderful editor and friend Charlotte Mursell for doing such a brilliant job on the edits, answering my many questions and being so enthusiastic and supportive every step of the way. Roll on our trip to Sheepwash! Thank you too to agent extraordinaire Camilla Bolton – you have helped me achieve my dream and I will always be so grateful to you for taking a chance on my writing back in 2014.

Huge thanks to the rest of the wider team at HQ Stories – I am very lucky to be in such safe hands, you're all such superheroes. Thanks to Anna Sikorska for designing me another knock-out jacket – I love this one even more than my first book, which is saying something – and to the lovely Lucy Richardson for handling my publicity, and to Jennifer Porter for doing a stellar job with the marketing. Thanks too to Sarah Goodey, Lisa Milton, JP Hunting, Georgina Green, Clio Cornish and Celia Lomas for all your energy and enthusiasm – you're an amazing team. Thank you to Laura Gerrard for your eagle-eyed copyediting skills and to Clare Wallis for doing the proofread.

Thank you to Mary Darby, Kristina Egan, Emma Winter, Rosanna Bellingham, Philippa Archibald and Roya Sarrafi-Gohar at Darley Anderson for selling my books into foreign territories, advising me to spend my advance on shoes and wine, and dealing with endless queries. You are all stars.

Thank you to everyone at Team Avon for being so supportive of my writing – I promise I'm not doing it at my desk! Thanks to Anna Derkacz for all the mentoring, wine and advice.

Special thanks to my girlfriends: Anna Garrett, Delphine Gatehouse, Lizzie Ashley-Cowan, Gigi Woolstencroft and Flo Gillingham for being so incredibly supportive – and to Remi, for being the cutest baby I ever did see.

Thank you to Sabah Khan for being my moonlight publicist, to Helena Sheffield for your continuous advice and friendship, Eloise Wood for always being there to listen, and to all the amazing authors who so kindly provided endorsements. I really appreciate it.

This writing journey would be a whole lot less fun without the Doomsday Writers – thank you for everything, and long may we continue!

Thank you to Alex, for giving me plot ideas, celebrating everything with me, and making me so happy.

Thank you to my family for their amazing love and support – my brothers Owen and Fergus, my dad, my grandma and my mum. You are the best.

And finally, thank you to my readers! To everybody who bought my first book, *The Doll House*, and took the time to message me, review the book, or recommend it to their friends – THANK YOU. It really does make it all worth it, and I hope you like *The Girl Next Door* just as much!

Don't miss *The Doll House*, the gripping psychological thriller from Phoebe Morgan...

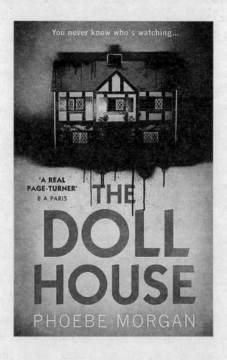

Then

'Can we go now?'

I am tugging on Mummy's coat, my fingers clutching the thin black fabric of it as though it is a life raft. Mummy's eyes don't move; her gaze doesn't falter. It is as if I have not spoken at all.

Minutes pass. I begin to cry, small, quiet sobs that choke in my throat, sting my cheeks in the wind. Mummy takes no notice. I push my palms into my eyes, blotting out the last remnants of light in the shadowy garden around us. The darkness continues to fall, but still Mummy stares, glassy-eyed. She doesn't comfort me. She just stares. I bite down hard into the flesh of my cheek, harder and harder until I can taste a little bit of blood on my tongue. I'm trying to be quiet, trying not to make a sound. Mummy tells me that I shouldn't complain, that we're just playing the game. But it's too cold tonight, and I'm hungry. The chocolate bar I had at school is swirling around in my stomach. I don't think I'll get anything else tonight, not if we don't see them soon.

In the winter time it's always cold like this, but Mummy never lets us leave. In the summer time it's better, sometimes the game is almost fun. The garden is the best part, I like the way the grass feels against my knees, and the way the hole in the fence fits me perfectly, like it's been built just for me. I'm really good at getting through it now, I never even snag my clothes any more. I'm almost perfect.

Now though it's freezing and my hands are red, they burn like they're set on fire. I squeeze my eyes tightly shut and pretend that it's summer time, all nice and warm, and that I can feel the rays of sun on my back from where I'm hiding. In summer I get to see animals. They have rabbits in cages but I don't go near those any more. One time I did, I crept right up to the cage and put my fingers through the gap, touched one of the bunnies on his little soft nose. But when Mummy realised, she got very angry, she said I had to stay back in the shadows. She says the bunnies don't belong to us. So I don't see them any more, but I do get to see the little hedgehog that lives near the fence, and all the creepy-crawlies; the worms and the beetles that Mummy says I oughtn't to touch. I do touch, though. I push my fingers into the dirt and pick them up, lay the worms flat on my hand and watch them wriggle. I don't think they mind. It's nice to have things to play with. I'm usually by myself.

Mummy suddenly leans forward, grabs my frozen hand in hers. I can feel the bones of her hand against mine, clutching me tight. It hurts.

'Do you see them?' she says, and I open up my eyes, blink in the darkness. It's almost fully dark now but I look at the golden window, and I do see them. I see them all. My heart begins to thud.

1

Now

Corinne

The house is huge. It sits like a broken sandcastle in the middle of the lawn, strangely out of place amongst the remnants of construction, discarded hats and polystyrene cups left by over-caffeinated builders. I cling to Dominic's hand as we pick our way through the site. Two fold-up chairs are positioned mid-way across the lawn, their silver legs wet with cold condensation.

'Dominic? You're here early!' A man is striding towards us, hand outstretched. I let go of Dominic and step backwards, feel the immediate rush of anxiety as we disengage.

'You must be Warren.' Dom smiles, reaching out to grasp the bigger man's hand in his own. 'This is my girlfriend, Corinne Hawes.' He propels me forward slightly with his left hand. 'She's got the day off work so I thought I'd bring her along with me. Got a keen eye for a story too, so she might be of use!'

Neither of these things are exactly true. Dominic is a journalist; it's easy to twist the truth, blur the lines. He's good at it.

'Thanks for coming down,' Warren is saying, his voice loud and fast. 'We really appreciate the coverage.' Spittle connects the fleshy pouches of his lips, hangs horribly before separating itself into two sticky drops. He is moving as fast as he speaks, leading us both towards the house, raising a hand to builders as they walk past. The closer we get to the building, the worse I feel. It looms over us, white in the winter sun. There is something strange about it, something sad. It looks ruined. Forgotten.

'So, Dominic, Dom, can I call you Dom?' Warren continues without bothering to wait for an answer. 'Dom, the thing is, this building is going to be a beauty by the time we're finished with it. Yeah, it needs a bit of TLC, but that's what we're here for.' He looks at me suddenly and winks. I recoil. He reminds me of Dom's colleague Andy, the one who spent the entire Christmas party staring down my blouse, his eyes finding the gaps between the buttons on my chest. The memory makes me shudder. That man has never liked me since.

'Shall we start off with a few questions, I'll tell you what you need to know? Then you can take a few snaps, I know what you paparazzi are like!' Warren laughs. I want to catch Dominic's eye, share the horror of Warren together, but he's scribbling in his notebook, little squiggles of grey against the white page.

We sit down at the chairs, I feel the wetness of the cold plastic seep through my jeans. The sun hits my eyes and I close them momentarily; they feel dry, the tear ducts emptied. Dom made me come with him today, told me I needed to get out of the flat. He said a week is long enough. He's right, I know he is. I just can't bear the fact that we've failed again, that another round of IVF has led to nothing. I feel empty.

'Our readers love a good backstory,' Dominic continues, and I find a glimmer of peace in the familiar rise and fall of his voice. 'Especially with a building as beautiful as this.'

'Well, let's see,' Warren says. 'Carlington House – this is what's left of it – was originally built back in 1792. It was designed by a guy named Robert Parler—'

Something shifts slightly in my brain, a bell of recognition.

'I know Robert Parler,' I say. 'Well, not *know* him, of course. I mean I know of him; my dad told me.'

Dom smiles at me, his eyes flashing over the notepad.

'Corinne's dad was an architect too,' he tells Warren, and I feel that familiar sucker-punch at the use of the past tense. It's coming up to a year since Dad died. I miss him every single day. I miss him more than anyone thinks. I'm grateful to Dom for not saying Dad's name – Warren will no doubt have heard of him and I don't want to have to hear him start to suck up to me. People do that when they realise who my father was – one of the most well-known architects in London, famous in the industry and beyond. But it hurts to talk about him, and I feel fragile today, as though I'm made of glass that might shatter at any second.

'Got yourself a smart little lady here, Dom!' Warren grins. His teeth are too big for his mouth; I spy a piece of greenery stuck in his gums. 'So, Parler does a grand job with Carlington and it passes through the hands of local landowners, the few that were wealthy enough. But then the Blitz rolls around, and we suffer some pretty major damage. Family living in it at the time, the littlest of their kiddies is found under the rubble nearly three months later. Three months, can you believe. Tragedy.'

Warren shakes his head, presses on gleefully. I picture tiny bones, birdlike under the aftermath of a bomb.

'So, the thing is, the place never had the chance to shine until years later, must've been around twenty years ago.' He pauses, stares for a moment at the house before us. I follow his gaze; there is a sudden movement, a shower of white dust spills from the collapsing roof. A trio of rooks fly out from the left-hand corner, shooting into the light, their spidery legs trailing behind them like stray threads in the ashy grey sky. One of them calls out, fleetingly, a short sharp cry that echoes in my chest.

'Anyway, eventually someone spotted its potential. Employed a whole new round of builders, started work again. By that time, it was owned by the de Bonnier family, you know, they were a big deal in the jewellery business? Very wealthy back then.' Warren sucks his teeth and raises his eyebrows at me.

Dominic, in the midst of writing, pauses and looks up. 'You've not been at this twenty years though, surely?'

'Of course not, Dom, of course not.' Warren laughs. 'My men are quicker than that! No, the de Bonniers hired a new company, started to do the place up. Made some good progress—'

'So what happened?' Dominic leans forward. His breath mists the air; I watch the cloudy white of it disappear into nothingness.

'Whole thing got abandoned.'

'Abandoned?'

'Yep. Story goes that some pretty deep shit went down between the de Bonniers and the architect firm. All turned a bit nasty. Lot of money lost, from what I understand. That's what it always comes down to, isn't it? Money.' He waves a large hand in the air, it comes dangerously close to my shoulder.

'So then of course, lucky us, we manage to wangle the deal and get the go-ahead to renovate. One of my biggest commissions so far, Dom, pays for the kids' school fees, that's what I always say. You guys got kids? Bloody rip-off these days. My missus says the little buggers are bleeding us dry.'

He turns his head towards me, I feel the heat rise in my face as his eyes meet mine. How can he say that? Doesn't he know how lucky he is?

'What kind of trouble went down?' Dominic asks, saving me from answering his question.

'Oh,' Warren wafts a hand airily. 'It was all a bit hush hush—' I receive another wink '—I'm sure we can find out for you though! But isn't that more your department?' He laughs, the criticism veiled.

Dominic inclines his head. I sense his annoyance and my heart beats a little bit faster.

'So who owns the house now?'

'Oh, it's being sold,' Warren says. 'Woman who owns it can't afford to keep it, that's why it's in the state it's in. Been left to rot, really. But someone's finally come forward to buy it, pumped a load of money in – not that I care where the money's coming from, as long as it's coming!'

Dominic winces. 'Right, right.'

Warren grins at me. 'I can show you the house, if you like. Any excuse to show off our work, that's what I always say.'

We are treated to a few statistics on Warren's builders before we all stand up and Dominic takes a couple of photos. I close my eyes when the camera flashes; I hate cameras. Dad always said he hated them too, but I don't think he did. He loved the attention, the limelight he used to get in London whenever he unveiled a new design. Flash. Flash. Dominic sees me wincing and touches my hair, asking if I'm all right, and I force myself to smile at him. The house surrounds us. I feel like it's watching me.

Warren leads us both around the back, to where a hole in the wall gapes brutally, exposing the half-finished rooms inside. I remove a mitten and run my hand over the sturdy stone, enjoying the cold sensation. It is an off-white colour, *argent grey*, I think, the paint number popping into my head, an old habit from my first gallery days. A spider drifts downwards, its legs moving quickly like tiny knitting needles, spinning itself towards the soft padding of my outstretched arm. Drops of water glisten on its silvery web.

As we wander through the garden, around the crumbling walls, I feel the building enveloping me, touching me with its feelers, pulling me in. Cold fronds of air creep towards me from the dark holes where the windows should be. I stare up at the highest window, wondering who lived here, what secrets this house has held. As I turn away I see it – a flash in the darkness, a white movement. A face. There's a face in the blackness, ghostly pale. I can see it.

I scream, put a hand to my chest and stumble backwards, my heart thudding.

'No!' I am saying, the words bursting out of my mouth before I can stop them. 'No!'

'Ssh, Corinne, ssh now, it's all right.' Dominic is there, holding me, telling me to calm down, it's just him, just the flash of his camera. Nothing to see. There is nobody there. He holds me against his chest and I take deep breaths, my legs shaking, cheeks flushing as Warren stares at me. My heart is thudding uncomfortably. I can't keep doing this, living on my nerves, panicking at nothing. Dom continues to stroke my hair and tell me everything is fine, and I know he's right but I can't help it, I keep picturing the sight: a face at the window, looking out at me, staring straight into my eyes.

*

I run a bath that evening while Dominic goes to buy dinner for us both. My discarded boots sit by the radiator, their insides stuffed with old newspaper. We always have far too much of it; Dominic keeps his old copies of the *Herald* stacked up in the hallway.

I sit on the side of the bathtub, my legs cold against the white enamel, and turn the page of a book called *Taking Charge of Your Fertility*. I'm trying not to think about earlier, the way I panicked at the house. It's not good for me, these bursts of irrationality. Dom thinks it's to do with my dad, the shock of his death. He's said as much too.

I flip the book in my hands over. It has a picture of a serious-looking woman on the back and a photograph of a baby in a pushchair on the inside jacket flap. I have been hiding the book from Dominic since I bought it on Amazon. I'm embarrassed by it, I suppose, because actually I don't really believe in any of this stuff, never have.

I saw the fertility book in Waterstones the other day and found myself hovering, looking around to see if anyone was watching me research ways to have children the way other people look up hobbies. I picked the book up, started to carry it to the counter, but the woman in the queue looked at me sympathetically when she saw what I was holding. I left the shop in a hurry, cheeks flaming, unable to bear her pity, but that night I found myself on the computer with my purse open beside me, typing in my bank security details and our address.

I have forgotten that I am running a bath until I feel the ends of my dressing gown getting wet against my skin. The water has reached the rim of the tub and is threatening to overflow. Swearing, I reach for the tap and turn it off, plunging my hand down into the wet heat to release the plug. The book falls from my lap onto the floor, landing with a dull thud.

Once the bath water has resigned itself to an acceptable level, I undress, my dressing gown pooling on the floor. My stomach is flat, white. I imagine it stretched out in front of me, like Ashley's was with Holly, and the hairs on my body stand up against the cold air, only relaxing as I slide into the hot water. I put my shoulders back against the enamel, feel the points of my shoulder blades flinch at the sensation. I lean down to pick up the book. I should be more open-minded. Perhaps it will work. After all, I am fast running out of options.

Around me, the water goes cold but I stay in the bath, letting my body relax. I used to have baths when I was a little girl, I've always preferred them to showers. Images of Carlington House keep surfacing in my mind; the way I screamed, the darkness of the windows. I need to get a grip. I've always been a bit like this. When I was a little girl, I was always thinking I saw faces, ghosts in the dark. There was never anyone there. Dad used to say I had an overactive imagination. 'Seeing the spooks again, Corinne?' He'd laugh, ruffle my hair. He thought it was funny, but actually it made me feel scared. Still. I'm an adult now, I ought to know better.

My mobile rings twice, a sharp trill followed by a thudding vibration that echoes through the silent flat, but I don't want to get out of the water just yet. It's probably my sister. As the sound of the phone begins again, I give up and sink my head under the water, enjoying the cold rush enveloping me, my hair floating up and around me like a dark halo.

The next thing I know, Dominic is shouting, his hands are underneath my armpits, slipping and sliding, and there is water splashing everywhere. The bath mat is bristly under my feet and the towel as he rubs it over me is rough. My teeth are chattering and my fingertips are prune-like. He has pulled the plug and the water is draining out, forming rivulets around the sides of the sodden paperback lying on the floor of the tub.

'Jesus Christ, Corinne,' Dominic says, and his voice is shaky.

I blink, focus on his hands as they wrap my dressing gown around me. I can't quite work out why he's so worked up. Did I close my eyes in the bath?

Dominic is still staring at me, shaking his head from side to side. There is a funny gasping sound that I realise is coming from me. I need to think of something to say.

'Did you pick up the dinner?'

2

Ashley

Ashley shifts her daughter from one hip to the other so that she can bend to pick up the mail on the doormat. Holly lets out a cry, a short, sharp sound followed by a wail that makes the muscles in Ashley's shoulders clench. Every bone in her body is aching. Her hands clasp Holly's warm body to her own; her daughter's soft, downy hair brushes against her chest and she feels the familiar aching thud in her breasts. *Please, not now.*

She feels exhausted; even on days when she's not at the café it's as though she's on a never-ending treadmill of nappies and tantrums, homework and school runs. It's not as if James is around to help her; her husband has been staying at the office later and later, leaving early each morning before the children are even out of bed. He is pulling the sheets back usually around the time that Ashley is starting to drift off to sleep, having spent the night rocking Holly, trying to calm her red little body as she screams. She has never known anything like it; her third child is by far the most unsettled of the three. It has been nine months and still Holly refuses to sleep through the night; if anything she is getting worse. Ashley doesn't think it's normal. James stopped waking up at around the four-month mark, has been sleeping lately as though he is dead to the world. She doesn't know how he manages it.

Ashley had woken yesterday to find his side of the bed empty and the sound of the tap running in their bathroom. She had put her hand to the space beside her, sat there mutely as her husband gave her a brief kiss on the cheek and headed out the door. As he had leaned close to her, Ashley had had to fight the urge to grip his shirt, force him to stay with her. She hadn't, of course, she had let him go. Then she had been up, bringing Benji a glass of orange juice, placing Holly in her high chair, making coffee for her teenage daughter Lucy. On the treadmill for another day.

Working a few shifts a week at Colours café is her one respite, her only time when she is no longer a tired mother or a wife, she is simply a waitress. James had laughed at her when she decided to start working at the little café on Barnes Common, with the ice creams and the till and the tourists. He had been amazed when she insisted on continuing work a few months after having Holly, strapping her daughter carefully into the car and driving her across the common to their childminder.

'You don't need to now, honey,' he used to say, before giving her little pep talks on the latest figures of eReader sales, on how well his company was doing. She knows they don't need the money any more. But the waitressing isn't for the money – most days she even forgets to pick up the little tip jar that sits at the edge of the counter, ignores the dirty metal coins inside as though they are nothing more than

20

the empty pistachio shells that Lucy leaves in salty piles around the house. Ashley has always been happy to give up her publishing career for her children, but she craves this small contact with the outside world. The easy days at the café give her insights into other people's lives, a chance to be in an adult environment. Just a few times a week, when she becomes someone else, someone simple, leaves her daughter in the capable hands of June at number 43 and walks back to her car alone, her arms deliciously light, weightless. It isn't about the money.

June has been a godsend to Ashley in the last six months. A retired schoolteacher, she had been recommended to them a couple of months after Holly was born. Neither of them had been coping very well and the offer of a childminder seemed like a golden ticket, a chance opportunity that might never come again. Neither Benji nor Lucy had ever had a babysitter. Ashley had stayed at home all hours of the day and night, playing endless games of peek-a-boo and living her life on a vicious cycle of nappies and tears. Not that she'd minded at the time, not really, but now that she is older she finds her mind wandering, her energy limited. To be able to work in the café is bliss.

June is unwaveringly kind, and Ashley is overwhelmingly grateful to her for stepping in a few days a week. As far as she knows, the woman lives completely alone, has never had children of her own. Ashley can sense the sadness there, is happy to see the joy in June's eyes when she drops off Holly. Yes, June really has been a blessing.

Ashley has thought about asking Corinne to mind Holly, but she has the gallery, and besides, Ashley doesn't want it to upset her. Her sister's emotions are so close to the surface at the moment, spending all day looking after someone else's child rather than her own might have been too much.

It took Ashley seconds to make the decision last week. When Corinne had called with the doctor's news Ashley had gone straight to her laptop and transferred her sister the money for her final round of IVF, thousands of pounds gone with a wiggle of the mouse. Still, it's for the best. The money would only have been accumulating dust in their joint account. She hasn't told James yet, has barely had the chance. She can hardly tell him at midnight, when she is half asleep, trying to catch one of her half-hour bursts between the baby's cries and he rolls into bed next to her, pulls her towards him in the dark and wraps his arms round her stomach. There never seems to be the time.

'Are you worried?' her friend Megan had asked her last week. They had been sitting outside Colours café, taking a break from their waitressing duties, huddled against the cold with a pair of creamy hot chocolates.

'Am I worried?' Ashley had repeated the question out loud, the words misting the January air.

Megan had nodded, pushed her strawberry blonde hair behind her ears, tucked the ends underneath her purple wool hat.

'About what?' Ashley knew what her friend meant, had pretended not to.

'Well, you know.' To her credit, Megan had had the grace to look slightly uncomfortable. 'Why do you think he's staying late so much?'

'He's working, Megan,' Ashley had told her, and they had finished their drinks in silence, drunk them too fast so that the cocoa burned the top of Ashley's mouth and scorched the taste buds off her tongue. Megan had apologised later, put her arm around Ashley as they stood behind the counter together.

'Ignore me,' she said, 'I haven't had any faith in men since Simon left. James is one of the good ones. Don't worry.'

Ashley had squeezed her friend back, allowed herself the warm flood of relief. The feeling hadn't lasted. The hot chocolate she'd had coated her mouth, she felt the thick sweetness of it on her tongue, looked down at herself in shame and felt the bulge of her stomach, the way it pressed against her jeans since having Holly. It never used to.

In the kitchen, Ashley sets Holly down in her high chair, humming to her until she begins to quieten down. Holly's chubby hands reach out for the wooden spoon on the work surface and Ashley hands it to her obligingly, closes her ears to the noise of the daily drumbeat beginning, the sound of her baby hitting the spoon on the table. She begins to sift through the pile of mail, catches the edge of her finger on an envelope and closes her eyes briefly as a slit appears in her flesh. She is so tired; as she squeezes her hand she thinks momentarily how nice it would be to sink onto the sofa and blot everything out, just for an hour, just for five minutes. Three children have knocked the wind completely out of her sails. She thinks of herself as a child, and wonders at how well behaved she was. She and Corinne were good as gold, would spend hours sitting cross-legged in front of the big doll house their dad had made, playing endless games of families in the light of the big French windows that overlooked their garden, the sprawling green jungle that was home for so many years.

At fifteen, Ashley would never have spoken to her dad the way Lucy sometimes talks to James. She would never have wanted to let him down – the disappointment in his eyes if she came home with a less than perfect grade was always heartbreaking, though he'd always pull her into his arms and tell her it didn't matter. By contrast, Lucy can be so insolent, the harsh words fly out of her mouth like bullets. She apologises, of course, most of the time. Ashley has seen her curl up next to James, rest her head against his shoulder, put on her pink piggy socks so that she looks like a ten-year-old again. With Ashley she is closed off, on guard. Perhaps it's just a phase. Her friend Aoife's daughter had come home the other night with a shoe missing, vomiting up vodka in horrible swirls of sick. At least they are not there yet.

Ashley checks her watch. Ten to five. Her eyes meet Holly's, as though her daughter will speak to her, will offer some advice. Instead she smiles, a big, round-cheeked smile that makes Ashley's heart melt. Neither of them blink and the moment stretches out, and, just for a second, Ashley feels the rush of love, the energy she used to have. It is all worth it, the exhaustion, it is worth it for this. These moments. Then Holly's eyelids swoop down to cover her eyes and the moment is gone, lost. The kitchen is humming with everything still to do. Ashley has to pick Lucy up from the school bus in ten minutes, which leaves her about forty-five seconds to spoon some coffee granules into her mouth. She doesn't bother with the kettle and water ritual any more, there never seems to be time. Still, she'd never eat granules in front of James; it feels shameful, like a dirty secret. As she unscrews the jar of the coffee, the phone

24

begins to ring; Ashley reaches for it automatically, using her other hand to dip a spoon into the brown granules.

'Hello?'

There is a silence on the other end of the line. Ashley listens, straining to hear. Being a mother always gives telephone calls a new level of anxiety: the children, the children, the children.

'This is Ashley?' she tries again but there is still nothing, just the steady sound of the house around her, the receiver pressed to her ear. Behind her, Holly gurgles, she hears the sound of a spoon hitting the floor. Ashley thinks of her husband, wonders where he is, who he is with, what he is doing right this second. There was a time when the only place he'd ever be was right next to her. She puts the phone down, crunches the coffee between her teeth. The taste is bitter in her mouth.